## SHE WANTED TO MARRY A HERO

Maximillian Wells, the Earl of Trent, couldn't believe his ears—or his eyes. Before him stood beautiful, unattainable Pandora Effington, the *ton*'s most scandalous beauty. Max believed the fiery heiress would make a *most* satisfactory bride, and now she was making him a most tantalizing offer. If he wanted to take Pandora's hand—and the rest of her irresistible body—in marriage, he had to play a game of her devising—one he had no intention of losing . . .

After seven glorious seasons, Pandora knew it was time to wed, but most of London's eligible bachelors left her cold. She longed for a true hero . . . a man who would do anything in his power to win her love. Maximillian's very touch sent shivers down her spine and made her dream of long nights spent in his arms. But was he willing to risk everything to prove his love?

*Other Avon Books by*
**Victoria Alexander**

THE HUSBAND LIST

# VICTORIA ALEXANDER

# The WEDDING BARGAIN

*An Avon Romantic Treasure*

## AVON BOOKS
*An Imprint of HarperCollinsPublishers*

This is a work of fiction. Names, characters, places, and incidents either are the product of the author's imagination or are used fictitiously. Any resemblance to actual events, locales, organizations, or persons, living or dead, is entirely coincidental.

AVON BOOKS
*An Imprint of* HarperCollins*Publishers*
10 East 53rd Street
New York, New York 10022-5299

This book is dedicated with love to
Lorie Knudsen Canno,
who showed me that the bonds of best friends
forged on an Air Force base at age thirteen
can last forever

# THE TWELVE LABORS OF HERCULES
### *as interpreted by Pandora Effington*
### *from the writings of*
### *Lord and Lady Harold Effington*

1.  Defeat the lion of Nemea.

2.  Defeat the nine-headed Hydra.

3.  Capture the gold-horned deer of Diana.

4.  Defeat the wild boar of Erymanthus.

5.  Clean the Augean Stables.

6.  Drive away the carnivorous birds of Stymphalis.

7.  Capture the wild bull of Crete.

8.  Tame the man-eating mares of Diomedes.

9.  Capture the cattle of Geryon.

10. Obtain the girdle of the Queen of the Amazons.

11. Retrieve the golden apples of the Hesperides.

12. Defeat the three-headed hound guarding the gates of Hades and rescue Theseus from the Chair of Forgetfulness.

# Chapter 1
## *The Opening Gambit*

*Spring, 1818*

"You, my lord, are a rake and a rogue. A scoundrel." Pandora Effington leveled a gaze filled with every vile thought she could marshal at Maximillian Wells, the Earl of Trent. "In short, sir, you are a beast."

Trent stepped into the secluded salon, within easy distance of the crowded ballroom of the Marquess and Marchioness of Rockingham, yet far enough away to provide a discreet meeting place for a private assignation. "Am I?"

"You are indeed. You should probably be shot."

"I scarcely know what to say." He snapped the doors closed behind him.

A twinge of apprehension stabbed at her. Perhaps it was not a good idea to be alone with a rake, a rogue, a scoundrel, and a beast.

"Except, of course," amusement glimmered in his eye, "thank you."

"Thank you?" Why, the man *was* as arrogant as she had heard.

The corners of his mouth twitched as if he struggled to hold back a grin. "It is not often that one receives such a compliment."

"It was in no way intended as a compliment." In the space of a few moments, Trent had managed to turn the conversation completely around. Why was she surprised? She should have expected that he wouldn't believe her comments were criticism of the highest order. His reputation preceded him.

Trent leaned against the carved fireplace mantel in a manner at once casual and challenging. "Perhaps it was not intended as such, but it was indeed high praise. Although I must admit, I did not expect flattery when you lured me in here."

"Oh?" Pandora was never particularly given to caution, but the same instinct that kept her from straying too far past the bounds of proper behavior warned her now to take care. Still, curiosity was as integral to her existence as the beat of her heart. "What did you expect?"

Trent raised a brow.

Pandora laughed in spite of her annoyance. He did indeed have an inflated opinion of himself. "Surely, you did not presume—"

Trent nodded, a slow smile spreading across his face. "What would you have me believe? I am enticed into a private setting—"

"I did not entice you."

"—For reasons completely unknown to me—"

"I intend to make those perfectly clear."

"—By a woman who is no longer a green girl, and by all accounts should know what she is about. I believe this is your eighth season, is it not?"

It should not have bothered her, this reminder that in a life filled with the excitement of following her own rules, her inability or unwillingness to marry was a failure in the eyes of most. Yet it did. Always. Her amusement vanished and she gritted her teeth. "Seventh."

"Forgive me. One tends to lose track when a young lady passes a certain age. But then again, the term 'young' is relative, don't you think?"

"I am barely four-and-twenty. Hardly in my dotage."

"As old as that," he murmured. "One would consider most women of that age past their prime and firmly on the shelf."

"If I *am* on the shelf, it's because I *prefer* to be there." She settled on the edge of a perfectly appointed settee in the perfectly appointed salon and adopted a calm demeanor that belied her irritation at his condescending attitude. "I quite value my independence."

"Oh?" Skepticism rang in his tone. "I thought the wish of every unmarried young woman of notable family was to wed, preferably to a noble title and nobler income."

She raised her chin. "It has never been my particular desire to marry."

"Come now, my dear." The expression on his face verged on pity and her hand itched to slap it off. "One would have to have been blind and deaf not to have noticed the enthusiasm with which you've thrown yourself into

the festivities of the marriage mart the past
eight seasons."

"Six." Was he deliberately baiting her, or
was he really as sanctimonious as he sounded?

"The number scarcely matters; suffice it to
say, it is considerable. If you are not interested
in marriage, as you claim, what *are* you interested in?" He paused as if struck by the answer to his own question. "Forgive me, I
should have realized."

"Realized . . . what?" She did not like the
knowing look in his eye.

In two strides he was by her side, towering
over her in a most disconcerting way. Quickly
she rose to her feet. He stood nearly a foot
taller than she, and his eyes, gray and deep,
gazed down at her in an impertinent and assessing manner. No, she did not like the look
in his eyes at all. Unease fluttered in her stomach. He stood far closer than propriety dictated, and while she'd never cared about silly
edicts before, at once she comprehended their
worth.

"I take pride in being an intelligent man, but
tonight I seem to have forgotten myself." He
took her hand, turned it palm up, and lightly
brushed his lips against the sensitive skin of
her wrist, revealed by an unbuttoned gap in
her glove. Her breath caught. "I understand
completely now."

"You do?" Why didn't she? She too prided
herself on her intelligence. Yet at the moment
she could do little more than wonder why she
had never before realized gray was quite an
intriguing shade for a man's eyes.

"Indeed." He nodded soberly. "While in

most circumstances the daughter of a viscount would have to depend on marriage to secure her future, all of London knows your father has seen fit to ensure you not only a substantial inheritance, but funding enough to provide you with independence even now."

He still held her hand in his, only now his thumb traced lazy circles in her palm. Shivers skated down her spine. "It has long been rumored that's why you have not felt it necessary to pursue marriage. And at this juncture, as the possibility of a suitable marriage dwindles with the years, you have made another plan for your life."

"I have?" Why was he doing that to her hand? He studied her as if she were a delectable meal and he a discriminating connoisseur. Other men had, of course, regarded her in that way, but never had such a perusal seemed quite so personal, so intimate. Mesmerizing. And distinctly uncomfortable.

"Why, my dear, it's obvious." He leaned closer. Lightning flashed deep in his steely eyes. Her gaze drifted past a straight aquiline nose, a jaw square and strong, to lips firm and full.

"What is obvious?" An unbidden thought danced in her head: what would those lips feel like next to hers?

"You have, no doubt, decided on a different course. And for that you need a rake, a rogue, and a scoundrel."

"I do?" An intoxicating scent of spice and man wafted around her.

"Only a rake, a rogue, and a scoundrel, and—what else did you call me?"

"A beast." A beast with hypnotic gray eyes.

"Ah, yes. A beast. Only such a man would agree to flout society blatantly and take the granddaughter of a duke as his mistress."

The odd spell that had gripped her vanished. "His mistress?"

"Naturally. I assume that's the purpose of this rendezvous. You wish to offer yourself to me as my mistress."

"I do?" she said cautiously.

"I must admit, while it does come as something of a surprise, it also strikes me as an eminently sensible solution to the question of your future. After all, you simply cannot continue to go on season after season as you have." Trent shrugged. "And there are so few options available for unmarried—forgive me, *independent*—women, these days. No one in his right mind would ever imagine you as a governess. And beyond that . . ." He paused as if words were no longer necessary.

Her immediate impulse was to crack her hand across the confident smirk on his face. No man had ever had the nerve to suggest such a thing to her. She might well tread close to the edge of scandal, but she had never entirely crossed the bounds of respectable behavior.

"Your mistress." Pandora pulled her hand from his slowly and deliberately and crossed the room, affecting a thoughtful manner, as if she were actually considering his words. She paused before the mantel to study the portrait that glared from above the fireplace: an eminently proper painting of an eminently proper ancestor perfectly positioned in an eminently proper room.

There was nothing here out of place, nothing unexpected. The salon in the Rockingham mansion was as staid and unimaginative as everything else in the world of London society, or at least, the world open to well-bred young women of good family. Perfect and proper and boring.

"And precisely what would that entail, my lord?" She glanced at him over her shoulder. His smug smile slipped just a bit. She smothered a triumphant smile of her own. Just as she'd suspected: he'd been toying with her. Playing a game to ascertain just how far the Hellion of Grosvenor Square would go. Pandora relished nothing more than a good game.

"Well, the details, of course, would have to be decided upon."

Was there a slight hesitation in his voice? A man of his reputation was well used to dealing with women of the world. Actresses or demireps or widows at last savoring the heady excitement of freedom from their husbands. The last thing he would be expecting was for the daughter of a noble line to consider such an outrageous proposal.

"A great many details, I should think." Pandora turned and struggled to keep her sense of victory from showing on her face. Trent studied her cautiously for a moment, then his smile returned as if he realized she too was playing a game.

"A great many indeed." A wicked light shone in his eyes. "Perhaps we should discuss them?"

"Perhaps. But this is not the place for such a discussion. It is not yet midnight. I should think in an hour—no, two. I shall meet you in two hours' time. In the park. Near the Grosvenor gate."

His brows pulled together; his smile disappeared. "My dear Miss Effington, I daresay the wisdom of such a meeting—"

"You're absolutely right. Even at this hour, the park might not be the best place for our rendezvous." She thought for a moment. "I know. Behind Grosvenor Chapel, by the burial grounds. That should be more private."

"I had not planned on frequenting a graveyard in the—forgive me—*dead* of night until such time as it was unavoidable," he said wryly.

"Do you not wish to continue our discussion?"

"Indeed I do." A considering expression crossed his face. He stepped to the door, pulled it open, and bowed. "Two hours, then."

She nodded and swept from the room. A low chuckle drifted after her. Her step faltered.

By the gods, what had she done? She'd never before agreed to meet a man, any man, not to mention a virtual stranger, alone in a secluded spot in the middle of the night. What could she have been thinking? Indeed, was she thinking at all? This had not been her intention when she'd sought him out for a private conversation. The beast had simply caught her unawares. He was much more interesting and far cleverer than she'd ever expected. All that nonsense about her wanting to be his mistress. Still, perhaps this time she had gone too far.

She groaned to herself. Her impulsive nature and reckless disregard for the consequences of her acts had led her into a situation rife with unknown peril. Yet didn't peril go hand in glove with adventure? For good or ill, she did so long for true adventure.

Pandora slipped into the ballroom and hoped her absence had not been observed. Surely in such a crush no one would have missed her. Odd and unfair, how unmarried men could behave precisely as they wished, while women in similar circumstances were constrained by all manner of ridiculous rules. Her meeting with Trent would be considered quite improper.

Absently she accepted a dance with a vaguely familiar gentleman and allowed him to lead her onto the floor. Pandora had made it a rule of her own to ignore the rules of others whenever possible, while still avoiding the kind of scandal and censure that would make life rather unbearable. It was as difficult a path to tread as a fallen log across a raging stream, and just as challenging. And her life was anything but boring.

Trent strode into the ballroom, caught her gaze, and lifted a glass in a slight mocking toast. At once the spin of the dance took him out of her sight, much to her relief. She cast her partner her best flirtatious look and vowed to keep her attention on him—whoever he was—and away from Trent. A dazed smile was her reward. Quite pleasant. Quite flattering. And not in the least interesting. She

sighed. The earl was as present as if he danced
between them.

Resolve swept through her. She would not
allow Trent to consider himself a victor in
their encounter. No indeed.

She would keep their appointment, but she
would not be unprepared. And surely being
alone at the chapel with Trent would pose no
real danger beyond the ever-present possibility of discovery. Should that happen, no doubt
his sense of honor would then dictate salvag-
ing hers with an offer of marriage. That was
one trap she preferred to avoid.

When she married, *if* she married, she
would do it for love, as her mother had, and
most of her friends had not. Nothing less
would serve.

As for Trent and his little game, it would be
amusing to play, at least for the moment. She
laughed softly and her partner glanced at her
with a pleased expression. Her true purpose
in seeking out the earl tonight had nothing to
do with any desire to become either his mistress or his wife.

Why, not once during her seven seasons had
the man even asked her for a dance. Admittedly it rankled, through the years, knowing
this one eligible lord had failed to so much as
cast his eye in her direction. Not that she
cared. She'd scarcely been aware of the man
herself.

However, he was right in one respect: she
did want to speak to him about matters of the
heart. But not her heart. She beamed at the
very idea of Trent's surprise. Her partner

grinned back and hope lit in his eyes. Pandora paid it no heed.

The Earl of Trent, Maximillian Wells, might indeed be a rake, a rogue, and a scoundrel, not to mention a beast, but he'd never before pitted wits with the Hellion of Grosvenor Square. Poor man probably didn't even realize the truth before him.

The game had begun.

"Another deadly ball, another wasted evening." Lawrence, Viscount Bolton, pronounced the observation with his usual air of studied indifference.

And as usual, Max ignored him. "I would scarce call it wasted, Laurie."

"Come now, haven't we spent enough time in this purgatory on earth? Can't we now be allowed to leave without incurring the wrath of a host of well-meaning female relatives intent on cutting short our lives by shackling us in marriage?"

"Not quite yet, old man," Max murmured. He directed his words to his friend, but his attention was fixed on Pandora. She moved about the dance floor with the grace born of generations of excellent breeding, but there was more in her step than mere heritage. The woman had a spark about her. Life with the incomparable Miss Effington would never be dull.

Laurie deftly lifted a glass from the tray of a passing waiter and downed the champagne in one gulp. "Why on earth not, Max? It's still a reasonable hour. We can try our hand at the gaming tables, or—"

"Later." After his meeting with Pandora.
Not in his most farfetched dreams had he expected her to suggest such a thing. But nothing
in their first face-to-face encounter had gone
quite as he had anticipated. He certainly
hadn't planned on accusing her of a desire to
become his mistress. He smiled to himself. It
seemed the Hellion did indeed bring out the
beast in him.

"Who are you staring at?" Laurie glanced
from Max to the whirl of dancers, then back
to his companion's face. "Max?"

"Yes?" He'd been vaguely aware of Pandora in her first season, when she was a green
girl straight out of the schoolroom. Who
hadn't been? But he had just been back from
the war, and an innocent, no matter how
lovely, held no appeal for him. He'd missed
her second season entirely. It was only in the
last few years that he'd noted her activities.
Wondering what she would do next. What
rule she would flout. Which heart she would
break. Wondering as well if any man could
conquer her. None had. Until now.

"Don't even think it."

"Don't even think what?" Max said absently. It was not until the start of this season
that he'd realized that what had begun as simple curiosity had evolved to fascination and
finally to desire. Intense and undeniable.

"Think about *her*." A note of alarm sounded
in Laurie's voice. "That's who you're staring
at, isn't it? Pandora Effington? The Hellion?"

"She is lovely," Max said in an unconcerned
manner. It was past time he chose a wife. For
good or ill, the only wife he wanted, the only

woman he wanted, was Pandora Effington. And he would have her.

"Quite lovely. All that black hair and those remarkably blue eyes." Laurie studied the dancers with annoyance. "For some odd reason, the woman's charms seem to develop with each passing year. And she has a great deal of money. But she's trouble, Max."

"Is she?"

Laurie eyed him for a moment. "Do you know how many times her name has appeared in the betting book at White's?"

"Twenty-three, to be exact." Max grinned and raised his glass to his lips. "She's been extremely busy."

"She's been the cause of at least one duel in any given year."

"Not at all. She missed last year and 1815, I believe."

"The year 1815 was not my best, either." Laurie shook a warning finger. "The chit skates on the edge of scandal."

"As do we all. But she's yet to fall." Max handed Laurie his glass. "I believe I should like to dance."

"Stay away from the Hellion, Max. When and if either of us decides it's time to sacrifice freedom to the demands of producing an heir, we shall require a bride far different from Miss Effington. A lady of unquestionable behavior and unblemished reputation. A young woman of the highest standards."

"Standards you yourself have not seen fit to abide by." Max raised a brow. "And what does such a model of respectability get in return?"

Laurie smiled smugly. "Me."

"A bargain at any price." Max laughed and started in the general direction taken by Pandora and her escort.

Laurie groaned. "Have you heard a single word I've said?"

"Each and every one."

"And you're still going to approach the Hellion?"

"Not at all." Max adjusted the cuff at his wrist and cast Laurie a sly smile. "I am going to approach her dearest friend."

Even with the light of a full moon, the burying grounds were distinctly unnerving. Pandora rested her back against the cold stone wall of the chapel and shivered, the weight of the pistol she held hidden under her cloak scant comfort. This was certainly no way for the Hellion of Grosvenor Square to behave.

She sighed. It was not easy to live up to such a title. Particularly when she hadn't really done all that much to earn it, save refuse to curb her temper and her tongue. In point of fact, it all stemmed from a simple misunderstanding in her second season involving a race to Gretna Green with a young lord, whose face and name now escaped her, and two other couples, only one of which was seriously intent on marriage. The others had been far more interested in the excitement of a late-night adventure and the lure of a forbidden lark.

Unfortunately, between carriage accidents, a brief stop at an overcrowded inn, and hot pursuit by angry relations and spurned suitors, the incident had spiraled completely out of hand, the ensuing scandal quite out of proportion to the actual event. The other couples had dutifully agreed to wed, one eagerly, the second more reluctantly, to avoid society's eternal condemnation.

Pandora, however, had flatly refused to marry the gentleman who had accompanied her on the escapade, her refusal loud and long and in no uncertain terms. She saw no reason to be condemned for life to a man she barely knew when she'd scarce done anything truly wrong. Besides, the man was a twit.

The couples involved vowed to keep her participation secret, although word leaked out, as word always did. Still, her part in the debacle was not quite so public as was the others'. That, plus the fact that she was descended from dukes and her family possessed considerable wealth and the power to match, kept Pandora's reputation intact, if a bit tarnished. However, the twit—she did wish she could remember his name—was rather taken with her, and her vehement rejection did not sit well. It was he who'd bestowed the title "the Hellion of Grosvenor Square." Secretly she had to admit she quite liked it.

A twig snapped in the distance.

Pandora tensed and squinted into the black shadows of the graveyard. *Trent?* No. Trent would not slink silently into sight. Rather, she was certain he would stride onto the grounds in the manner of a conquering hero. He had that air about him. He also seemed to have a rather disturbing effect on the pit of her stomach.

No doubt the sound came from Peters, her family's butler, or one of the two footmen she'd had the good sense to bring with her and hide strategically among the gravestones.

Surely Trent should have been here by now, if indeed he was coming at all. A creature skittered across the grass and she started, tightening her grip on the pistol. It was probably nothing more menacing than a squirrel out for an evening stroll. Still, if Trent wasn't here soon, she'd have to leave. She could not wait all night. Why, that was simply inviting trouble. And she'd had more than her share of that, due in great part to the actions of men.

In any given season, at least one youthful lord would declare his undying love. Inevitably there would be a chance remark, usually in reference to her hellion title, and a duel would ensue in defense of her honor. No one was ever killed. Even the occasional wound was scarcely worth mentioning. If these gentlemen, the cream of British manhood, were such incredibly bad shots, Pandora wondered how England had ever managed to defeat Napoleon at all. Perhaps the incompetence evidenced on the dueling fields explained the sheer length of the war with France.

Something brushed against her hand; she bit back a scream. It was but a spring breeze, nothing more menacing than that. What else could it possibly be? Surely she did not believe in ghosts or other creatures that came out only at night to terrify little girls unable to sleep, or test the bravery of little boys too young to know danger, or terrorize foolish young women determined to live up to a reputation not all well earned, or—

A heavy touch fell on her shoulder. Panic ripped through her. She screamed, jerked the pistol from beneath her cloak, whirled, and fired into the night.

# Chapter 2
## *The Stakes are Declared*

"**W**hen you said I should be shot, I did not realize you planned on doing the deed yourself tonight." Wry amusement rang in the familiar voice.

"Trent?" Her voice trembled.

"Were you expecting someone else?"

"Not at all." Her heart hammered against her ribs and she attempted a calm manner she did not possess. "You are late."

"I am precisely on time. Were you trying to kill me?"

"Not yet." She lowered the weapon.

"Excellent. It would not be the ideal way to begin our arrangement."

"Ah yes." She pulled a deep steadying breath. "Our arrangement. I have given it a great deal of thought." As bright as the moonlight was, his face was still obscured by shadow. She would much prefer to see his expression. "My lord, it seems to me there are only two reasons why a woman would agree

**18**

to give up her virtue to a man: money or protection. I have no need of either."

"No indeed. You have money and a pistol. Do you know how to use it?"

"Certainly," she lied.

He snorted. "Not well. I was right behind you and you missed me."

"I'm English," she murmured.

"I must say, I am disappointed." He sighed. "If you have no need of my money or my protection, although I could give you a few pointers on handling a firearm, then we have nothing to discuss."

"We have a great deal to discuss." Her voice was firm, in the manner of a stern relative. "I wish to know what you intend to do about Miss Weatherly."

"Miss Weatherly?" A question sounded in his voice. "Why should I do anything at all about Miss Weatherly?"

"You have shown her a great deal of attention this season. You have led her to believe you have an affectionate interest in her." Pandora poked a finger at his chest. "You, my lord, have broken her heart."

For a moment Trent stood silent, as if he could not quite believe her charge or her nerve in charging it. Then he abruptly laughed, a rich, deep sound that echoed inside her. "What did you expect? You said it yourself." She could hear the smug grin in his voice. "I am very much a rake, a rogue, a scoundrel, and let's not forget, a beast."

"You needn't be so proud of it."

"Oh, but I am proud. I have spent much of my life working for the titles you so kindly bestowed on me. But even as I deserve them, and have well enjoyed their acquisition, I cannot take credit where your friend is concerned."

Pandora scoffed. "No?"

"No." His tone was unyielding. "As much as I hate to risk the ruin of my hard earned reputation, I have done nothing to encourage Miss Weatherly."

"But she—"

He held up a hand to forestall her words. "If she has interpreted my minimal notice to denote any affection on my part beyond that of acquaintance, it is a mistaken assumption. In addition, if I were in the market for a wife, I should certainly not choose someone of Miss Weatherly's ilk."

"Whyever not?"

"She is a paragon of virtue."

Annoyance on her friend's behalf surged through her. "She is a lovely girl."

"Perhaps." Trent shrugged. "And as a wife, I've no doubt she would be quite biddable and easy to manage, yet . . . where would be the challenge in that?"

"Challenge?" Pandora cocked her head and studied his dark figure.

"Indeed. If I were to choose to be leg-shackled for life to a woman, any woman, I should prefer the experience to be an interesting one. I would want a wife with a spark of fire in her eyes and spirit in her soul. She should be not unpleasant to look upon with a pretty face and a fine figure. She should be able to produce children—"

"Sounds very much like the requirements

for a good brood mare," she said under her breath.

He continued as if he hadn't heard her. "—Heirs one could hand one's estates to with confidence in the future. In addition, I should like a fair amount of intelligence in a wife. I have no intention of spending my days in the company of a simpering imbecile."

Pandora drew her brows together. "It seems you wish the attributes of an accomplished mistress in the guise of a respectable wife."

"I suppose I do." He chuckled. "You see, when I wed, I do not intend to seek pleasure elsewhere. A radical idea, but there you have it."

Pandora shook her head. "You set impossibly high standards, my lord."

"Do I?" He turned his head and his eyes caught the moonlight. His voice softened. "I thought so once, but now . . ."

She swallowed the lump that abruptly rose in her throat. "Now?"

"Now, I believe I have found a wife to meet my requirements.

A knot to match the lump settled in her stomach. "You have?"

"Indeed." His voice rang with a determined, businesslike manner. "I think we shall suit very well together. I shall call on your father first thing in the morning."

"You will call on my father?" Was this presumptuous creature planning her future without even a thought as to her wishes? Why, she was right in the first place: he chose a wife with the same attitude he'd use to select a horse.

If this was a jest on his part, he had gone far beyond the bounds of a mere joke. The man needed to be taught a lesson. Perhaps she should simply shoot him after all and be done with it. "I gather your intention to talk to my father makes this conversation a proposal of marriage?"

"That is my desire."

She tilted her head to glance at him through a fringe of lashes she knew were dark and lush and irresistible. She quirked up the corner of her mouth in a hint of a smile designed to deepen the dimples in her cheek. Her glance, her expression, her demeanor—all perfect. Exactly as she'd practiced them. Her voice was as low and seductive as she could muster. "Would you care to hear of my desire?"

"Your desire?"

"My desire." She sighed the words. Pandora hadn't spent seven seasons in London society without learning a thing or two about handling rakes, rogues, scoundrels, and the occasional beast.

"And . . . er . . . what is your desire?" His words were cautious.

"Well, my lord, my desire . . ."

"Yes?"

"My heartfelt desire . . ."

"Yes, yes?"

She bit her lip to hold back a laugh. The man sounded so frightfully expectant. "That is, I should like nothing more . . ."

"Go on."

Pandora favored him with her sweetest tone. "—Than to be tortured at the hands of naked savages in the wilds of America before I should consent to marry you."

For a stunned moment, silence hung in the air. Triumph swelled within her.

Without warning his laughter rang through the night. "I was right. You will make a delightful wife."

"Indeed I will," she snapped, all sense of victory lost. "But not for you."

"I daresay, we'll make an extraordinary couple."

"Which part of my declaration did you not understand, my lord?"

"Come, come, Dora—"

"Do not call me Dora!" She raised the pistol. "Only my parents are allowed to call me Dora."

"And," he said pointedly, "your betrothed."

"You are not my betrothed!"

"I'll permit you to call me Max." He grabbed the firearm and twisted it from her hand.

"I don't want to call you Max. I don't want to call you anything!"

"Dora and Max, I quite like the sound of that," he murmured.

"It sounds like a pair of matched hounds." She raised her chin and glared in his direction. "Now, if you would be so kind as to give me my pistol, I believe our discussion is at an end." She tried to pull it out of his grasp but he held it tight.

"Now, now, my dear, the single shot has been spent and it can do you no good, save to accidentally drop it on my foot and cripple me for life."

"I can assure you, it would be no accident!"

"Furthermore, our discussion is just beginning." The brute was obviously enjoying this. "And I daresay I prefer you unarmed."

"Very well. Keep the blasted thing." She turned on her heel and stalked off.

"Where are you going?"

"Home." She strode toward the graveyard.

He laughed. "Nothing lies in that direction but the dead."

Her step slowed. Damn the man. He had her completely turned around. "I should rather be among those enjoying eternal rest than spend one more moment in your company."

"Pandora." His footsteps sounded behind her. He caught her arm and spun her to face him. "Don't be a fool. I cannot allow you to go traipsing through a graveyard alone at night."

"I am not afraid," she said, with a defiance spurred more by annoyance than courage. "The dead are scant threat."

"It's not the dead who concern me. It's the living who haunt London in these late hours that threaten the safety of a woman alone. Even a hellion." Amusement sounded in his voice. "Life with you will never be boring, will it?"

"Life with me will never be your concern." She tried and failed to shake off his grip.

"Oh, but it will be." He whirled her around and half led, half dragged her toward the church. "My carriage is in front of the chapel. I will take you home." He raised his voice. "The rest of you can go now."

Pandora groaned. "How did you know—"

"Beg pardon, my lord." Peters stepped out

from behind a nearby tree. "Miss Effington's safety is our responsibility."

"And are you armed as well?" Max stopped, his tone resigned.

"Of course, my lord," Peters said without a moment's hesitation. Pandora doubted he carried so much as a kitchen knife.

"Very well, then." Max sighed. "You may ride with my driver. As for you," he steered her toward the street, "you will accompany me. Our chat is far from over."

"I have nothing more to say to you," she said in as lofty a manner as she could manage.

"I doubt that," he muttered, as they entered his landau.

In a few mercifully short minutes, it rolled to a stop before her door. Max stepped out and turned to assist her. She ignored his hand, scrambled out of the vehicle and marched to the front entry, Peters a scant step ahead of her. The door opened as if by magic; no doubt an unseen servant on the other side had watched for their return. "Shut the door, Peters. Do not allow that beast inside."

"Indeed, Peters, close the door. The beast is already inside."

Pandora whirled and leveled an angry glare at Max. "You have seen me safely home." She waved at him in an imperious gesture of dismissal. "You may leave now."

Even in the dim candlelight in the massive front foyer she could see the twinkle in his eye. "We are not yet finished."

"I believe I have already—"

"Peters." Max held out her pistol to the butler. "If you would take this out of the range of Miss Effington I believe we can all rest a little easier. She's likely to throw it at someone. Probably me."

Peters studied him for a considering moment, then nodded, as if he'd taken the measure of the man and found him up to snuff.

"Miss?"

"Very well." Pandora heaved a resigned sigh. "Leave us."

Peters accepted the weapon and disappeared into the shadowed recesses of the house, although she knew he would not go far.

"Now, *Max*"—she said his name as though it left a bad taste in her mouth—"what could we possibly have left to say to each other?"

He grinned. "I love it when you call me Max."

"A hound would love it as well. But at least a hound would know when the hunt was at an end." She nodded toward the door. "As is our conversation."

"Not at all." Max seemed in no hurry. He meandered around the impressive receiving area, one of the few spots in the huge house that Pandora knew was quite comparable in furnishing and style to any other home. He paused by a cherrywood table and picked up a small marble fragment. It was a carved face of a young boy, a cupid, perhaps, the rest of the statue long lost to the ravages of man and time. He turned it over in his hand. "Interesting," he murmured. "Classical period?"

"Probably," she said cautiously,

"Very nice." He studied the piece closely. "Part of your parents' collection, I assume."

So he knew about her parents. Of course, who didn't? Still, few in the social world of the *ton* took her parents' work at all seriously. It was only among academics that her father, and surprisingly, her mother as well, received the recognition they deserved for their studies of Greek antiquities. For Max to appreciate the marble spoke well of the man. Her annoyance eased. "It was one of the first pieces they discovered together. My father had long been—"

"Pandora." He glanced at her, his look and his voice surprisingly intense. "What do you want?"

"What," her voice faltered, "what do you mean?"

"What do you want in a husband?" He replaced the sculpture with care, his demeanor once again unconcerned. "Come now, I explained what I wished in a wife. The least you can do is tell me what you wish in a husband."

"I told you," she said, at once relieved by his change of manner and somehow disappointed. "I don't want a husband."

"But if perhaps you did?" He continued his survey of the room, nodding appreciatively at the broad, sweeping stairs leading to the gallery above and the soaring marble columns. His movement triggered a matching restlessness in her and she clasped her hands together in an effort to keep still.

"If I did, which I don't, but if I did," she searched her mind, absently biting her bottom lip, "I should, like you, prefer a spouse who is not unpleasant to look upon."

"Very practical. It would not do to tie oneself for life to a man whose visage would scare small children." He paused before an ancestral painting, inspecting it with the knowing air of a collector or a critic.

"But that's not the most important quality." For some obscure reason, she did not want this annoying man to think she was quite so flighty as to choose a mate for appearance alone. "I should want a husband who is intelligent."

"That goes without saying."

"A gentleman who has great moral fiber. Strength of purpose, if you will. Courage."

He nodded his approval. "Courage is an excellent quality in a spouse."

"I should look for honor."

"Of course." He moved to yet another table and examined a rather ugly porcelain shepherdess. A gift not to her mother's liking, but which had found a home nonetheless.

"Loyalty."

"Naturally." He slanted her a curious glance. "And what of wealth?"

She frowned and considered the question. "Wealth is much like appearance. Pleasant, but not a definitive requirement. I have a significant fortune myself. Still, I should prefer any potential husband to have his own resources. I'm not certain one can ever have too much money. I have never been without funds and shouldn't think I would like poverty at all."

"No, it's definitely against your nature to be poor." He set the shepherdess down and moved on. "So that's it, then? Your specifications for a spouse?"

"Yes. Except I should like it if he stood

still!'' She blew an exasperated breath. "If I were looking for a husband, and I remind you once again that I am not—"

"No question about that." He leaned against a marble column and crossed his arms over his chest.

"—Those are the qualities I would insist on."

"In short, my dear, you are looking for a hero."

"A hero?" What an intriguing idea. "You mean like Achilles or Odysseus?"

"Or the Earl of Trent." He smiled modestly.

"You." Pandora snorted in a most unlady-like way. "You, my lord, are no hero."

He shrugged in a matter-of-fact manner. "I do meet all the qualifications."

"You do not."

"I most certainly do." He inclined his head toward the darkened end of the foyer. "Peters?"

"Yes, my lord." Peters' voice drifted in from the shadows.

"Do you think I have the qualities of a hero?"

"I am in no position to ascertain that, my lord."

"Max," Pandora snapped. Max grinned. "I meant to say *my lord*. Leave Peters out of this."

"I would, but I believe we need an objective opinion. Now then, my good man," Max angled his head in the direction of the unseen butler and raised his voice, "not that this is at all significant, mind you, but would my appearance scare small children?"

"You are quite handsome, my lord."

Pandora smothered a smile. This was absurd. Still, there was no denying the man was indeed handsome and quite dashing, with his dark hair and smoky eyes, broad shoulders, and impressive height. Peters had excellent taste. "As you said, that's not important."

"Not important, but preferable. Peters?"

"Yes, my lord?"

"Am I not perhaps even wealthier than Pandora's father?"

"So I have heard, my lord."

"Again, not important." She waved away his words and struggled not to laugh. What was it about this man? One moment she wanted to thrash him and the next she wanted to laugh aloud.

"Ah, but once again, preferable. What say you, Peters?"

"Yes, my lord, preferable." The butler paused. "She would not take well to poverty."

"Peters!"

"Have you ever heard my courage questioned, Peters? Did you know I served with Wellington?"

"No, my lord."

She had no idea he'd been in the war. It certainly cast him in a somewhat different light.

"Should I show her my commendations?"

"An excellent idea, my lord."

"No, no," she said quickly. "That's not necessary."

Pandora knew little about the workings of the military, but she was fairly certain commendations were not given merely for a nicely laundered uniform. She couldn't help but be the tiniest bit impressed.

"I see. If you accept my word without proof, then you trust that I am telling the truth. Therefore you obviously do not doubt my moral fiber. Wouldn't you agree, Peters?"

"Indeed, my lord."

Pandora shrugged. "I suppose that—"

"As well as my sense of honor."

"Hah! I have you there. What of your dealings with women? Vast numbers, if rumor serves." She nodded with the satisfying sense of a point well scored. "Peters? Haven't you heard that?"

"His lordship has quite an extensive reputation, Miss."

"He's already admitted he's a rake," she said pointedly.

"Don't forget a rogue, a scoundrel, and a beast." A note of pride sounded in Max's voice.

She scoffed. "I have not forgotten anything."

"But perhaps your memory is not entirely accurate. Ours is a small society fraught with rumor and innuendo. In all the talk about me through the years, have you ever heard of me ill-treating a woman?"

"Well, no."

"Peters?"

"Not that I have heard, my lord."

"Have I ever exposed a lady to scandal?" Max moved toward her.

"I don't think—"

"No, my lord," Peters called.

"Have I ever caused the ruin of an innocent?" He stepped closer.

"Probably not, but—" She resisted the urge to step back.

"No, my lord."

"Therefore you cannot doubt my honor." He grinned down at her triumphantly. Only a few bare inches separated them. "At least where the fairer sex is concerned. As for the rest of my behavior, my word is my bond and I have never broken it."

"Regardless, all that does not make you a hero." Was he to make it a habit of standing too close?

"Doesn't it?" He raised a brow. "Peters?"

"You do appear to meet all the qualifications, my lord."

"Thank you, Peters." His gaze drifted to her lips and back to her eyes. "You may leave us now."

"As you wish." The servant's voice seemed to fade.

"He hasn't left, you know." She stared up at him. Why was it so difficult to breathe?

"I know," Max said softly. Was he going to kiss her? "I could be your hero."

"No, you could never be my hero." Could he? Not that she cared. How could she possibly care about a man who had never once glanced her way? Or asked her to dance? Or risked his life to defend her honor?

"I could prove it." He bent his head toward hers. "Test me, Pandora. Let me prove it to you."

"What kind of test?" Her voice was barely a whisper.

"Whatever you wish."

"And if you should pass my test?" She

could feel the heat of his body close to hers.

"Then you shall be my wife and I shall spend the rest of my days being your hero." His lips were a scant breath from hers.

"And if you fail?" she blurted.

He hesitated then shrugged. "I will not fail."

"But if you do?" It wasn't as if she hadn't been kissed before.

"I have no idea," he said impatiently.

"There should be a forfeiture, don't you think?" Why did her heart hammer at the thought of his kiss?

"Not particularly."

"I do." If he was going to kiss her, what was he waiting for? "And since you named the prize if you win, it's only fair that I name the penalty if you lose."

"As you wish." He straightened and a pang of regret shot through her. It was probably for the best. She certainly didn't want him to kiss her.

His tone was dry. "What do you suggest?"

"Let me think." Pandora pulled a steadying breath and tapped her finger against her bottom lip. His gaze followed the movement. Heat burned her cheeks and she snatched her hand back to her side. At once she knew he suspected she would not have been at all averse to his kiss.

She wrenched her mind away from the thought of his lips on hers. What would the appropriate penalty be for a man like Max? "If you fail to pass my test, you shall still have to marry—"

"Excellent." He grinned.

She grinned back. "But the bride will be someone of my choosing."

Max's forehead furrowed with annoyance or worse. "Of your choosing?"

"Exactly. Oh, I would not pick a serving girl or an aged crone. I would select someone suitable, although perhaps not meeting of your standards." She raised a questioning brow. "So, my lord, is it agreed?"

He considered for a moment, then nodded sharply. "Agreed. And you agree to marry me if I win."

It was her turn to hesitate. What if he did indeed win? What if she was forced to marry him? And why wasn't she more upset by the prospect? "Very well."

"It's settled, then."

"Indeed it is." She stepped to the door, pulled it open, and turned. "Good evening, Max."

"Well?" He stood unmoving in the foyer. "The test. What is it?"

"You can't expect me to declare it right now, this minute. A test of this nature requires a great deal of thought and planning. And," she waved at the street, "I cannot do that in the middle of the night with you by my side."

"I quite like the idea of being by your side in the middle of the night." He narrowed his eyes. "I warn you, Pandora, I am prone toward impatience."

"You shall have to curb that tendency."

"I think not." He smiled, a satisfied expression that did not bode well. "I shall give you twenty-four hours."

"I couldn't possibly—"

"Regardless. Twenty-four hours. No more. If you do not have your test for me devised by then . . ."

"Yes?" No, she did not care for the look on his face one bit.

"I shall consider you in default. I will pronounce myself the victor—"

Pandora gasped. "I don't think—"

"—And will at once declare myself to your father—" He started toward her.

"You would not!"

"—And will furthermore put a notice in the *Times* as to our impending nuptials." He stepped past her to the open door and stopped.

"You could not!"

"I could, I would, and I shall. It has taken me a very long time to select a wife, and now that I have found one who meets my," he cleared his throat, "specifications, I do not wish to let her go." He smiled confidently. "I always get what I want, Pandora. I am quite used to winning, and I do not intend to lose this particular match."

"It seems we are agreed on that as well, then." She couldn't resist a smug smile of her own. "Neither do I."

# Chapter 3
## *The Players are Positioned*

**"D**evil take you, Max, you are insane." Laurie pulled himself to his feet. "As your closest friend I consider it my duty, no, my responsibility, no, my obligation to try to save you from yourself." He raised his chin and squared his shoulders in a less than steady manner. "But I cannot do it alone."

"Laurie." A warning sounded in Max's voice.

Laurie ignored him and scrambled to stand on the seat of his chair, then stepped agilely onto the table by its side. He surveyed the room in the private men's club like a general taking measure of his troops. "Gentlemen, may I have your attention?"

The sparse, late night gathering of those still seeking yet another hand of cards or simply too deep in their cups to attempt to return home regarded him with idle curiosity. Laurie lifted his glass in a dramatic sweeping gesture.

"I ask you. Does this man look sane to you?"

Max groaned. Even as a youth, Laurie had had the alarming tendency to climb on furniture and address crowds, large or intimate, when he felt the occasion warranted. Apparently the state of Max's mind now called for just such a display.

"He is mad, I tell you. I taught him everything I know about women. I made him the envy of each of you here today. Why, his exploits are legion."

Max rolled his eyes toward the heavens in a silent prayer of thanks that few of the men here tonight would remember Laurie's declaration.

"Now he is ready to cast all that aside. He is contemplating," Laurie's voice lowered, "marriage."

A low murmur circled the room. Most of the men here were no doubt married, and many no doubt unhappily. Max smiled to himself. He would not share their lot.

"Why?" Laurie shook his head in a mournful manner. "His head has been turned by a pretty face and a fine figure and—"

"An excellent dowry," a gentleman called from the back of the room.

"It would take a damned sight better dowry than the one my wife brought me to get me to shackle myself to any woman again," another grumbled.

An elderly lord snorted in disdain. "I haven't had a day of peace since the day I wed."

At once the clubroom erupted in a chorus of complaints against the fairer sex.

Laurie grinned down at Max. "Behold, my friend. The happy state of wedded bliss."

"I suspect any man still here at this late hour remains because bliss is precisely what he lacks. You would need to address those who long ago left for the comforts of home for a true assessment of marriage."

"Still," Laurie gestured at the gathering, "I would wager each and every one of them is married to a women far more biddable than the one you want."

"Perhaps that is the problem." Max's gaze skimmed the room. "There is no excitement, no passion in their lives."

"If excitement and passion are what you wish, there are far less painful ways to achieve them than with marriage." Laurie stepped off the table and slid back into the depths of his chair without spilling so much as a drop of the liquor from the glass he still held. Regardless of how many times Max had witnessed this particular feat, it never failed to amaze him. Laurie pulled a long swallow and shook his head. "Pandora Effington."

"I gather you believe this is a mistake?"

"A mistake?" Laurie scoffed. "The first war with the Colonies was a mistake. The great fire of London was a mistake. But they are a picnic in Hyde Park compared to this."

Max struggled to contain his laughter. "So your answer is yes?"

"That is an understatement." Laurie glowered at Max over the rim of his glass. "Is there any hope I can talk you out of this?"

"None whatsoever. I am two-and-thirty, and it's past time to marry and start a nursery.

Besides," Max swirled the amber liquid in his glass, his voice level, "she fascinates me. I've never wanted a woman as I want Pandora."

"I think this will be a disaster of biblical proportions." Laurie's voice was grim with the specter of doom. "And allowing her to propose a test..." He lifted his glass in a half-hearted toast, "I wish you luck. You shall surely need it."

"Perhaps it's Pandora who will need it. You see, my friend," Max grinned and lifted his own snifter, "this is one game I do not intend to lose."

"You what?"

"You heard me."

"I did indeed, but even for you, Pandora, it's quite beyond imagining." Cynthia Weatherly sank onto the settee in the cluttered parlor of the grand old Effington mansion. She sprang back to her feet with a shrill shriek. "What on earth..."

"Sorry." Pandora plucked the small shard of pottery from the damask upholstery and eyed it thoughtfully. "Mycenaean. Very nice."

"To be sure," Cynthia said weakly, and felt the back of her frock for rips in the fabric.

"Cynthia, do sit down. You're quite safe now."

Cynthia inspected the settee for any other hidden threats to her backside. Gritting her teeth, she lowered herself gingerly on to the edge of the sofa and cast a suspicious glance around the room. "Is he...?"

Pandora shrugged. "I have no idea."

Cynthia nodded in long-suffering resignation and turned her attention back to Pandora, fixing her with an accusing eye. "I don't know what you could have been thinking."

Pandora pushed aside the jumble of artifacts, small chunks of statuary, and various unidentified antiquities that littered the top of a nearby table and placed the piece of pottery in the newly found space. "Frankly, I was thinking of you."

"Of me?" Cynthia's typically startled expressed grew even more pronounced.

Pandora sighed. What was she going to do with the girl? She'd taken the younger woman under her wing two years ago during Cynthia's second season. She'd hoped the friendship of an older, hopefully wiser, and definitely more assured woman could help Cynthia cope with life on the marriage mart. Unlike Pandora, Cynthia wanted nothing more than the dubious bliss of wedlock.

But Pandora's influence hadn't done a great deal of good. Cynthia refused to assert herself. And assertion was sorely needed if Cynthia was to overcome the handicap of being a— how did Max put it?—a paragon of virture. Pandora had made it her mission to find the spark hidden inside her quiet blond friend.

"Yes, your future and your happiness."

"Oh dear." Cynthia's voice was faint.

Pandora picked her way past haphazard stacks of books, large pieces of elaborately carved marble, and the assorted odds and ends that made up her parents' studies to the only chair in the room relatively uncovered by the antique debris that filled nearly every nook and cranny of her home.

She tossed the handful of scribbled notes left abandoned on the seat into a wicker basket filled with what might have looked like rocks in another household but here were probably significant remnants of a long ago civilization. A few brilliant green feathers drifted to the floor. Pandora plopped into the now vacant chair.

"I asked him what he planned to do about you. I told him he broke your heart."

"You told the Earl of Trent he broke my heart?"

Did Cynthia's porcelain complexion actually grow paler? "If you faint on me, Cynthia, I promise you I shall let you lie here among the ruins until you are an antiquity in your own right."

"No, no. I'm fine." She gripped her hands tightly together in her lap. Cynthia's tendency to swoon was one of her more annoying habits. However, in this particular circumstance, her faint might well be justified. "How could you, Pandora?"

"It was not at all difficult." Pandora shifted uncomfortably in her chair at the memory of last night and how very little of the discussion had been about her friend. "Max has been paying you a great deal of notice this season."

Cynthia's eyes widened. "Are you certain?"

"I am."

"Well, what did he say?" Excellent. Wasn't that even a bit of color in Cynthia's cheeks?

"Actually, he denied it."

Cynthia's expression fell.

"I am sorry, dearest," Pandora said quickly.

"But I am still convinced of his interest in you."

"He was being polite. Nothing more." Cynthia slumped back on the settee. "I suspect it's past time you and I faced some rather unpleasant facts. I am nearly two-and-twenty. This is my fourth season—"

"But I am four-and-twenty and this is my seventh season and I do not consider those facts at all unpleasant."

"For you, they're not. You've never had the mildest interest in marriage. Your father has settled a handsome income on you. You have been doing exactly as you've wished ever since you came out in society. You're extremely pretty and very witty and you don't seem to care who knows you're clever."

"I have always thought a woman should be intelligent and I see no reason to hide what I consider an attribute."

"I know." Cynthia heaved a heartfelt sigh. "You're unique. Practically a legend."

"Am I?" Pandora smiled with pleasure. "How delightful."

"Most women wouldn't think so."

"I am not most women."

"That's exactly the point." A rare glimmer of determination sparked in Cynthia's eye. "I am very much like most women. Not unique at all. At least, not in the ways that count. I am too tall and too thin. My complexion is far paler even than fashion decrees. I have a rather sickly nature and a timid disposition."

"Nonsense. You're quite lovely. We shall simply have to—"

"Pandora, stop." Cynthia's tone was surprisingly firm. "Don't you see? Lord Trent is used to clever, sophisticated, beautiful women. Why, the man is a rake."

"A rogue, a scoundrel, and a beast." Pandora nodded.

Cynthia shook her fair head. "I'd hardly go that far. He has a sizable reputation, but given his title and wealth he is considered quite a catch. A man like the earl could never be seriously attracted to someone like me."

"Of course he could."

"Put that clever mind of yours to work for a moment, Pandora. Does that make any sense at all?"

"The nature of attraction is not at all sensible," Pandora said primly.

"Be that as it may, I suspect that if indeed Lord Trent was paying attention to me, it was his way of getting to you."

"To me?" Surprise and more than a touch of satisfaction coursed through her.

"For a women who is so proud of her intelligence, you certainly seem lacking in it today," Cynthia said with an unaccustomed sharpness. "How many proposals have you had?"

"A few."

Cynthia raised a brow.

Pandora lifted her shoulder in a casual shrug. "Very well, dozens."

"And how many have you accepted?"

"None, of course."

"And what do all those suitors have in common?"

"Despair and disappointment, I suppose." Pandora grinned.

"Beyond that."

"I have no idea."

"Every one of those discarded admirers wanted you much more than you wanted them. You are always the fox and they are always the hounds. Already Lord Trent has turned the tables. You approached him."

"But I wished to talk about you."

"Regardless, you ended up agreeing to this ridiculous game." Cynthia smiled in an altogether too smug manner. "He turned you into the hound. *You* went to him. *You* started it."

"Well, perhaps I did, but I had no intention . . ."

Or had she?

Max was indeed nearly the only eligible man in all of London who had not paid her heed. Of course, she had been aware of him through the years. Who wouldn't be? The man cut a wide swath through society. She could even vaguely recall seeing him during her first season. Dark and reckless, with eyes that smoldered and a swagger that proclaimed he was intent on having a far better time than he could expect from a green girl.

In recent years, perhaps, she had noticed him with increasing frequency. Wondering why he had not married. Why some charming young thing with a determined mother and an impressive dowry had not snatched him up long ago. Wondering what he was really like and what he really wanted. He had seemed no more interested in her than she was in him.

And why on earth not? The question nagged at her each time she happened to see the dashing Earl of Trent across the room at a ball or riding in the park or kissing the hand of her dearest friend. Was Pandora somehow not to his liking? Not lovely enough or wealthy enough? Even if her parents were a bit unusual, their ancestry was impeccable. Why had he never cast his attention in her direction?

He himself said he wanted a wife with fire in her eyes and spirit in her soul. Who better fit that description than the Hellion of Grosvenor Square? Who and who alone could meet the requirements of the rakish earl as perfectly as if they'd been designed with her in mind?

The answer slammed into her with the vengeance of a summer storm. How could she have been so blind? She rose to her feet, a touch of awe in her voice. "By the gods, the man tricked me!"

Cynthia's face took on its familiar dazed-rabbit expression. "How?"

"Never mind how." She flicked a dismissive hand. It was all so clear now. She pushed away the persistent thought that last night's confrontation was due as much to her own desire to have an encounter with a man who'd never sought her out as any overt effort on his part. "He is a beast. And I'm Dora. A hound! Bloody hell."

"Pandora!" Cynthia clapped a hand over her mouth.

"Sorry." Pandora grimaced. She'd used the occasional satisfying obscenity since she was twelve, when she had dropped a small bronze statue on her foot. "I shall not let him get away with this."

"Away with what?"

"You said it yourself. He was flirting with

you to attract me. That's truly vile."

"He hardly put any effort into it," Cynthia said under her breath. "I hadn't even noticed."

"I did, and that's all he wanted. The scoundrel."

"But why—"

"Because I'm perfect for him." Pandora glared at her friend. "I'm everything he wants in a wife. Everything he's ever wanted."

"But I thought—"

"And this test nonsense! Oh, he is clever all right. Wanting to be my hero—"

"He wants to be your hero?" Cynthia's expression brightened with delight. "How romantic."

"How devious!" Pandora scoffed. " 'Let me prove it to you,' he said. 'Test me,' he said. And I believed him. Oh, I am a fool."

"But I thought you got to devise the test?"

"That's what makes it so much more appalling. He wants to make me think this is all my idea. He's an intelligent beast, I'll grant him that." Pandora shook her head slowly. "If I can't devise a way to outwit the blasted man by tonight, I'll be the next Countess of Trent before you can snap your fingers."

She stalked past a bronze figure of some god or other, skirted a large earthenware urn, and stepped over an untidy mound of loose papers to reach the fireplace and the magnificent Chinese gong positioned to one side. A wooden hammer dangled by a leather thong. Today, it was particularly gratifying to lift the matching wooden hammer, haul back, and let it fly. The thunderous *bong* echoed through the house.

The double doors to the huge receiving hall

swung open almost at once. Peters stepped into the room. "Miss?"

"Tea, please." Peters never failed to amaze Pandora. He was the quintessential proper British butler, and yet he refused to abandon the Effingtons' strange abode even for tempting offers from households boasting bigger incomes or loftier titles.

The butler nodded and turned to leave, stooping quickly in a motion so fluid it took Pandora a moment to realize just what he'd done and why.

"Oh, botheration. Cynthia, perhaps you'd better—"

A small blur of greenish-blue soared into the room, diving low over Cynthia's head. She screamed and lunged off the settee to the relative safety of the floor, upsetting a precarious pile of books and overturning a box of pottery fragments in the process. The crash of the volumes and clank of the crockery clashed with the distinct sound of the poor girl's dress ripping and the unmistakable *meow* of a cat.

"—Duck?" Pandora said in a faint voice.

"How on earth can you people live with that—that—that *creature* running amuck in your home?" Cynthia crouched amid the ruin on the floor.

"He doesn't run amuck. He simply enjoys a certain amount of freedom. Hercules." At once the parrot settled on her hand.

Cynthia scrambled back onto the sofa. "That bird hates me."

"Nonsense. He loves people, don't you, sweeting?" Pandora turned to the gong and Hercules hopped onto the crossbar. "Why, he practically saved Father's life on one of his trips to Greece. Distracted a thief intent on Father's purse."

"The bird's a vicious menace," Cynthia said under her breath.

Hercules cocked his head and fixed her with a single beady, black eye. "Meow, auk."

Cynthia glared back. "And stupid as well. He thinks he's a cat."

"He's just a bit confused."

Cynthia examined the tear in her dress, her voice low. "He should be roasted for supper."

Hercules meowed.

"Cynthia! Hercules is very much a member of the family."

"I daresay Lord Trent won't appreciate him once you're married."

"I am not going to marry that man!"

"Of course you are." Cynthia stared her straight in the eye. "You want to marry him."

"I most certainly do not." Pandora lifted her chin in indignation. "I should rather be boiled alive by tribes of ill-mannered cannibals in the South Seas than marry him."

"Oh? You've never risked marriage before with any man. And," Cynthia paused in an unusually dramatic manner, "you call him Max."

"Max is his name." Even as she said it she was aware of the impropriety.

"Everyone else calls him Trent."

A sinking sensation settled in Pandora's stomach. "I don't see—"

"You call him Max."

"I simply like the sound of it. There is nothing more to it than that."

Cynthia smirked. "Except that you want him to win."

"I do not," Pandora said with a lofty air. Cynthia couldn't possibly be right. Oh, certainly Max—Lord Trent—was intriguing. And she did have an odd desire to know him better. And the thought of marriage to him wasn't quite as repulsive as the thought of marriage to anyone else. Still . . . she sank into a chair. "And I shall prove it with a test he will never pass."

"You haven't much time."

She sighed. "I have to think of something . . ."

Hercules preened on the gong.

". . . Something clever . . ."

Hercules swung upside down and dangled from the crossbar.

". . . Something inspired . . ."

Hercules meowed.

"Hercules, be still." Pandora cast the bird a threatening glare. "I will admit, sometimes he is annoying, but my father has always called him his hero. That's why he named him Hercules, after the Greek . . ." Pandora caught her breath, ". . . hero."

Cynthia eyed her cautiously. "What are you thinking?"

"That's it! I've got it!" Pandora laughed with the sheer delight of victory. "The perfect test. He may well give up before he even starts."

"It won't kill him, will it?" Cynthia's forehead furrowed in an anxious frown. "Or ruin him financially? Or destroy his good name?"

"His life, his finances, and his honor should

remain intact. But his arrogance—" Pandora cast her a wicked grin, "—that's another matter."

"Are you certain you really wish to defeat him?"

"Absolutely." Now that she realized how he had manipulated her, she could not allow him to win. "It's a matter of principle."

"Oh dear." Cynthia's voice was faint. "I should probably pray for the poor man."

"Indeed you should." Pandora settled deeper against the back of the chair and smiled sweetly. "He shall need it."

# Chapter 4
## *The Gauntlet is Thrown*

"**W**hat is this?" Max drew his brows together and studied the neatly written page.

"It's your test." Pandora's voice was light.

He'd been supremely confident when she'd asked him to meet her in the library, away from the crush of guests at Lady Harvey's rout. Now . . . Max looked up from the paper and stared at her. "*This* is the test?"

"Indeed it is, my lord." She was a perfect image of charming innocence. Judging by the sheet in his hand, it was a forged likeness.

"Surely you are not serious?"

She tilted her lovely head in feigned surprise. "Surely I am."

"But this," he waved the sheet at her, "this is impossible!"

"Then you concede defeat? You forfeit the game and I win? With all the benefits due the victor?" A charming smile played on her lips, but a spark of wicked triumph shone in her eye. Damn the woman, anyway. He had never even considered going through this kind of trouble for a mere female before. "My lord?"

Pandora Effington was no mere female.

"No, I am not conceding defeat." His words were slow and measured. "I simply did not expect anything like this."

She shrugged. "You did seek a challenge."

"A challenge is one thing. This is something else altogether. This is a legend straight from your father's studies."

"Indeed it is."

"But it's—"

"That's right, my lord, it's for a hero."

"I scarcely think—"

"You said you wanted to be my hero." Her gaze meshed with his. "Didn't you mean it?"

"I meant it, but—"

"And you said test me. I remember that distinctly. A test of my own choosing." Challenge rang in her voice. "Do you wish to rescind your words?"

"No." His tone was sharp and firm.

Surprise flitted across her face, followed by a touch of unease. Did the chit really think he'd give up without a fight? He smiled and the smug expression on her face faded slightly. Confidence again surged within him.

"Not at all. We have made a bargain—and I, for one, intend to hold to my part of it." He quirked a brow. "I assume you are still willing to adhere to your agreement?"

"Of course. But you can't win, you know."

"Oh really? Why not?"

"Well, did you read it?" She stepped to his side and plucked the sheet from his hand.

"I read enough. If I remember my lessons accurately, these are the labors of Hercules."

"The twelve labors of Hercules, to be exact. They are not easy."

"I never expected your test to be—"

"I do hope I am not interrupting." Laurie pushed open the door.

Max sighed. "You are. Now, if you don't mind—"

"Oh, but I do." Laurie's voice lowered. "I must speak with you on a matter of the utmost urgency."

Pandora glanced up from the list in her hand with a polite smile fading almost at once to a puzzled expression.

"Allow me to introduce—"

"Not now, Max," Laurie said sharply. "We have to talk. At once."

"Very well." Max turned to Pandora. "If you will excuse me?"

Pandora waved him off and returned her attention to the test.

Max nodded to Laurie and they stepped into the hall, Pandora's muttered voice trailing after them. "The first test alone could well kill him."

Max grinned. She was concerned for his safety, or perhaps she preferred not to have his blood on her hands. Either way, it was a good sign.

"Now then, Laurie." Max raised a brow. "What is so urgent?"

Laurie grabbed his elbow and steered him down the hall toward the back of the house, his pace brisk, his step resolute. "I have given your problem a great deal of thought. And I have a solution."

"I do not have a problem."

"You may not have realized it yet, but you most certainly do." Laurie pushed open a side door leading to a servants' hall and stepped inside. "Follow me."

"What on earth are you up to?"

"I'm saving you, Max." His voice was grim.

Max bit back a laugh. He couldn't remember the last time he'd seen his friend quite so determined. The least he could do was play along for now. "Saving me from what?"

"Marriage, of course. And the Hellion. Separately, a fate worse than death. Together—" He shuddered. "Your only salvation lies in escape."

"Sounds rather cowardly to me," Max said mildly.

"There is nothing cowardly about a man's efforts to save his life. And I have a plan." Resolve furrowed Laurie's forehead and he pushed past a footman in the narrow passageway.

"Have you, indeed?" Max struggled to keep a straight face. Just how far would this rescue of Laurie's go?

"Everything is arranged." Laurie nodded and hurried along the hall, turning abruptly to the right and pulling to a stop before an outside entry, obviously for servants and deliveries. He yanked open the door and nodded for Max to precede him. "Come along, Max, I have a carriage waiting."

"Where exactly are we going?" Max stepped past him into the night. A closed carriage waited beside a shadowed gate.

"I'm not entirely certain. I thought I should leave the final destination up to you."

"Bloody decent of you," Max murmured.

"I checked this afternoon. There are at least three ships due to sail within the hour. One should suit to get you as far away from the Hellion as possible."

The driver opened the carriage door.

"What are you waiting for?" Laurie gestured at the open door. "Get in."

"I think not."

"Well, think again, man!" Laurie grabbed his sleeve and tried to pull him into the carriage. "You can go to the continent. Or India. Better yet, America. I'll go with you. We'll have a grand time. Recreate the days of our youth. Think of the adventures we shall have, the excitement. And the women, Max, think of the women. Dark-skinned and exotic, or fair-haired and delicate—"

Max jerked his arm free and smoothed the wrinkled fabric of his jacket. This scheme of Laurie's was rapidly losing its humor. "I think I have had quite en—"

"You'd forget about her in no time, and she'd never track you down."

"I'd rather want her to track me down."

"Pandora Effington?" Laurie scoffed. "You have obviously lost your mind. As your oldest friend, it is up to me to save you in spite of yourself." Laurie pulled his shoulders back and stared down his long nose, no mean feat, as he was an inch or two shorter than Max. "I do not have the same experience in warfare as you do, but I have had to use firearms on occasion. I am not without some experience on the dueling field."

"You've yet to kill a man. I don't believe you've ever even inflicted a wound."

"I assure you, that was always my intention. Nonetheless, I am armed, and if you do not get in the carriage, I will not hesitate to shoot you in my effort to save you."

"That seems to be a common desire lately." Max sighed and held up his arms in a gesture of surrender. "Very well, shoot me."

"Shoot you?"

"If you must. I'm not getting in the carriage. I'm not leaving the country. And I'm not giving up my pursuit of Miss Effington."

"Bloody hell, Max, I could never shoot you. I did hope, however, just this once, you would see things my way." Laurie crossed his arms over his chest and slouched against the carriage. "I fail to understand any of this. I told you the woman is trouble. Equal to flood, famine, pestilence. No." He narrowed his eyes in a sinister manner. "Flood, famine, and pestilence pale in comparison to Pandora Effington. Of all the females in the world, why have you set your sights on the one guaranteed to wreak havoc with your life and no doubt break your heart?"

"She won't break my heart." Max grinned. "And a life of her wreaking havoc sounds like an interesting way to spend the rest of my days."

"It's not just your life that will be in ruins, you know. Think about me. Why, I shall hardly have any fun at all without you along." Laurie brightened. "Remember the widow of that Italian count and those two energetic actresses—"

"Twins." Max chuckled. "We did enjoy ourselves."

"It was bloody glorious. And it can be again."

"It will be. For me. With her."

"I knew my attempt to bring you to your senses was futile." Laurie heaved a heavy sigh. "Yet I had hoped . . ."

"And I do appreciate your efforts, old man, and your concern, but it is misplaced. I have nothing to fear from Miss Effington . . ." Max turned to reenter the house and smiled to himself.

*And a great deal to gain.*

"I assume, given the length of your absence, you have returned to concede defeat." Pandora sat behind the large desk in Lady Harvey's library, the test on the polished mahogany surface before her. "I am prepared to be gracious in victory, however—"

"I concede nothing of the sort." Max smiled pleasantly and crossed the room to one of the floor-to-ceiling bookcases lining the walls. "Although I do admit it will indeed be a challenge."

"I'd scarce call it a mere challenge." Her brows pulled together. "Most of these could well do you in."

"Then I shall have to take care." He kept his voice light and struggled to hold back a grin at the annoyance in her manner.

"I don't think you have given this the

proper amount of thought." She drummed her
fingers on the desk. Irritation underlay her
words. "You have to best the lion of Nemea—"

He examined the volumes in an effort to
look as though he hadn't a care but watched
her out of the corner of his eye. "Where is Nemea, anyway?"

"Somewhere in Greece," she snapped. "It
scarcely matters, a lion is a lion."

"I just wondered . . ."

"And here, you have to defeat a Hydra."
She shook the page at him. "That's a beast
with nine heads."

He shrugged. "That will be awkward.
Damned hard to find a Hydra in London today."

"Max!" She rose to her feet and grit her
teeth. "You are not taking this at all seriously."

"No?" Max favored her with his best innocent gaze.

"No! Look at what I'm asking you to do.
Why, in animals alone, this requires you to
stock a small zoo."

"I hadn't thought of it that way." Why was
she so overwrought? The selection of Hercules' labors was her own brilliant idea. Did she
now regret it?

"Then perhaps you should." She pursed her
lips and picked up the paper. "You have to
catch a deer with gold horns, best a nasty boar,
capture a bull from Crete and cattle—"

"Cattle as in horses, or cattle as in roasted
beef?"

"It just says cattle!" She shot him a quick

glare. "You have to tame mares that eat men. Man-eating horses, Max."

"I daresay that will be difficult."

"Difficult? Hah! Impossible."

"Still," he pulled a book from the shelf and paged through it, "a bargain is a bargain."

"Max." She groaned. "We're only halfway through. There's the cleaning of the Augean Stables—"

"Ugh." Max shuddered. "Nasty chore, cleaning stables."

"—Eliminating the Stymphalian birds—"

"Is that like a sparrow, do you think?"

"—Defeating a three-headed hound who guards the gates to Hades, and rescuing a friend from the Chair of Forgetfulness—"

"I should think forgetfulness would be appreciated down there."

"Wait," she studied the page, "those last two are actually part of the same labor."

"That certainly relieves my mind. I was beginning to worry."

She ignored him. "You have to retrieve the girdle of the Queen of the Amazons—"

Max glanced at her with a wicked grin. Pandora looked up from the sheet, a note of sarcasm in her voice. "Perhaps that one is not as dangerous as the others."

"One never knows." Max's grin widened. "There could be hazards I wouldn't dare imagine."

"No doubt," she said wryly. "And finally, you have to find the golden apples of Hesperides."

"Is that it, then?"

"Yes." She hesitated as if coming to a decision, pulled a deep breath, and stepped around the desk. "And I apologize. It wasn't at all sporting of me. No mortal man could possibly do these things. I simply wanted to beat you, and this seemed the easiest way to do it."

"I see." He studied her for a moment. "I gather this means you forfeit the game."

"Forfeit?" Surprise flashed across her face. "Why, not at all."

"But if you do not have a test for me . . ."

"I have a test, it's just not reasonable. I can devise something else," she said quickly.

"I think not." He snapped the book closed, replaced it on the shelf and turned to face her. "We agreed that if you did not have a test for me by tonight, then you lost."

"I have a test," she said sharply.

"But you don't want to put me to it."

"I don't want to see you killed."

"Why, Pandora?" He stepped toward her.

She stood her ground and stared up at him. "It's rude to attempt to murder a man who has done little to deserve it."

"I don't believe you." He moved closer.

"It is rude." She huffed. "Ask anyone."

"Not about that. About why you don't want me to attempt your test." There were but a few meager inches between them.

"Guilt, Max. I do not want to be responsible for your death. There's nothing more to it than that. Why, I would have the same concern about a dog in the street." Defiance flickered in her blue eyes. Deep and azure and entrancing eyes.

"Would you?" He could see the pulse beat

at the base of her throat. "I still don't believe you." And her scent. What was it? Some kind of exotic flower? Some type of rare spice? He couldn't quite place it, but it seemed to seep into his very soul.

"I would. I am exceedingly fond of animals." Her voice was faint, as if she too knew their spoken words had little to do with what they were saying.

"No doubt." His gaze drifted to her lips, full and ripe and the color of summer berries. She bit her bottom lip and his stomach tightened.

"And that alone is reason to halt this nonsense." Her breath seemed to come a little faster, as if she couldn't get enough air.

"Perhaps. But it's not your reason." His gaze met hers.

"It's not?" Her words were a bare whisper.

"No." He stared into her eyes and knew he was lost, knew they were both lost. He could take her in his arms at this moment and she would not resist. He could make her his. Now. Without the nonsense of this ridiculous test, this silly game.

No. He could not allow her to withdraw her challenge. It would be tantamount to failure, and he could not, would not, accept failure.

"No, my dear." He drew a long calming breath. "You're simply afraid I will win."

The burgeoning desire in her eyes vanished and fire snapped in its place. She stepped away from him. "I most certainly am not. You cannot possibly succeed."

"I see." He considered her thoughtfully. "In that case, you must be afraid I'll lose."

"Of course you'll lose!"

"But I should then end up wed to someone else. And *that* is what you're afraid of. That, and only that, is the reason you do not want me to undertake your test."

Astonishment washed across her face.

"Nothing to say? I didn't think so. It is in your hands now. Either I attempt your test, risking my life in the process—which I am more than willing to do—or you withdraw it. In which case I shall consider us betrothed and procure a special license tomorrow for a wedding as soon as possible."

Pandora's fists clenched at her sides. "Why, you arrogant—"

"Beast?"

Her eyes narrowed. The line of her tempting mouth was firm and set. "Good luck, my lord. I suspect you will need it even more than Hercules did."

"I daresay it's possible. Although I believe my reward is much greater than his was."

Suspicion colored her words. "What do you mean?"

"Hercules' prize was merely immortality. Mine," his gaze trapped hers, his voice intense, "is you."

She stared at him for a long moment as if unsure of his sincerity. "You do turn a pretty phrase, Max."

"Thank you." He shrugged in a modest manner.

"Regardless, our discussion is at an end. I shall wait to hear from you." She paused, then pulled a deep breath. "I do not wish to marry you, Max. Nothing will change that."

"I understand." He gazed at her solemnly,

struggling not to smile at the sincerity in her tone.

"I would prefer, however, if you managed not to get yourself killed. The guilt, you know. Nothing more."

He nodded. "Nothing at all."

She held out the list of labors. "Do not forget this."

"Never." He stepped closer and took the paper, his hand lingering near hers. Once again her presence surrounded him. Intoxicating. Captivating. She gazed up at him, eyes wide with apprehension and desire.

"Max?" Her voice rang with a dry note. She moistened her lips in a nervous gesture that snapped something inside him.

"Damnation, Hellion." He pulled her into his arms and pressed his lips to hers. She hesitated, then her arms wrapped around his neck. She tasted of sweet champagne and promises and all the flavors he'd ever loved. He shuddered with the unmistakable knowledge that she would fit with him as though they were made one for the other. Destined to be together.

But not tonight. He pulled his lips from hers.

She gasped. "By the gods, Max. What—I—you—we—"

He laughed in a shaky voice and relaxed his hold on her. Still, she did not step out of his embrace. He drew back and grinned down at her.

"I believe, Hellion, we just sealed our bargain."

# Chapter 5
## *A Point is Scored*

A small pool of light cast by the brace of candles held by her father illuminated the gathering at the foot of the stairs. Peters stood beside her parents, apparently explaining whatever it was that had routed them all from their beds.

"What is it?" Pandora started down the stairs, clutching her wrapper tighter around her. At once three pairs of eyes turned in her direction and she stopped short. At least she hadn't done anything to cause yet another middle-of-the-night uproar. This time, her conscience was clear.

"Come down here, my dear," her father said, in his most authoritative manner.

Her heart sank. Her conscience wasn't that clear. She drew a deep breath and descended the stairs.

"Harry. Grace." Pandora reached the bottom and approached her parents with all the dignity she could gather. She didn't have to look at Peters to know he gazed imploringly at the heavens when she called her parents by their given names. But Lord and Lady Harold had very distinct convictions when it came to child rearing. They believed if child and parent were friends as well as relations, there would be much more harmony for all concerned.

"Pandora, darling," Grace said brightly. "It appears you have a delivery."

"Most thoughtless," Harry grumbled. "Damned inconvenient. Bothersome business, middle-of-the-night deliveries."

Peters handed her a small box. A note of censure underlay his words. "A rather loathsome boy brought this, Miss."

"How very exciting." Grace's eyes gleamed in the dim light.

Pandora pulled the end of the cord tied around the box and noted with annoyance a slight tremble in her hands. Curiosity, perhaps, nothing more. She pulled off the lid and stared.

It was a brooch: gold and delicate, fashioned in the shape of a hunting horn.

"This accompanied the parcel." Peters passed her a card. It bore the crest of the Earl of Trent and four words written in a strong, bold hand.

*"My dear, your horn,"* she read aloud.

"Whatever does it mean, darling?" Excitement sounded in her mother's voice.

"I really have no idea." She flipped the card over and read: *Test number three.* "Test number three? How could this . . ."

*You have to catch a deer with gold horns.*

She sucked in her breath. "It's a horn! A gold horn. He's calling me 'dear,' and this is my horn, therefore this is the gold horn of a dear. What nerve the man has!"

She crumpled the card in her hand. "He shall not get away with this. Peters, did the boy who brought this say anything about it?"

"Only that he was instructed to deliver it and make as much noise as possible in the process." Peters raised a brow. "I believe he also muttered something about his employer being roused out of bed and made to open his shop."

"Aha! I knew it." She stalked to and fro across the foyer. "If Max thinks he can toss his wealth around to win this game he's sadly mistaken."

"What game? Who is this 'Max'?" Harry said to his wife.

"Max is Maximillian Wells." Pandora paused for the inevitable reaction.

"The Earl of Trent?" Grace's eyes widened in surprise.

"Who?" Puzzlement rang in Harry's voice.

"Trent, darling," Grace said. "He is one of the most eligible men in the country. His title is distinguished, although I've always thought his mother a bit stuffy, his fortune impressive, and," she cast her daughter a wicked grin, "he has the look of Apollo about him."

"Grace!" Pandora glared.

"Bravo, darling." Grace beamed. "I have never been prouder."

"There is nothing to be proud of!"

"I quite disagree." Grace plucked the box

from her daughter's hand and picked up the brooch, studying it with the expert eye of a collector or a jewel thief. "This is lovely. Excellent craftsmanship. I would expect nothing less from the Earl of Trent." She passed it back, her voice soft. "What game are you playing with this man, Dora?"

"He wants to marry me." The horn glittered in her palm, reflecting the candlelight almost as if it had a life of its own. As if a touch of magic lingered amid the warm glow of its golden surface. As if it were indeed made to call restless seekers to the hunt. A hunt charged with promises of adventure and romance.

Harry groaned. "Damnation, girl, not again. What are you going to do with this one?"

"Do?" Pandora started and shook her head to clear the distant sound of a hunting horn from her ear.

"Dora, sweet." Grace grabbed her daughter's hands and gazed into her eyes. "Tell us about the game."

Pandora drew a deep breath. "Well, I'm not quite sure how it started. One minute I was telling him what I wanted in a husband—"

"I can tell you what *I* want in your husband," Harry said under his breath.

"—And he said I wanted a hero—"

"A hero?" Harry snorted.

"—And he could be my hero—"

"Utter nonsense," Harry muttered.

"—And challenged me to test him—"

Harry groaned. "Man's a fool."

"—And if he won I'd marry him and if he

lost I'd choose his bride. And naturally I wanted to win—"

"Lord help us all," Harry said morosely.

"—So the test I gave him . . ." She paused and chewed her bottom lip.

"Yes, darling, do go on." Grace nodded her encouragement.

Pandora braced herself and released her words in one, long, fast gasp. *"Igavehimthelaborsof Hercules."*

Grace gasped. "Dora, you didn't."

"Did what?" Harry's face was turning a definite shade of frustration red.

"Do you really think that's quite sporting of you?" Grace's tone carried a chastising note.

Pandora jerked her chin up. "He asked for it."

"Asked for what?" Harry's roar echoed through the house.

"Harry." Grace directed her voice to her husband but pinned her daughter with a steady gaze. Pandora resisted the urge to squirm. "Your daughter has set this young man a test no mortal could possibly master: the twelve labors of Hercules."

"You didn't?" Harry's mouth dropped open in astonishment.

"Well, yes, actually I did. However, I also gave him the option of calling the entire thing off." She gritted her teeth at the memory. "But he said he would consider that a forfeit on my part and he would win. I could not allow that."

Grace shook her head. "But, darling, this—"

"You heard the girl, Grace, she couldn't allow it." Harry laughed. "By Jove, she's an Eftington, all right. Most stubborn, pigheaded family in the whole of England."

"Thank you, Harry." Pandora grinned.

"It is not something to brag of." Grace folded her arms over her chest. "The man could be very well be killed."

Pandora snorted in disdain. "I'd wager the bloodshed at the jeweler's shop alone was impressive."

"Dora," Grace said sharply. "Hercules had the help of the Gods. Lord Trent—"

"In point of fact, Grace," Harry said in his most scholarly manner, "Hercules received no help whatsoever from the gods. However, as the son of Zeus—"

"Hush, Harry." Grace considered her offspring. "I gather you do want him to lose."

"I most certainly do." Pandora nodded firmly, ignoring the odd twinge that stabbed through her. "If given a choice to marry Max or be torn limb from limb by wild animals in the jungles of Africa, I should choose the beasts gladly. And I'd go to my death with a smile on my face and a song of thanksgiving on my lips."

"She doesn't want him." Harry heaved a resigned sigh. He could see the day of his daughter safely wed drawing farther and farther away.

"Very well, then," Grace said, a considering note in her voice. She brushed her lips along her daughter's cheek, then turned to her husband. "Come along, dear. It is high time to retire."

"Past time," he grumbled, and headed to-

ward the stairs. "Past time she found a husband, too, isn't it?"

Grace took his arm and they started up.
"That's why you gave her all that money, my
love, so she could marry whom she wanted,
when she wanted."

"Even so . . ." The couple climbed the stairs,
their figures blending with the shadows but
their words still clear. "She calls him Max,
Grace. Highly improper, I'd say."

"That's the other reason you gave her
money, so she could do as she pleased."

Harry scoffed. "Damned intimate, though."

"I've always called you Harry." Their voices
grew fainter.

"That's different."

"Oh?" A bare moment later a peal of her
mother's laughter rang out in the hall.
"Harry!"

Pandora glanced at the butler, trying his
best not to smile, then gazed at the horn in her
hand. "Peters."

Peters sighed in resignation. "Beg pardon,
Miss, but if we are to have one of our late-
night discussions on what you shall do with
your life, I shall have to summon Cook and
Mrs. Barnes. If they are not included, meals
will more than likely be served raw or black-
ened, and Mrs. Barnes will command her parlor maids not only to clean the collections of
your parents, but to organize them as well."
He shuddered. "Do you remember the last
time?"

"Of course," she said faintly.

"Therefore, I would suggest—"

"Never mind, Peters." She sighed. "I understand."

He hesitated for a moment, then rolled his gaze toward the ceiling, as if even his words were against his better judgment. "You like this one."

"I *don't*—"

"You do. It is quite obvious that you regard this man differently than the others. Do not let your competitive nature or your pride overrule your instincts." A bare hint of a smile seemed to light in Peters' eye. "And do try not to kill him."

"No doubt Max can take care of himself," she said dryly.

"Can you?"

"Of course." Pandora tossed her head with a confidence that was perhaps a bit less than she'd had only a few days ago. Before a mere kiss had rocked her senses and gray had become a mesmerizing shade for eyes. "I daresay he'll fail both miserably and quickly."

"And that is what you want?"

"Yes," she said firmly, then heaved a heartfelt sigh. "I only really want what they have, Peters." She glanced toward the stairway, a wistful note in her voice. "Is that so very wrong?"

"No, Miss. It's simply extremely difficult to find."

Her gaze dropped to the tiny horn in her hand, gold winking with the flicker of the light. The metal as precious and rare as the affection shared between her parents. Love, actually, if the truth were told. The idea of a marriage without love, the kind so common among her friends, empty of the joy she'd witnessed all her life, terrified her somewhere in the depths of her soul. Bargain or no bargain, she would marry no man without love.

She flashed the butler a weary smile and turned toward the stairs. "Good evening, Peters."

She climbed the wide staircase and barely noted her upward progress. Max hadn't mentioned love in his list of requirements for a wife. Of course, a man like him was more used to baser emotions—lust primarily, she suspected—in his dealings with women. He obviously wanted her. She moistened her lips and the memory of his mouth covering hers fired a hot flush up her cheeks and a tremor through her blood.

*What do you want?*

The question halted her in mid-step. Two days ago she would have said she wanted life to be adventurous and exciting. She would have said she wanted independence and the freedom to do exactly as she pleased. And she would have said she wanted someday to share with a man what her parents shared.

Had anything at all changed since then? Or had everything?

How very odd. Right now, she could think of but one answer to the question of what she wanted. The only thing Pandora Effington, the Hellion of Grosvenor Square, really and truly wanted.

She wanted a hero.

# Chapter 6
## A *Canny Strategy*

～⌒のⅭ⌒～

**"S**ix days. It's been *six full days*," Pandora said over her shoulder, making her way up the great staircase, through the mad crush that always marked Lady Locksley's galas. "Nearly an entire week."

She smiled and nodded as she progressed up the broad stairs, tossing a pleasant comment to a young lord here and waving a flirtatious flutter of her fan to a noble gentleman there, all the while moving upward relentlessly with a single-minded determination. And all the while searching the crowd for the one figure she wished most of all to see.

"Pandora." Cynthia's voice trailed behind her.

"I tell you, Cynthia, if I am to be a hound, I shall be a good one. And a good, determined hound will never fail to flush out its quarry."

If Max was here (and if he wasn't, he was the only one in town not directly in her path at the moment) his height alone would make him stand out above the crowd of heads. His confidence might well raise him a few inches more.

"I can scarcely keep up with you."

"It's not easy to flush a fox," she said grimly. "I cannot do it properly if I am forced to stay in one place."

Lady Locksley was a typical hostess who did not consider her entertainments successful unless the crowd was large enough to prohibit movement and prevent the breathing of air that had not already been exhaled by any number of celebrants. It was uncommonly stuffy and overly warm, and tomorrow would be considered a high point of the season for precisely those reasons.

"Pandora, if you do not slow down at once I shall be forced to swoon right here on the spot!"

Pandora stopped and swiveled so quickly that Cynthia nearly stumbled into her. "You'll do no such thing!"

"I will, I swear it." A stubborn light gleamed in her friend's eye. Pandora noted it with a measure of satisfaction. Perhaps Cynthia was finally developing the fortitude needed to navigate the tumultuous waters of society. "I shall collapse on this stairway with half of London above me and the other half below if you do not explain yourself right now."

"Very well." Pandora hooked her arm through the younger woman's and urged her upward. "The first thing one learns when one hunts is to give the hounds the freedom to pursue their quarry."

Cynthia stared in confusion. "What hounds? What quarry?"

"You said it yourself. I am the hound and—"

"Trent is the fox." Understanding dawned on Cynthia's face.

"Exactly."

They reached the top of the wide staircase and turned into the gallery. Here, too, scarcely an inch of space remained unoccupied. Pandora quelled her impatience and managed to greet one and all with a fair amount of feigned charm and a well-practiced smile. She had learned well the lessons taught through seven seasons: leave every lady with the impression of friendship, and each and every gentleman with an unrealistic hope of much more.

The few moments it took to reach the balustrade overlooking the crowd below stretched to a lifetime, but at long last Pandora reached the vantage point. She scanned the crowd, assuming her gaze would light on Max like a pigeon on a statue.

"Do you see him, Cynthia?"

Cynthia gazed downward, gripped the stone railing and closed her eyes. Her voice was weak. "I don't think so."

Pandora shot her a quick glance. Her porcelain complexion was perhaps a shade more porcelain than a moment ago. And just a touch green.

"I am sorry, I quite forgot about your fear of heights." Guilt twinged through her. "I never would have made you look over the edge had I remembered. Here." Gently she grabbed her friend's shoulders and directed her steps until she was a few feet back from the edge, settling her against a column that hid the view of the ballroom. "Now you may look." Cynthia's eyes flickered open. "Better?"

"Yes. Thank you." Cynthia heaved a heavy sigh. "I always feel I am somehow disappointing you. You never seem to be cowed by anything."

"Nonsense. You are my friend, and I don't care about your fears or weaknesses. They are not at all uncommon, you know." Pandora studied her for a moment. Cynthia was indeed her truest friend. Oh, she had any number of acquaintances and a host of Effington relatives, but Cynthia was the one person with whom she shared her secrets. Ironic, to realize she had befriended the girl to help her, when Pandora herself had gained so much from their relationship.

"Even I have my limits. Personally, I cannot abide," she drew a deep breath, "being trapped in carriage in the rain. I simply cannot sit still in a closed carriage with the rain pounding down." Pandora shrugged in an off-handed matter as though her admission was of no real concern.

It was, of course. Cynthia was right about Pandora setting high standards, and she set none higher than those she set for herself. This illogical fear was a weakness she refused to dwell on and hated to acknowledge. No one outside her immediate family knew of its existence . . . until now.

"Admittedly, it sounds ridiculous." Pandora grimaced. "But the walls seem to close in on me and I feel trapped."

A bemused smile lit Cynthia's face.

"I see my confession has improved your spirits and your color."

"I do feel much better." Cynthia's grin widened and she shook her head. "Wet carriages."

"Carriages in the rain." Pandora said in a firm, this-is-the-end-of-this-discussion manner. "Now, while I am searching below, you can keep watch here. It's always possible the fox has managed to escape detection long enough to reach the gallery."

"You can never really trust a fox," Cynthia murmured.

"They are cunning creatures. And we must be just as cunning." Pandora turned to peer over the balustrade. "Try to appear natural, as if we are simply chatting."

"Oh, I daresay that will look natural. I often stand against columns at gatherings and chat to my companion's backside."

Pandora ignored the sarcasm while noting Cynthia's newfound boldness.

"Do you see him?" Cynthia said.

"Not yet." Pandora studied the milling crowd. "One would think a man that tall . . ." Colors of every hue imaginable swirled and mingled like a jeweled kaleidoscope. ". . . With shoulders that broad . . ." Laughter mixed with murmurs of conversation and the odd squeal, and rose from the ballroom. ". . . And eyes like an oncoming storm . . ."

"Really?" There was a definite grin in Cynthia's voice. "I imagine that alone would make him stand out in a crowd. Especially a crowd viewed from a bird's vantage point."

Pandora paid no heed to Cynthia's amusement. Max did indeed have the most remarkable eyes. The memory of the knowing looks they'd harbored lingered at the back of her mind and had intruded at unexpected and altogether too frequent moments in recent days.

"It is possible he isn't here, you know."

"I know." Pandora leaned forward slightly. "It's just the sort of annoying thing he'd do."

"I believe there as many people up here as there are in the ballroom," Cynthia said idly. "Lord Chalmers is at the far end of the gallery, chatting with Lady Simpson-Atwood, who looks as lovely as always. Of course, she is standing beneath a portrait of a remarkably unattractive ancestor."

"An attribute we can forgive in those long dead."

"And over there, the Earl of Latham appears intent upon peering down the rather daring bodice of Lady Pentworth."

"Lady Pentworth's bodices are always daring and men are always trying to peer down them," Pandora said absently, wondering if, again tonight, Max would fail to appear. "I believe it's become an accepted sport on a par with racing or gaming."

Cynthia snorted in a manner that would have caused her to faint with embarrassment only a year or two ago. Pandora bit back a smile. Cynthia was indeed coming out of her shell.

"And there are Lady Everly and Lady Jersey." Cynthia paused. "I believe Lady Jersey is looking in our direction."

"I doubt that." Pandora sighed and straightened. If indeed Max was amid the humanity clogging the room below her, locating him was proving to be a feat no less difficult than the tasks she had set him.

"You're right. She's signaling to a servant. No, wait—she's looking at us again." Cynthia gasped and tugged on Pandora's gown. "Dear Lord, she's coming toward us."

Pandora brushed her hand away and paid no attention to her words. There, at the far end of the ballroom, a tall dark-haired man stood talking to a group of gentlemen. His back was to her but his height and build were right. Her heart beat faster.

"Pandora." Panic edged Cynthia's voice. "What on earth do you think she'd want with us? No, not us . . . you alone. I'm no doubt little more than an innocent bystander."

A corner of Pandora's mind acknowledged that she should respond, but if that figure was indeed Max . . .

"A mere leaf caught in the whirlpool of your escapades."

And if it was, she had never imagined he would be the type of man to wear a coat of such a brilliant shade of magenta.

"Doomed by simple association to suffer your fate."

Even so, regardless of the taste of his questionable, though admittedly fashionable, attire . . .

"I shall surely have to swoon after all simply as a manner of escape."

The gentleman turned, dashing Pandora's hopes, yet providing a tiny measure of relief. She much preferred the dark blue and back evening attire Max usually wore to the jewel tones so in favor with gentlemen these days.

"Pandora," Cynthia said in an urgent whisper, and tugged harder.

"Blast it all, Cynthia, if you don't stop that at once, you may well tear my gown, and that will certainly not improve what appears to be a tedious and probably boring—" Pandora whirled to face her friend in time to see her bob a quick curtsey to a figure just out of Pandora's sight. Pandora's heart sank as quickly as her mind engaged. "—Evening since nothing can ever quite compare with the joys of a few hours spent at Almack's."

"Well done, my dear."

Pandora turned and feigned surprise at the presence of an Almack's patroness and the undisputed queen of fashionable society. "Why, Lady Jersey," she curtsied demurely, "I didn't see you."

"Indeed." Lady Jersey laughed, and a measure of Pandora's confidence returned. No matter what stringent rules the Lady held sacrosanct within the confines of the Almack's assembly rooms, it was known, although rarely discussed aloud, that the countess appreciated the humor in the world around her. She turned toward Cynthia. "You are looking lovely tonight, Miss Weatherly. I suspect this season may well be a successful one for you."

"You do?" Cynthia's eyes widened and her mouth opened. Pandora nudged her with a discretely placed elbow. "I mean . . . thank you."

"You're quite welcome. And as for you." Lady Jersey pinned Pandora with a firm gaze that would have made her cringe, if not for the amused look she saw there. "I gather your eighth season—"

"Seventh," Pandora said quickly, then groaned to herself at her impudence.

"—Seventh, of course, is as, shall we say, eventful as ever." A smile flashed across Lady Jersey's face and vanished, lingering only in her eyes. It would not do for this paragon of social correctness to be seen finding Pandora's lack of deference entertaining.

"Well, it is rather interesting," Pandora said cautiously. What on earth could she be referring to? So far this season Pandora's life had been relatively free from anything even mildly untoward.

"Beg pardon, my lady." A liveried servant stepped up behind Lady Jersey and handed her a neatly wrapped packet. She nodded in dismissal and turned her attention back to Pandora.

"I have been entrusted by an old and dear friend to deliver this to you." She handed Pandora the package.

"What is it?" Pandora's brows pulled together. The parcel was wrapped in tissue and tied with a blue satin ribbon, a card tucked beneath the knot.

"I would suggest you read the note first."

An odd, heavy feeling settled in Pandora's stomach, a cross between anticipation and dread. She pulled the card free. The crest of the Earl of Trent stared up at her. Her heart beat faster. Beneath the crest, the familiar hand read: *Test number eleven.*

She sucked in a sharp breath.

*Given the times we live in, this should suffice*

*for the girdle of the Queen of the Amazons.*

She jerked her gaze from the card to meet Lady Jersey's amused eyes. "Is this—"

"There's no need to open the package here, it merely contains a personal article of mine. However, I believe you will wish to read the note on the other side."

Pandora turned the card over, not certain if the tremble in her hand was due to surprise or annoyance or excitement.

*Test number six: The patronesses of Almack's have been known to devour men whole on occasion, the modern equivalent of man-eating mares. You may consider them tamed.*

Pandora shook her head. "I don't understand."

"It's quite simple, my dear." Lady Jersey smiled. "The Earl of Trent has enlisted my help, and through me the rest of the Lady Patronesses."

Shock coursed through her. "He told you about—"

"Your little game?"

Pandora swallowed hard and nodded.

"Indeed he has. I find it quite delightful."

"Delightful?"

"Most certainly. I have always been rather fond of Trent—and rather fond of you as well." Lady Jersey leaned toward her in a confidential manner. "Watching you career through society these last eight—"

"Seven."

"Seven years has been most entertaining. However, while your independence is a trait that will serve you well, it is not the sort of thing I would like to see other young women emulate." She glanced pointedly at Cynthia, who smiled weakly. "It is past time you were safely wed. You and he will be the match of the season, perhaps the match of any season, and I shall have had a hand in it."

Pandora drew a deep breath. "I beg your pardon, Lady Jersey, but there is a very distinct possibility Trent will not win."

Lady Jersey laughed. "I doubt that. He has always been quite resourceful. In addition," she raised a brow, "I have always considered you to be rather intelligent, and I cannot imagine why any woman who was not a complete ninny would want Trent to lose."

"I've tried to tell her that," Cynthia said.

"Splendid." Lady Jersey nodded approvingly. "It appears *you* have a fair amount of good sense. Hopefully, your influence will rub off on Miss Effington."

Cynthia's chin raised and she looked for all the world like a soldier accepting a dangerous assignment from his commander. "I do try, but she is exceedingly stubborn."

Pandora gasped. "Cynthia."

"She is an Effington," Lady Jersey said under her breath, and exchanged a knowing look with Cynthia.

Pandora nearly choked from indignation. "The fact that I am an Effington has noth—"

"On the contrary, my dear, your heritage, on both sides of your family, I might add, has everything to do with it. Which is precisely why I am confident all will turn out well. I had feared this season might not be as enjoyable as those of past years, but now I am confident it will be quite lively after all. Good evening."

She turned and swept down the gallery, the crowd parting before her like a well-dressed, and properly behaved, Red Sea.

"She said I have good sense." Cynthia's awed gaze followed the countess's retreating form. "She thinks my season will be successful and—"

"And she knows about the game." Pandora's voice was grim. "If *she* knows, *everyone* knows. If it hasn't already, it's bound to become the talk of the *ton*."

"Surely you didn't expect it to remain a secret?"

"Quite frankly, I hadn't considered it at all." Pandora thought for a moment. "But I daresay I don't relish the idea of everyone watching my every move."

Cynthia raised a brow. "Everyone is always watching your every move."

"But this is entirely different. This is serious. No doubt wagers are already being laid as to the outcome of the contest."

"Forgive me, Pandora, but if I were to bet, I'd place my money on Lord Trent."

"Why would you do that?" Pandora pulled her brows together in annoyance. "You are my dearest friend. Where is your sense of loyalty?"

"Apparently, it's overshadowed by my good sense." Cynthia grinned. "Don't forget, he has already passed three of the twelve tests."

"He has not," Pandora snapped and waved the packet at her friend. "This cannot count for more than one test. Those are the rules."

Cynthia laughed. "The rules? You, of all people, are insisting upon rules?"

"There simply has to be rules."

"Does Trent know of these rules?"

"Not yet." She narrowed her eyes. "But the moment the irritating fox comes out of his den I shall inform him exactly how this game is to be played."

"I should like to see that." Cynthia studied her for a moment. "Lady Jersey was right you know. You have provided a considerable measure of entertainment through the years. And this game you're playing with Trent may well be the most amusing of them all."

"I'm so pleased my fate will provide the world with a bit of entertainment," she said wryly and turned back to gaze once more at the crowd on the lower level. There was no need to continue to search for Max. Lady Jersey had obviously done his work for him this evening.

Pandora stared unseeing at the eddy of bodies below her. Whether he knew it or not, by involving Lady Jersey—and therefore all of society—Max had upped the stakes. It was now a question not just of her future, but of her pride. Despite any disturbing feelings he might stir within her, she could not now allow him to win.

Regardless of how she had unwittingly earned it in the first place, the Hellion of Grosvenor Square had a position to maintain, and no mere man, no matter how charming and handsome and clever would be allowed to best her.

Her reputation was at stake, and with each passing day, she suspected, so was her heart.

# Chapter 7
## *A Foul is Charged*

"**This—**" A delicate chemise drifted softly on the papers spread before Max on the floor. He looked up in surprise. Pandora stood glowering down at him. "—Is not in the spirit of the game."

"It's *not?*" He picked up the undergarment and studied it curiously, trying to resist a triumphant grin. He knew if he waited long enough she'd come to him. She was not used to being ignored. "I thought of all your tests this one was precisely in the spirit of the game."

"You were wrong." She folded her arms over her chest and glared. "Whatever are you doing on the floor? That's certainly not a position I expected the Earl of Trent to be in."

"Oh, I don't know." He leaned back on his elbows. His gaze wandered from the toes of her boots peeking from beneath her skirts, up the length of her leg to the curve of her hip and higher, appreciating the intriguing way her crossed arms underlined her breasts, and still higher, past the creamy skin of her throat to her lips, full and inviting, to settle on her eyes, flashing with annoyance. "I find this position quite delightful."

"Do you, indeed?" she said, in a tone a shade less haughty than that of a moment ago and just a touch breathless. "You look like an undisciplined schoolboy."

"I feel rather undisciplined at the moment." His gaze dropped back to her mouth and she bit her bottom lip in a nervous gesture. "Although I don't recall my studies being quite so interesting as they are now."

"Interesting?" Her voice rose.

"Very." He wondered if she'd resist if he reached out and pulled her to the floor.

"What exactly are you studying?"

He smiled wickedly.

"I mean, what is all that?" she said quickly, waving at the books and papers scattered over the carpet.

The information he'd compiled thus far on the legends and myths of Greece had overtaken his desktop and spilled onto the floor and he'd discovered it was easier to be organized with everything spread out. He'd found numerous versions of the labors of Hercules, ranging from the writings of the ancients to those of obscure Oxford scholars to Lord and Lady Harold's works. He patted the carpet beside him. "See for yourself."

"I would prefer to stand, thank you."

"As you wish." He shrugged.

"A well-mannered gentleman would get to

his feet at this point." Unease sharpened her words.

"A well-mannered lady would never drop an article of feminine underclothing in the face of a man. Besides, you yourself have proclaimed me a rake, a rogue, a scoundrel, and a beast."

"You could at least be a well-mannered beast."

"Could I?" He got to his feet in a leisurely manner. "What, then, would be the point of being a beast?"

"The point?" She stared at him nervously.

"Indeed. A well-mannered beast would never meet an unmarried, unchaperoned lady in a secluded parlor or a graveyard—or," he stared down at her, "in the privacy of his own home."

She swallowed hard. "Well, perhaps I was mistaken. Perhaps you are not a beast after all. Perhaps—"

"Oh, but I am." He was close enough to note the rise and fall of her breasts with every breath. "Beasts disregard the dictates of society much as hellions do."

"Do they?"

Close enough to see her blue eyes darken with—what? Desire? "They do. And beasts don't hesitate to use every advantage to get what they want."

"They don't?" She fairly sighed the words.

Close enough to bend his head and touch his lips to hers. "And beasts never play games they do not intend to win."

"They . . ." She caught her breath. His lips brushed across hers and she jerked back, as if burned by the contact between them. He suppressed a resigned sigh. She stepped out of his reach. "You will not win this one."

Pandora drew a shaky breath. "However, that's precisely what I wish to talk about."

"Ah yes." He hid his disappointment with a chuckle. "I rather expected to see you before now, given your eagerness to speak with me."

"Eager?" At once her tone sharpened. Apparently, any lingering effects of their near kiss had vanished. "Not at all."

"Really? I got the distinct impression from your notes that you were most anxious to meet with me."

"Notes?" She widened her eyes as if she had no idea what he was talking about.

"Surely you remember? Your brief, but nonetheless demanding messages insisting I call on you?" He paused and looked thoughtful. "Of course, I could be confusing you with some other woman eager—"

"I wasn't eager," she said sharply. "I do seem vaguely to remember dashing off a letter—"

"Or four."

She lifted a shoulder in an offhanded shrug. "Regardless, impressions can often be misleading."

"From the notes you barely remember, I gather you wish to discuss rules for our game—or was that another mistaken impression on my part?"

"Rules are essential," she said, without looking at him. She wandered the fringes of the library glancing at a book here, an object there. "Without rules, why, anarchy will prevail."

"We can't have that." He struggled to keep his expression solemn. Through the years she'd disregarded the rules of society. Her insistence on them now was both amusing and an indication of her concern over his ultimate victory. "What did you have in mind?"

She tilted her head and cast him a pleasant smile. " First, you cannot pass two tests with one accomplishment. You cannot claim to have acquired the girdle of the Queen of the Amazons *and* tamed man-eating mares at the same time."

"Why not?"

"Because it's not fair."

"Not fair to whom?"

"Not fair to the spirit of the game," she said primly.

"As I said before, I think it's entirely in the spirit of the game."

"Well, you're wrong." She wandered to his desk and idly glanced at the writings littering the desktop. "Second, you cannot purchase your way through the tests."

He raised a brow. "The spirit of the game again?"

"Exactly." She picked up a paper and a frown creased her forehead. "This is what you've been studying? Greek myths?"

"Specifically, the labors of Hercules. It's been most enlightening." He'd found discrepancies rampant; some accounts referred to the hero by different names, and many did not even agree on the specific tests themselves. To his delight, he realized if there was no definitive reference, he was free to interpret the challenges in any way he wished.

"I see." Her frown deepened. She dropped the paper back on the desk and turned to face him. "In addition, there must be a limit on the time you have to complete the tasks. I cannot allow you to go on forever."

"That too would probably promote anarchy." He nodded solemnly.

"No doubt."

"Still," he said with a deep sigh, "this game may take forever."

"It may. Would you prefer to forfeit now and save yourself the humiliation of defeat?"

"Absolutely not, as I foresee neither humiliation nor defeat." *At least not for me.* "However, if you would like to concede at this point . . ."

"Never," she said sharply. "I would prefer to be eaten whole by jungle beasts in the darkest corners of Africa before I would allow you even the merest glimpse of victory."

"As you wish." He shrugged as if he didn't care one way or the other whether jungle beasts ate her whole.

"I propose to set a time limit of, oh, say, a fortnight."

"A fortnight? Impossible. I refuse to agree to any condition that virtually guarantees failure. Three months seems more appropriate."

"Entire civilizations have risen and fallen in three months." She paused. "I'll allow you three weeks."

"I'll take two months."

"One month, then. Or rather, four weeks."

"Agreed."

"With time commencing from the moment we agreed to our bargain."

"That puts us back to around three weeks."

"Yes, but you already passed two challenges." She smiled in a deceptively sweet manner.

"Very well," he said casually, although he still had no idea how to accomplish most of her tests. "Anything else?"

"Since this is a game, I propose each test passed will receive one point, simply as a way to keep track."

"And I need twelve points?" She nodded. "I have no difficulty with that. So is that the extent of your rules?"

"Not entirely." She glanced at her hands and plucked at the fingers of her glove. "There is one more thing."

"Yes?"

She drew a deep breath and raised her gaze to meet his. "I don't think there should be any more, well, affection between us."

"Affection?" He lifted a brow.

"Yes. Affection." She heaved a sigh. "Kissing?"

"Oh." He bit back a grin. "That kind of affection."

"It's highly improper and not entirely fair."

"To the spirit of the game?"

"Exactly." She smiled with relief.

"We wouldn't want to violate the spirit of the game. Still . . ." He adopted a studious air, clasped his hands behind his back, and paced the room. "I must confess, I am a bit confused."

"Confused?" Irritation crossed her face. "It's

a simple, straightforward rule. No kissing."

"So it would appear at first glance." He shook his head solemnly. "However, nothing is ever as simple as it seems."

"It's not?" she said with caution.

"No indeed. I have a problem with the definition of your terms."

"My terms?" She scoffed. "A kiss is a kiss. It's not difficult to define."

"Oh, but it is." He stepped to her side. "For example, should I meet you at a social gathering, would it break the rules to take your hand," he took her hand, "raise it to my lips," he brushed his mouth across her glove, "and place a polite kiss upon it?" His gaze never left hers.

"I suppose that would be acceptable," she said reluctantly.

"Excellent." He released her hand and moved closer. "If a kiss on the hand is allowed, then would a kiss, say, on the cheek be allowed?" He placed two fingers under her chin, raised it, and leaned forward to feather a light kiss on one cheek, then the other. "The French consider it no more than a polite greeting."

"But we aren't French." Her voice was just a bit breathless.

"No, but we do put great store in being polite." He gazed into her eyes and saw what was surely a reflection of his own desire. "Is such a well-mannered kiss acceptable?"

"I shall have to consider it." Her gaze darted to one side, as if she was considering escape. But the desk was behind her and she had no place to run.

"Very well. And if you decide it is permissible, then all we need to determine is what isn't allowed."

"We do?"

"Say, again merely as an example, I were to put my arms around you." He matched his actions to his words. "And you were to put your arms around me—"

"I don't think—"

"I want to make certain I understand the rules."

"Very well, but only for the sake of clarity." Tentatively she placed her hands on his shoulder, then around his neck. Her fingertips touched the nape of his neck and a jolt of heat shot through him. Without thinking, he pulled her tighter against him. Her eyes widened but she didn't protest.

"Clarity is crucial when it comes to rules. Now then, I would imagine this—" He lowered his head and placed a delicate kiss just below her ear, then trailed kisses down the side of her neck. She gasped. "—would be against the rules." He whispered against her warm, fragrant skin, then ran his lips along the annoyingly high collar of her pelisse to the notch in the fabric and the hollow of her throat. Her body seemed to melt against his.

"Oh my, yes." Her eyes were half closed and she angled her head to allow him better access to the other side of her neck. "That's definitely not permitted."

"I didn't think so. I suspect this would not be allowed either." He met her lips in a kiss barely more than a breath, fully intending to do no more than tease. For a moment she froze, then her arms tightened and her mouth pressed against his.

All restraint within him shattered and he crushed his lips to hers, holding her body tighter against his. Her lips parted and his tongue met hers in a mating of greed and wonder. Her hands clutched at the back of his head and she clung to him as if life itself were at stake. He slanted his mouth harder over hers and one kiss blended into another and another, the very taste of her intoxicating and addictive. His hands slipped lower to cup the enticing curve of her derriere, holding her yielding body tighter against the heat of his own arousal. How could he bear another moment, another day, let alone the remainder of a month without her?

He wrenched his lips from hers and tried to catch his breath. "Hellion." He nuzzled her ear and she moaned softly. "Forget this silly game. Marry me now."

"Max, I . . ." She ran her fingers through his hair, her chest heaved against his.

"I want you and you want me. We were made for each other." He could barely choke out the words. She was all the delights of heaven and the fires of hell at once in his arms. "You're all I require in a wife." He could not get enough of her and barely noticed she'd stilled in his arms.

She drew back. Her gaze searched his. "And?"

"And . . . what?" Confusion meshed with the fog of desire hazing his mind and he marveled he was able to think at all.

"And is that it?" Her tone was cool.

"Yes?" What had he said? "No?" She pushed free and stepped back. "No, of course not."

She folded her arms over her chest. Her face was flushed, her lips were swollen, and she looked very much like a woman tasting passion for the first time. The desire that had ebbed for an instant swept through him once again and he wanted nothing more than to take her back in his arms.

"I mean . . ." What on earth did he mean? "It seems pointless to continue when the outcome is inevitable."

"Inevitable?" Her eyes narrowed. Perhaps he was mistaking anger for passion.

"Certainly. I have every intention of victory, and according to the terms of our bargain, you will then marry me. Given what just occurred between us, it's obvious you want this match as much as I do." He stepped toward her.

Her hand shot out to stop him. "Unless you are willing to forfeit—"

"Which I'm not."

"I didn't think so." Her expression was as noncommittal as her tone. "Therefore the game will continue."

"If that's what you want," he said slowly.

"It is." She adjusted her gloves and smoothed her clothing, avoiding his gaze. He noticed with satisfaction a slight tremble in her hand. "I have told you more than once and I will tell you over and over if need be: I do not wish to marry you."

"That's not the impression I got."

"You do need to work on that, Max. Once again your impression is mistaken. What happened here was a momentary lapse in judgment, nothing more than that. And it will not happen again." She raised her chin in a haughty manner and started toward the door.

"As you wish."

She paused and turned toward him, her eyes wide with surprise. "You don't believe me?"

"Not for a moment."

"You are a beast, Max."

Her eyes flashed and he realized the passion of her anger was rivaled only by the passion of her kiss. Either way, it stirred his blood. By God, even if he had to face all the trials devised by ancient Greeks or stubborn hellions, she would be his.

"But I will grant you this. While it is definitely against the rules." A faint smile danced across her lips. "You are a bloody fine kisser."

She swept out of the room in as grand an exit as he'd ever witnessed. He shook his head and grinned. Pandora had obviously forgotten the tenet by which she'd long lived her life.

The best thing about rules was breaking them.

# Chapter 8
## *The Players Increase*

**L**ord Trent sat at a large desk, studying a book that lay open before him. He casually turned a page and addressed her in a smug tone without so much as looking up. "I didn't expect you to return so soon. Have you changed your mind?"

Surprise caught Cynthia up short. "I don't think so."

Lord Trent's head jerked up and he stared in disbelief. "Miss Weatherly?" He jumped to his feet. "I did not . . . what I mean to say . . ." He craned his neck to peer around her. "Are you alone?"

She glanced over her shoulder. "I believe so."

He rounded the desk. "I must say, this is an unexpected pleasure."

Cynthia smiled weakly. The butler who'd shown her in stepped out of the room and quietly shut the doors behind him. Her gaze shot to the entry and at once she knew the feelings of a trapped animal. She wished nothing more at this moment than for the ground to open up at her feet and swallow her whole.

Lord Trent stepped forward, a touch of sympathy in his eyes as if he sensed her apprehension. "To what do I owe this honor?"

"I really shouldn't be here at all," she murmured. How had she ever imagined she could summon the courage to say what she wished to say to the earl? What on earth could have possessed her? If she was caught, she could be ruined. It was outrageous. Improper. And no doubt a result of Pandora's influence.

"Do sit down." He smiled, and Cynthia realized Pandora was right: his eyes were indeed an interesting shade of gray. "Please forgive the disarray."

"The disarray . . ." She glanced around the room, noticing the clutter for the first time. "Oh my, it looks like the Effington parlor in here."

He laughed. "As well it should. I have been diligently studying Greek myths."

"How thoughtful." Her tension eased. "Of course, I would expect no less from a fox."

His brow shot up. "A fox?"

"It's of no consequence." She sank onto a leather couch and clutched her gloved hands tightly together in her lap. She was not a woman used to visiting a man alone and was not entirely certain where to begin.

"Miss Weatherly?" Her gaze jumped to his. Curiosity glimmered in his eyes and a smile lifted the corners of his lips. "How can I help you?"

At once she knew that, his reputation aside,

this was a kind man. And any man willing to go to the effort evidenced by the work scattered about the distinctly masculine domain was a man worthy of her dearest friend.

"In point of fact, my lord," she drew a deep breath, "it may well be I who can help you."

"Oh?"

"I want you to know," her voice rang with determination, "should you need any assistance in your match with Pandora, you may count on me."

"I may?" His eyes narrowed. "Why?"

"Why?"

"Yes, why?" He crossed his arms over his chest and leaned back against the desk. "Forgive me, Miss Weatherly, but Pandora accused me of leading you to believe I had certain intentions toward you, and I can only assume you believed the same thing. Therefore your willingness to help me now is somewhat suspect."

For a moment Cynthia could do little more than stare mutely. Then unexpected laughter bubbled through her lips. "My lord, I assumed nothing of the sort."

"You didn't?" he said cautiously.

"No indeed." Was it the humor of his suspicion or realizing he thought she was capable of spinning a web of revenge for a meaningless flirtation that vanquished her unease? "You did nothing at all improper, and in the handful of dances we shared, we scarcely spoke more than a dozen words."

"My apologies then," he said with relief.

"Accepted, although I do suspect the minimal attention you directed toward me was not aimed at me at all."

"Yes, well . . ." A distinct look of discomfort passed over the earl's handsome face.

She'd never caused discomfort in a gentleman before. An odd sense of accomplishment flared within her. So this was what it was like to have a man under your control. No wonder Pandora relished the manner in which she lived her life.

"Now then, my lord," she said with a new-found strength of purpose. "Pandora is like a sister to me. I wish to see her happy." She stared him straight in the eye. "I believe you are the man who can do that."

He gazed at her with an expression of bemused admiration. No man had ever looked at her like that.

"I appreciate your expression of confidence. Pity Pandora doesn't agree with you."

Cynthia frowned and debated how many of her friend's secrets to reveal.

"She doesn't agree, does she?"

"Not aloud." Cynthia resigned herself to doing what she must to ensure Pandora's happiness, even if she would not see it quite that way. "You have annoyed her, my lord. She finds you irritating and arrogant."

"And this has convinced you I'm the right match for her?" Again his dark brow raised.

Cynthia laughed. "Indeed it has."

"I'm afraid I don't understand."

Cynthia favored him with the kind of look she would give a small boy and relished bestowing it on a grown man. "I know it sounds illogical, but I have never seen Pandora react quite like this before. She finds men amusing in general and annoying on occasion, but she's never particularly been concerned enough about any one man to let his actions bother her." For the first time, Cynthia understood precisely how amusing men could be. "Does that make any sense at all?"

"Yes, I believe it does," he said slowly.

"Good." She heaved a sigh of relief and stood. It hadn't been nearly as bad as she'd feared. Indeed, the entire encounter had been almost pleasant. She started toward the doors. "I am quite certain—"

Without warning, the doors flew open and a tall, fair-haired man burst into the room. She took a quick step back, into the shadows of the room, and out of his way.

"Max, you're right. Absolutely and without a doubt. What was I thinking? Escape is not the honorable way out."

The stranger paced the room, brow furrowed, steps rapid, an image of concentration and barely restrained energy.

"Nonetheless, it remains the easiest answer and the most effective, and perhaps the most enjoyable as well. I hate to see you dismiss it." He glared at the earl, who watched him with the kind of tolerant smile worn by one who has seen such behavior before. "Still, you have my word I will not rest until I find a solution to this mess."

Passion radiated from the man, and she wouldn't have been at all surprised to see him jump onto a table and deliver a fiery speech equal to anything given by an overzealous parson or a wild-eyed orator.

"I vow here and now: I will save you, Max."
The man's promise rang in the room with the
power of a blood oath. She'd never encountered anyone like him. "Whether you like it or
not."

Who was he? They hadn't met, she was certain she'd remember . . . and equally certain a
man like this would be completely unaware of
her.

"Laurie," Lord Trent said, but his guest si-
lenced him with an impatient wave.

"No, Max, I cannot in all good conscience
allow you to go through with this ridiculous
bargain."

He was the most fascinating man Cynthia
had ever seen.

"You're certain to win, and then you'll be
stuck for the rest of your life. It's a fate worse
than death! She'll—"

"Laurie." Lord Trent tried again.

"Protest all you wish but you haven't
thought this through." He crossed his arms
over his chest. "You haven't considered the
consequences. *Dire* consequences. You—"

"Laurie." The earl's voice sharpened. "Have
you met Miss Weatherly?"

"Miss who?" He turned and caught sight of
her. "Damnation, Max, why didn't you tell me
we weren't alone?"

"I believe I tried," Lord Trent said wryly.

"Weatherly, did you say? No, I don't believe
we've met." His gaze flicked over her as if he
were assessing her fitness for harness and a
hot wave washed up her cheeks.

"May I present Lawrence, Viscount Bolton."
Lord Bolton stepped toward her, took her

hand in an expert manner, and brushed his lips across it. His gaze lingered on hers, and for a moment she thought she might well drown in eyes the rich, deep color of chocolate. She smiled hesitantly.

He straightened and stared down at her. She was tall, but he was taller. It wasn't so much that he was an attractive man, although she considered him such, with fine regular features and hair the color of sunlit wheat; it was rather his presence that held her enthralled. For the space of a heartbeat, she completely forgot how to breathe.

"By God, you're the friend, aren't you?"

"The friend?" He still held her hand. Terribly improper, yet she had no desire to pull her hand from the warmth of his.

Lord Bolton nodded at Lord Trent. "She is the Hellion's friend, isn't she? I daresay I didn't—" He stopped as if struck by sudden inspiration or a flash of genius and grinned with triumph. "Of course, that's the answer."

"What's the answer?" Cynthia's gaze slid from the viscount to the earl.

"Bolton feels Miss Effington is not the right woman for me," Lord Trent said.

"Oh?" Perhaps this man was not quite so fascinating as she'd first thought.

"No indeed. But this is perfect. Since you're the friend he paid such attention to—"

"One moment, Laurie," Lord Trent said quickly. "I never—"

Cynthia jerked her hand away and stepped back. "He most certainly did not."

Lord Bolton shrugged. "Regardless, it brought him to the Hellion's—"

"Pandora," she murmured. No, he was not fascinating at all.

"—Attention. And no doubt, should she win, the Hellion—"

"Pandora," she said again in a firm tone. In fact he was extremely annoying. It was all well and good for Pandora to be pleased with her hellion title, but Cynthia found it more an insult than a compliment. Especially the way this beastly man said it.

"—Will chose you as Max's bride. You will naturally decline, and Max will be free." He finished with a flourish.

"I will not lose," Lord Trent said mildly.

"No doubt the Hellion says the same."

"Her name is Pandora!" Cynthia resisted the all-too-appealing urge to bash him over the head with the nearest breakable object. "Miss Effington to you. And I would appreciate it if you had the courtesy to address her as such!"

Lord Trent choked back a laugh. Surprise colored Lord Bolton's face. Obviously neither man expected her to stand up for her friend or for herself.

"Now then, my lord." She met the viscount's gaze with an unflinching stare. "The earl is determined to win this match with Pandora. And I am equally determined to make certain he succeeds."

"You?" He gazed down at her in a condescending manner.

"Yes." She stared up at him with a stubbornness she didn't know she possessed. What an infuriating, arrogant creature this man was! Cynthia couldn't remember being this angry with anyone ever, let alone a tall, handsome lord. "I am quite willing to do whatever is necessary."

"Are you?" Lord Bolton's gaze traveled over her once again, a long, lazy look that carried the force of a physical caress. A shiver skated down her spine. "You know, Max, on further consideration, you could accept Miss Weatherly after all."

Cynthia gasped. "I cannot believe—"

"Laurie." A warning sounded in Lord Trent's voice. "Be careful you do not go too far."

"You could do much worse." He circled around her. Shock stole her voice, and it was all she could do to catch her breath. "She's younger than the Hellion, of good family, I believe, and not at all unpleasant to look at." He paused before her, an appreciative light in his eyes. "Personally, I prefer tall golden-haired beauties to short dark hellions, but we aren't discussing me. And I daresay she's much better behaved than—"

Perhaps it was the comparison to Pandora that snapped some long-held dam of restraint within her. Perhaps it was the culmination of the tiny triumphs of the last few minutes. Or perhaps her friendship with Pandora had indeed altered the mildness of her manner over time to a point where now only a spark was needed to ignite a raging inferno.

Viscount Bolton was without question a spark.

"I would not wager on it, my lord." Her words were cold and controlled. "You would lose."

He laughed. "Would I?"

"That's enough, Laurie." Lord Trent snapped and turned toward her with an apologetic expression. "I must beg your forgiveness for my friend. I'm afraid he's rather—"

"What he is is rather a . . . a . . ." *A what?* "A prig!"

"Am I?" Lord Bolton grinned.

Good Lord, the vile man was pleased! Apparently, "prig" was not strong enough. *What would Pandora say?*

"Indeed, you are. A prig." She stiffened her back, raised her chin, and fixed him with a defiant glare. "A bloody prig!"

An odd strangled sound came from Lord Trent, as if he wasn't sure whether to applaud or chastise.

Lord Bolton's grin widened. "Excellent, Miss Weatherly, you certainly proved me wrong. You're not nearly as well behaved as I'd thought."

"Oh?" Sarcasm colored her voice. "I was under the impression you did not think at all."

"Would you care to know my thoughts now?" He leaned toward her and trapped her gaze with his. His nose was but a few inches from her own. In a corner of her mind she marveled at her stubborn stance and realized that not once since this man had entered the room had she felt even the tiniest inclination to swoon.

"I can't imagine your thoughts to be of any interest."

"You may well be interested in this." His brown eyes gleamed with intensity. "Max is my oldest friend, and I will not allow him to ruin his life with marriage to the Hellion."

"Miss Effington," she snapped.

"*The Hellion*," he said through clenched teeth. "And I shall do all in my power to prevent him from succeeding in this game of theirs."

"I would wish you luck, my lord, but as Miss Effington is my dearest friend and I wish only for her happiness," her voice rang with all the conviction of one who knows she is in the right, "I shall do all in my power to ensure Lord Trent's victory."

Lord Bolton scoffed. "That's all well and good, Miss Weatherly, but what exactly can *you* do?"

What could she do? She'd offered her help to the earl, but she had nothing specific in mind. Still, there was no need to reveal that now.

She smiled slowly. The kind of secretive smile that Pandora had perfected and encouraged her to attempt. The kind of superior feminine smile that had always been uncomfortable for her. The kind of all-knowing smile that now fit her like a well-made glove.

Confusion tinged with suspicion and something else she didn't quite recognize flitted across Lord Bolton's face.

"We shall see, my lord. We shall see." She nodded at Lord Trent, who grinned back at her, turned, and swept through the doorway without hesitation.

"We shall indeed, Miss Weatherly," Lord Bolton called after her. "Bloody hell, Max, she's an apprentice hellion."

Masculine laughter rang behind her.

The butler held the front door open and she murmured a word of thanks. Only then did she notice the trembling in her hands, a paltry price to pay for the remarkable elation that filled her. She'd done battle and emerged unscathed. No wonder Pandora said what she wished and acted as she pleased. This exquisite, heady sensation of being for once the current in the stream and not a mere leaf subject to the whims of any and all other forces was well worth any risk.

She climbed into her carriage and settled back for the brief ride home. There was still the matter of exactly what form her help would take. Pandora's tests were difficult enough, but now that obnoxious viscount was determined to thwart his friend's efforts. She had no doubt if left alone Lord Trent would certainly triumph.

Abruptly the answer flashed in her mind and she laughed aloud. She knew precisely how she could lend the greatest assistance to the earl. It was an idea worthy of Pandora herself.

Perhaps on one point Lord Bolton was right.

Perhaps she was indeed an apprentice hellion.

# Chapter 9
## *The Rules Defined*

"**O**h, it's you." Pandora adopted her loftiest tone, as if she hadn't known full well Max was already in the parlor waiting for her.

"Good evening," he said, without looking at her. He stood beside the Chinese gong, staring at Hercules, who stared back.

"Interesting bird." He extended his hand. Hercules studied it for an instant, then hopped on.

"Do be careful. Hercules is not always pleasant with people he doesn't know."

"Hercules?" He chuckled and brought the parrot closer, bird and man surveying each other with interest. "I believe he likes me."

Hercules cocked his green head. "Meow."

"He's a bit confused," she said with a sigh.

"Very interesting indeed." Max brought his hand back to the gong and Hercules obediently hopped onto the crossbar.

*He has the look of Apollo about him.*

Her mother's words echoed in her head just as they had this afternoon. She'd nearly forgotten how handsome, tall, and overwhelming Max was. The cluttered room was fuller with his presence.

Max examined the gong with an air of concentration. He ran his hand over the carved ebony in an appreciative caress. At once she remembered the feel of his hands on her back and an odd longing surged through her.

"Remarkable piece," he murmured.

"Remarkable," she said under her breath.

"Is it very old?" He glanced at her, genuine interest in his eyes.

"Very." For the briefest moment she wondered why she didn't accept his offer to forget the game, declare him the winner, and throw herself into his waiting arms.

He straightened and studied her as if he could read her thoughts. Her breath caught. A taut silence hung in the air. Why didn't he say anything? What was he waiting for? It was as if she balanced on one side of a rickety bridge and he on the other and the simplest move would send them tumbling into the raging waters below. He smiled slowly.

"I didn't know you were here." She struggled to sound aloof and unconcerned.

"Odd." He raised a brow in disbelief. "I asked Peters to announce me. He doesn't strike me as the kind of servant to disregard a request."

"No doubt an oversight on his part." Of course Peters had announced him. But Max had thoroughly ignored her in recent days, and she refused to give him the satisfaction of thinking she had nothing better to do than wait for his attention. "He probably assumed I had no desire to suffer your company and thought if you were ignored you would go away."

Max laughed. "I doubt that. Peters seems rather too perceptive to jump to such a wrong conclusion."

"In this case, he would have been correct."

"Would he?"

"Yes." Any lingering inclination to throw herself in his arms vanished. The man was infuriating. "Why are you here?" She nodded at the bundle of fabric he held under his arm. "And what is that?"

"This?" Max looked at it as if he hadn't seen it before.

"Yes." Suspicion sounded in her voice. "Is it for me?"

"More or less."

"Then—"

"In due time." He glanced around in a futile search for available space.

Abruptly she saw the parlor as others might, well aware most people did not live among the remains of long-lost civilizations. She refused to apologize to anyone for the unusual nature of her family and her upbringing, although just once it would be pleasant if life in the Effington home was a bit more organized.

She waved at a chair. "You may put it there."

"It feels like home," he muttered, stepping around a large marble fragment, part of a frieze, probably, and avoiding a precarious stack of books to drop the bundle on the chair. What on earth was in it?

"Now then." He turned toward her. "First of all, I wish to discuss your rules. All of them."

"I believe we settled that this afternoon. You have the rules and I am to attend Lady Farnsby's soiree. Good evening." She nodded in dismissal and started toward the door.

"Not quite yet, Dora." The stern command rang through the room.

She stopped in mid-step and whirled to face him. "Do not use that tone with me. And do not call me Dora!"

"We are not finished." He strode toward her with a gleam in his eye and a tremor of panic shot through her. Without thinking, she stepped back. Good Lord, what were the man's intentions?

He brushed past her and closed the doors to the hall.

"Whatever are you doing?" Her hand rose to her throat.

He stepped toward her. "I do not wish to be disturbed, and I would prefer that Peters, and whoever else might be lingering outside the doors, not be a silent witness."

She gasped. A silent witness to what? Had she pushed him too far? Had he completely lost his senses? He had an odd look in his eyes. The look of a man who knew precisely what he wanted and was prepared to get it.

And what he wanted was her.

Surely he was not about to ravish her? To finish now what they had begun today?

Not while she had a breath left in her body. "I absolutely will not permit it, Max. Regardless of whatever feelings I may have for you, regardless of how, well, interesting this afternoon was, I will not allow it. Not now. Not ever!"

"What are you babbling about?" His brows pulled together in confusion.

Her chin jerked up in a manner worthy of a Greek shepherdess defying the advances of a god. "I will not allow you to ravish me!"

He hesitated. Good. Obviously he was reconsidering his actions. His eyes narrowed and his voice was cautious. "You won't?"

"Never!" Her voice rang fearlessly. No heroine of myth or legend had ever said it better.

"Never?" he said mildly.

He certainly didn't look at all distraught over her pronouncement. She planted her hands on her hips. "No, never."

"Not even a little?"

*Maybe a little*, a traitorous voice whispered in her head. She pushed it away. "No!"

"Not even when we're married?"

"We're not going to be married."

"Oh, but we are." He moved closer and a wicked light snapped in his eyes. Her stomach fluttered. Perhaps he wasn't distraught because he had no intention of heeding her protest.

"Only if you win, and you're *not* going to win." Even to her own ears she didn't sound entirely confident.

"Oh, but I am." He stood barely a hand's width away from her now. So close she could see the rise and fall of his chest with every breath.

"No." She shook her head. So close she

could feel the heat of him through his clothing and hers.

"Now about these rules."

"Rules?" So close she could reach out and touch him if she so desired. Feel the hard planes of his body beneath her fingers and the warmth of his flesh against her hands.

She tilted her head back and gazed up at him. He stared down at her. His gaze shifted from her eyes to her mouth. At once her throat was parched and dry, and without thinking she licked her lips.

Lord help her, she so desired.

He lowered his head to hers. Slowly. Deliberately. She strained upward to meet his mouth. She braced her hands against his chest and his muscles tensed beneath her touch. Her breath caught. His lips brushed hers and an odd weakness stole her strength and her will.

Her eyes closed. Her blood roared in her ears. Her heart thudded in her chest and there was nothing in the world save the barest touch of his mouth to hers. He whispered against her lips, his words dim, distant.

A sweet growing ache filled her, and she clutched at his coat. This afternoon his kiss had been firm and demanding. Now his lips teased, carrying only the vaguest memory of what had come before and a subtle promise of what was yet to come. And she wanted more.

"Hellion." His voice drifted somewhere in a haze, muffled and indistinct. "Did you hear me?"

"Umm ..." Why didn't he kiss her, *really* kiss her? Now. What was he waiting for? She opened her eyes. "What did you say?"

His lips were still against hers, his nose nearly touching her own. "I asked if you heard me."

"Before that," she said slowly.

"Hellion?"

"Previously."

"Oh, I simply asked if this was a permissible kiss. Not against the rules."

She stared into his eyes, only inches from her own, and a dozen scathing comments flew through her mind, but only one question rose to her lips: "You did not intended to ravish me, did you?"

"Not today." He grinned. "However . . ."

"Well, I wouldn't have allowed it, at any rate." Annoyance battled with frustration and the indisputable knowledge that she would have indeed allowed it. And with a fair amount of enthusiasm, to boot. She did not doubt he knew it as well. "Not now. Not ever."

"No?" He accented his question with a hard, fast kiss.

She gasped. "No."

"Really?" He kissed her again, longer and harder, and her very bones seemed to melt, until finally he drew his head back. "Are you certain?"

"Quite." Her voice had an annoying breathless quality.

"Then perhaps you should let go of my coat."

She jerked her hands away from him as if he was on fire. She certainly was uncomfortably warm. "I'd simply forgotten I was holding it."

Pandora crossed the room in an effort to put as much distance between them as possible. Her knees shook and she was amazed she could stand without assistance. Blasted man. How could he make her feel as if all that existed in the world were him and her? She'd always prided herself on her ability to keep her wits about her. How could he do this to her?

"Be aware, Pandora, that I fully intend to kiss you as often as possible. I do not promise to abide by that particular rule, or any of the others."

She turned in surprise. "But you must."

"Hardly. There were no rules when we made our bargain, and I see no need to alter our agreement now. I am well willing to risk anarchy."

"But—"

He held up a hand to silence her. "However, I am also willing to compromise, in the spirit of the game. I will agree perhaps that I have not tamed man-eating mares as of yet, but given the difficulty of the challenges you have set before me, from this moment, if I can accomplish two with one stroke I shall do so."

She opened her mouth to protest, but he cut her off.

"Furthermore, I will not hesitate to use any means at my disposal, up to and including every pound I have, to achieve success."

He did have a point, and he was willing to sacrifice one of his successes. And his threat to kiss her as often as possible warmed her blood in a delightful and exciting way. Still . . . "What about the time limit?"

He shrugged. "I will give you that."

"Very well. Then tonight's business is concluded."

"Not entirely. I have a rule of sorts of my own."

"Oh? And what is that?"

"It is difficult to prove the passage of most of these tasks without the testimony of a witness, and I could quite easily lie about accomplishing them."

She scoffed. "Your sense of honor would never permit you to lie."

"Thank you for your expression of faith, but the stakes in this game are very high." His tone was abruptly intense. "I will do whatever I must to win."

His eyes darkened and his gaze bored into hers and touched her soul. The man would indeed do as he pleased, and at this moment she knew there was little she could do to stop him.

"You haven't won yet."

"But I will." His lighthearted manner returned. He stepped to the chair, scooped up his bundle, and tossed it at her. She caught it with ease. "You will find what you need for tonight in there."

"For tonight?" She shook her head in confusion.

"I am about to take on another challenge, and you will be my witness."

"I think not," she said haughtily.

"I think so." His voice brooked no argument. "I further think you will accompany me, when necessary, on my efforts to pass the remaining tests. And that, Hellion, is my rule."

She considered defying him, turning and

stalking out of the room, but curiosity, and the tempting idea of more time spent in his presence, plus the distinct possibility of breaking at least one rule yet again, overcame her. "Where are we going?"

"You shall see in due time. Now." He nodded at the bundle. "That contains clothing suitable for this evening's adventure."

"What kind of clothing?"

"Women are not permitted where we are going so you shall have to be disguised." A grin showed in his eyes. "As a boy."

Adventure or no adventure this was out of the question. "I will not!"

"Don't tell me you've never done this before."

"Never!" At least, not since she'd come out in society. Oh, there had been occasions when, as a girl, the temptation to wear breeches and ride across the countryside with all the freedom allowed males but forbidden the fairer sex had proved too much. But that was a very long time ago.

"Then this is your chance."

She looked at the loosely tied packet in her hands.

"I cannot believe the Hellion of Grosvenor Square can resist the opportunity to dress as a male and invade a purely masculine domain."

"It does sound vaguely amusing," she said grudgingly. No, it sounded exciting. A familiar sense of anticipation rose within her. This was exactly the kind of thing the Hellion of Grosvenor Square would do. And if she wasn't quite so daring as her reputation had led him to believe, he was right about the opportunity he'd presented her with. It was indeed an adventure.

"Of course, if you'd rather not accompany me, I shall consider that a breech of our bargain, a forfeiture on your part, and declare myself the winner."

Her gaze snapped to his. "Very well. I'll do it."

"I thought you would." There was a smug note of satisfaction in his tone, the beast.

She stalked toward the doorway, struggling to hide her growing excitement. It wouldn't do for him to know she actually wanted to go with him. "I don't consider this in the spirit of the game. It's almost as if I'm assisting you. Helping the enemy. It doesn't strike me as being at all fair."

"You said it yourself: the stakes are high. Fair is very much a matter of perspective. Everything is fair in matters of the heart and on the field of battle, Hellion.

"And this is both."

"Tell me this, Max, why is it you're dressed like a gentleman and I look like a stable boy?"

He couldn't make out her features in the dark of the closed carriage but the tone in her voice was unmistakable. He choked back a laugh. He should have known a woman used to wearing only the finest clothing in the height of the current fashion would not take kindly to the well worn garments he had provided, although she did look adorable in the knit cap she wore to hide her hair.

"We wouldn't want to raise suspicion. No

one will ever guess your true identity in those clothes."

She muttered something he didn't quite hear, and he thought it was probably for the best.

Her distaste for her clothing was an amusing distraction but only a momentary one. His idea had seemed so clever at first, but now he wasn't at all sure of the wisdom of this venture.

It had been nearly two hours since she'd agreed to accompany him. He'd expected them to be on their way long before now, but he hadn't counted on the seemingly endless amount of time it took Pandora to don her disguise. He could only assume she'd spent as much effort complaining as she had changing.

"When are you going to tell me where we're going?" she said for the hundredth time.

"Patience, Pandora."

The lateness of the hour was a concern. While their destination was respectable, even the most reputable establishment could grow unruly as the night wore on.

Still, while Pandora was not nearly so adventurous as she would have people believe, there'd been an unmistakable glimmer of anticipation in her eye and a note of excitement in her voice that did not bode well. Of course, he would not let her out of his sight. Should they be discovered, the damage to her reputation would be irreparable.

He'd done all he could to ensure success and anonymity. Why, even Laurie thought tonight's plan was a capital idea—going so far as to point out that Max's carriage was far too recognizable and offering to lend Max an older vehicle of his own, complete with driver.

He slanted a quick glance at Pandora. She sat staring out the window into the night, the faint glow from the gaslights in the streets outlining her lovely profile. His stomach clenched with a fresh wave of desire.

When had she become so important to him? Oh certainly, he'd decided well before their first meeting she was the perfect match. Her ridiculous tests were simply a means to an end. And lord knows he wanted her in his bed. He could indeed have ravished her tonight. Or today. Could have taken her and made her his own.

In spite of her protests, he didn't doubt she would have submitted. Didn't doubt she wanted him as much as he wanted her. Victory was there for the taking. Bargain or no bargain, she would have been forced to marry him—exactly as he wished.

When had it ceased to be enough?

She was in his thoughts day and night. In every waking moment and in every dream.

He wouldn't lose, of course. Wouldn't permit himself to fail. He'd seen what happened to men who failed on the field of battle or on the battlefields of their own lives. Men who'd let down those who depended on them, trusted them, and put their own lives, futures and fortunes in their hands. Men he'd admired, éven cared for.

His jaw tightened. Nothing, not drink, not gaming, not even poverty destroyed a man as surely as failure. Destroyed lives. Destroyed families. Destroyed souls.

No, he would win. There was no other option. Pandora was a prize beyond measure. But with every passing day, the disquieting thought grew: did he want Pandora if she did not want him? Was it enough to win her hand if he did not win her heart as well?

Odd thoughts for a man who had never considered a woman's heart before. A man who'd always enjoyed the pleasures of a woman's body but never appreciated her soul or her spirit. A man who knew only the value of the prize and never the worth of the quest.

The carriage rolled to a stop.

"By the gods, Max, tell me now. What have you planned?" Exuberance rang in her voice and caught at something deep inside him.

And he knew without question her hand was no prize at all without her heart. She was right: the stakes of this game were exceedingly high.

And for him, they'd just been raised.

# Chapter 10
## *A Dangerous Move*

**M**ax stepped out of the carriage and his heart sank. Bloody hell. This was not at all where he'd intended to go. He and Laurie had stumbled on this nefarious establishment during one of their infamous forays in debauchery. It could still suit those purposes, but disguised or not, he could never allow Pandora to set foot inside.

He called up to Jacobs, Laurie's driver. "Blast it all, man, there's been a mistake. This is the wrong place."

Jacobs was getting on in years and had been in Laurie's employ for as long as Max could remember.

"Wrong face? What do ye mean, 'wrong face'?" Jacobs said, in the irritated tone only a servant confident of the security of his position could adopt.

"Not 'wrong face,'" Max snapped. "Wrong *place*."

"Nope," Jacob said obstinately. "This is

where milord said to take ye. And here ye
are."

"Nonetheless, we are leaving." He turned
and collided with Pandora in the doorway of
the vehicle.

"Get in." He pushed her backward and onto
the seat. "We're leaving."

She craned to see around him. "Why?
Where are we?"

He knew he should never have trusted Laurie. His voice was curt. "It's called the Lion
and Serpent. It's a tavern of sorts. Disreputable
and dangerous. This is not what I'd planned."

"What did you plan?"

He blew a long breath. "I'd planned on taking you to the Lion's Lair. A very exclusive
club, run by a committee of nine gentlemen. I
thought I could, symbolically, of course, tame
the lion of Nemea and defeat the nine-headed
hydra in one fell swoop."

"It's rather weak." Her voice was thoughtful. "Not at all like encountering a real lion.
But, I suppose, acceptable."

"Bloody decent of you."

"And you can still accomplish one test. This
place has a lion in the name. Besides," excitement sounded in her voice, "I've never been
anywhere truly disreputable before."

"And you're not about to, either." He
rapped sharply on the roof of the carriage. The
vehicle started to move.

"Oh, yes I am." She reached up and repeated his knock. The carriage stopped.
"Don't be ridiculous, Max. After all, we're
here now. And frankly, this is your chance to
pass another test. You have a time limit, and

even symbolic lions are not all that easy to come by."

He shook his head. "This not the kind of place where a lady is safe."

"Perhaps not, but tonight," he could hear the grin in her voice, "I'm simply a scruffy boy."

"Hellion—"

"Now, Max, you'll protect me. You claim to be my hero, remember?"

"Yes, well, apparently I'm also something of a fool. I cannot believe I'm considering this." He was indeed well capable of protecting her. All he really had to do was get her in and out unscathed and he could claim another point. And they were already here.

"Max?"

"Very well." He heaved an apprehensive sigh. "But only under the conditions that we stay no more than five minutes, you remain by my side, you do exactly as I say, and you keep your mouth shut. Agreed?"

"Agreed."

"I hope I do not regret this," he said under his breath, and reluctantly climbed out of the carriage. Before he could help her, she'd scrambled down to stand beside him.

A wooden sign overhead creaked back and forth in the slight breeze, scolding him for the foolish nature of this venture. Every muscle in his body tensed, every nerve tingled. He directed Jacobs to take the carriage around the corner to wait for them in the alley and watched the vehicle pull away in the night.

"Why did he leave?" For the first time, Pandora sounded less than confident.

"I don't want to draw undue attention to the carriage. In addition, there's a back entrance we might need to use."

"Why might we need to use that?" she said slowly.

"One never knows in a place like this. It's wise to be prepared." He stepped to the entry and placed his hand on the heavy wooden door. "Remember, you stay by my side. Ready?"

"Ready." The enthusiasm she'd exhibited earlier had obviously dimmed, and he couldn't help a tiny surge of satisfaction. The Hellion of Grosvenor Square had spent years with a title she hadn't entirely earned. Tonight, she'd make up for that, even if no one but the two of them would ever know.

Perhaps they could tell their grandchildren about this adventure one day.

If they lived that long.

They stepped into the room and at once she thought it resembled everything she'd ever imagined about hell. No flames nipping at their feet, of course, but smoke hung over the place like a plague and stung her eyes. The light was dim, shadows danced on rough-hewn walls in a constant counterpoint to the din of voices and clanking tankards. The stench of tobacco smoke and the smell of cheap candles and cheaper oil lamps mingled with the odor of unwashed bodies and stale spirits. It was hell, all right, filled with obvious sinners who no doubt deserved to be here.

Max made his way past long tables to the back of the room, Pandora hard on his heels.

The room was full but not overly crowded.
There were a few well-dressed gentlemen here
and there, apparently sampling the darker
side of life, but most of the patrons were definitely not well bred. At once she was grateful
for the clothing Max had provided. While
there were occasional curious glances directed
at him, no one seemed to give her a moment's
notice. Ill-mannered, raucous laughter punctuated the general clamor. They passed one table with men disputing the play of a card and
another with a crowd two deep watching the
throw of dice in a game she was unfamiliar
with.

She well understood Max's reluctance to
bring her in here. Danger lurked in every
quarter. It was a world completely foreign to
her, at once crude and rather frightening.

And completely delightful.

Max found a half-vacant table and gestured
for her to have a seat. She lowered herself cautiously onto a hard wooden bench. He sig-
naled to a serving girl in some silent language
she did not understand and dropped onto the
bench across from her.

He leaned forward, his voice quiet. "It
would attract undue attention to leave without
so much as a drink. However, we will slip out
a few minutes after we're served."

"As you wish." She smiled obediently. As
exciting as this adventure was, she was cog-
nizant of the precarious nature of their presence. And as fascinating as she found their
surroundings, tonight she was more than willing to abide by Max's orders. Still, as long as
they remained unnoticed they would no doubt

be perfectly safe. The knot of fear in her stomach eased.

Pandora adopted a noncommittal expression, as if she frequented places like this all the time, and casually glanced around. She couldn't recall seeing such an outstanding display of mankind's more colorful-looking members in one place before.

She leaned toward Max. "Do you think there are housebreakers and thieves and even murderers here?"

"No doubt," he said glumly.

"Really?" A thrill of fear tripped up her spine.

He grimaced and drummed his fingers on the table. Was he impatient with her or the speed of the serving girl or both? He was eager to be off, but they were compelled to remain at least a few more minutes. Time Pandora could put to good use.

She surreptitiously cast her gaze at the other patrons. After all, her parents had spent their lives studying another civilization, and this world was as far from her own as the ancients were from today. The least she could do was make a few scholarly observations of her own. She was, if nothing else, her parents' daughter.

There were a few women in the room who, by appearance and demeanor, made no effort to hide their profession, but most of those here were men. Without appearing to stare, she studied them. Their ages and features varied, but they shared a commonality of class and manner. She considered their faces, rough, like wooden sculptures an artist had failed to complete or lost interest in, carved by lives of difficulty and deprivation. Their fate determined more by the ill luck of their birth than by any fault within themselves.

At once it struck her how very lucky she was to have been born who and what she was. And it struck her as well if one took away their fine clothes and social standing and wealth, there would be little difference between the men here at the Lion and Serpent and those who could be found at Max's Lion's Lair. The knowledge swept away any remaining fear.

" 'Ere ye go, yer lordship." The serving girl sauntered up to them, full hips undulating. Pandora could see she was hardly a girl, age and living and who knew what else was etched upon her face. She plunked a tankard down in front of them, ale splashing over the sides, and cast Pandora a dismissive glance, as if she wasn't worthy of further attention, then turned her gaze on Max.

She placed his tankard on the table with a slow, provocative movement and leaned toward him, thrusting her overlarge bosom nearly in his face. A bosom in immediate danger of escaping from an outrageously low bodice. Irritation stabbed Pandora and she stifled a curt comment.

"Anything else ye need, yer lordship?" Her voice was throaty and suggestive, and there was no doubt in Pandora's mind exactly what the wench had to offer. She rolled her gaze toward the ceiling.

Max's gaze lingered on the flesh presented him for a moment, far too long as far as Pandora was concerned, although she supposed he could scarcely help himself, since the ample offering no doubt obscured any other view. Max looked up at the woman and grinned. "Not tonight."

"Or any other night," Pandora muttered to herself.

"Name's Muriel. If ye need anything . . ." She was practically drooling over him. It was disgusting.

Max pulled a coin from beneath his coat and tossed it at her. She straightened to catch it, glanced at it with a look of appreciation, then propped her plump hindquarters on the edge of the table, directly in Pandora's face. She scooted down the bench a foot to avoid sure and certain suffocation.

"I ain't never seen ye in 'ere before."

"And you ain't never going to see him in here again," Pandora said under her breath. If she so much as touched him, Pandora would be forced to hit her over the head with the tankard.

Muriel ignored her but Max threw her a sharp glance.

Once again the tart leaned toward him, pushing her chest forward, and whispered something in his ear. Max's grin widened.

"Oh, that's quite enough." Pandora got to her feet.

"Sit down," Max said through clenched teeth.

"No," she snapped, and sat.

"What's the lad's problem?" Muriel glanced at her over her ample shoulder.

"He's too big for his britches." Max shot her a warning look. "He probably needs a sound thrashing."

Pandora resisted the childish urge to stick out her tongue.

Muriel got to her feet and turned to study Pandora.

" 'E's a fine lookin' lad. Maybe it's not a thrashin' 'e needs." Muriel rested her hands on the table and leaned toward Pandora, the position allowing full view of her barely confined bosom and beyond, practically clear to her toes. Max lifted his tankard and directed a quick toast at her, then brought the drink to his lips, no doubt to hide his grin. The beast was obviously enjoying this. Pandora clenched her teeth.

Muriel leered in a suggestive manner. "Maybe what the lad needs is a woman."

An odd sound exploded from Max and ale sprayed from his mouth. He started coughing and couldn't seem to catch his breath. It was the least he deserved.

Muriel skirted around behind him and smacked him on the back.

"Harder," Pandora said, and smiled sweetly at Max.

Max held up a hand. "No. Thank you. That's quite enough. I assure you, I'm fine."

"Oh, me poor lordship." Muriel clutched him tight to her, wedging his head firmly between her enormous breasts like a close-fitting bonnet. Under other circumstances Pandora would have found it extremely amusing, but at the moment she was not about to allow the bosom of a tart to entrap the head of the man she might well marry.

Pandora jumped to her feet. "He said he was fine."

She pushed Muriel's shoulders with all the force she could muster. Who knew how much suction was connected with that bosom?

Muriel stumbled backward a good three feet, lost her balance, and sat with a loud smack and a flesh-muffled crash on a table, scattering tankards and plates and bottles in all directions. The two men who had been sitting there in relative peace only a moment before shot to their feet with a roar, spewing a string of foul curses that singed Pandora's ears even as she hoped to remember them for their creativity alone.

A bench tumbled over in the process, tripping another serving woman who carried at least five tankards in each hand, a feat Pandora couldn't help but admire. Pity she couldn't hold onto them. The woman plunged forward, tankards flying as if shot from a cannon, flinging their contents over a remarkably wide area.

The room exploded around her in a kaleidoscope of noise and movement. She sprang backward, smacked into a wall, and ducked in an effort to avoid the pungent wave of spirits that sprayed over her head and splashed against the barrier at her back.

A bellow sounded above her and she snapped her head up. Her wall was a huge brute of a man, now glaring down with murderous intent in his eye. Her heart thudded hard in her chest and she tried to scramble out of his way. He yelled something she couldn't make out in the general chaos and the abrupt realization that she was in serious trouble.

*Where was Max?*

Frantically she scanned the room, searching the roiling sea of battling bodies. Panic surged through her, rising in her throat to propel a scream at the top of her lungs. "Max!"

"Here!"

She searched in the direction of his voice and spotted him in time to see him dodge a fist and throw one in return, the solid thunk of knuckle against flesh lost in the uproar engulfing the room. Max's gaze met hers, a deadly determination flashed in his eyes, and she knew he wouldn't let anything happen to her. He vaulted across the table toward her. Someone grabbed the fabric of her coat and yanked her back.

She fought to keep her footing and threw a quick glance behind her. Good Lord, it was the brute of a wall! By the gods, if he pulled off her coat, or worse her hat, the revelation of her gender would surely heighten the frenzy about her. She struggled to escape. Without warning the hold on her broke. She pitched forward, momentum sliding her under a table. For an instant she lay stunned. What was she supposed to do now?

She twisted around and peered from beneath the shelter. Max was embroiled in combat with the wall. He landed a well-placed punch, and without thinking, a cheer broke from her. Hercules himself could not have done it better. The next moment a fist seemed to come from nowhere and struck his jaw with a force that snapped his head back. She winced in sympathy.

From her protected vantage point she had an excellent view of the brawl. Max was doing

his best, but every time he laid low one ruffian, another would take his place. And he certainly was impressive, although she'd wager
he'd have more than a few bruises tomorrow.
The man did indeed have the spirit as well as
the skills of a hero. Still—a blow struck him
in the stomach and she sucked in a hard
breath—perhaps he needed to work on his de-
fensive strategies before they ventured into
anyplace like this again.

How were they going to get out of here? It
was obvious she couldn't hide under a table
until Max could rescue her. For one thing: he
was seriously outnumbered, although it did
appear the fracas was something of an every-
man-for-himself affair with blows raining in-
discriminately on friend and foe alike. She
didn't relish the idea of leaving her sanctuary
one bit, but at some point she'd be unable to
avoid it. The only question was when.

Max had barely recoiled from delivering a
staggering punch to a nasty brute with few
teeth when a blackguard leapt on him from
behind. She gasped in indignation. Why, that
wasn't at all fair! Not in the spirit of the fight!
He needed help. Somebody should do something. And apparently, she was the only somebody available.

She drew a deep breath for courage and slid
out from under her hiding place. Perhaps if
she kept low to the ground she could avoid
attention. With a speed she never suspected
she had, Pandora crawled on her hands and
knees toward Max. She ducked back under a
table once and dodged a falling body but at
last reached him. She scrambled to her feet.

The miscreant still clung to Max's back or perhaps it was a new one. How dare this nasty creature try to hurt Max!

Anger overcame her fear and she looked for a weapon. Any weapon. She spied two bottles on one table and a third on another, all still miraculously whole, grabbed them, and climbed up on the table behind Max, keeping one and setting the others down beside her, to stand about two feet above the head of Max's attacker. She gripped the neck of the bottle, aimed, raised it high, and brought it down as hard as she could.

Spirits splashed outward. Shards of glass stung her hands. For a moment, nothing happened. Then the man slid to the floor in a fluid move that would have been rather graceful under other circumstances.

Max whirled around. His gaze dropped first to the man at his feet then up to her. "What in the name of all that's holy are you doing here?"

"Helping you." She tossed what was left of the bottle neck aside and smiled, amazed by the sense of calm that pervaded her. "I believe a show of gratitude is in order."

"Gratitude?" He had to yell to be heard but he certainly didn't have to use that tone. A ruffian loomed at his back. "Max! Behind you!"

He turned and felled him with a single punch.

Pride surged through her but she had no time to enjoy it. Yet another scoundrel approached Max on his blind side. Without thinking, Pandora grabbed a second bottle and smashed it over his head.

Max pivoted fast and stared, shock on his face. "Good God, Hellion!"

She grinned. "I daresay, Max, I didn't know what I was missing."

He groaned but wasn't there just a flash of pride in his eyes as well?

"We're getting out of here." He grabbed her by the legs, threw her over his shoulder, and started for the door.

"Wait!" she yelled.

He paused just long enough for her snatch up her remaining bottle then took off. They made remarkable progress given his burden and the confusion around them. She tried to keep her head up to see what was happening, but it was damned awkward in this position. They reached the door and he yanked it open just as another reprobate lunged toward them and she used her last bottle to drop him in his tracks. At that moment she could have sworn Max's body heaved with laughter, but between the noise and his movement, she couldn't be sure. She certainly was enjoying it all.

He strode into the alley and found the carriage at once, barely a few feet from the exit. Max jerked open the door, threw her inside, yelled at Jacobs to go, and leapt in after her. The vehicle lurched forward. The driver's commands to the horses were dimly audible amid the staccato of the animals' hooves hitting the street and the clanking of the carriage itself. They careened around the corner of the alley at a breakneck pace. For a moment he feared the carriage itself would fall apart leaving them sitting in the street on a pile of rubble with an angry crowd behind them. Within minutes, the carriage speed lessened and he breathed a sigh of relief. Old or not, Jacobs was smart enough not have slowed unless they were out of danger.

Pandora's gasps for air beside him were the only sounds in the closed quarters. The euphoria that always seized him after a brawl like this vanished, replaced by remorse.

Damnation he wished he could see her face. No doubt she was frightened and furious with him for putting her in such danger even if it had been her own stubborn inability to keep her mouth shut and listen to anyone but herself that had landed them in this mess.

Still, the entire debacle was his fault. He never should have allowed her to talk him into entering that hellhole in the first place. But he'd been seduced by the idea of earning another point. He was a complete and total fool and he wouldn't blame her if she refused ever to see him again, let alone marry him, regardless of the outcome of the game. He deserved no less.

Abruptly he wondered if that wasn't precisely what Laurie had hoped. His jaw tightened. Friend or not, he would make Laurie pay for this.

A muffled noise sounded beside him. Blast it all, was she crying? No doubt she was terrified. Oh, certainly she had put up a brave front at the end and shown a great deal of courage, but now that the danger was past, she was obviously close to hysterics. Remorse and guilt gripped him. He truly was a rake, a rogue, a scoundrel, and a beast.

"Pandora," he said gently. "I am sorry. I was such a fool to allow you to go in there. I hope you can forgive me, but if not, well, I'll understand."

"Forgive you?" She threw her arms around his neck and kissed him hard and fast. "What great fun that was, Max. What a wonderful adventure." Her exuberant laughter filled the carriage. "I've never experienced anything so completely enthralling in my life. I want to do it again! And you, Max, you are indeed a hero! My hero."

"I am?" he said cautiously.

"You saved my life. You were absolutely magnificent."

Relief flooded him. She wasn't angry at all. In fact, apparently she'd enjoyed it. Cautiously, he wrapped his arms around her.

"And how was I? I think I did a bloody fine job of lending you assistance in there."

"You did a bloody fine job of starting the whole thing." He tried to keep his voice firm but he couldn't hold back a chuckle. He'd been prepared to lecture her thoroughly but her excitement and his relief at their escape relatively unharmed, plus the fact that she was now in his arms, tempered any annoyance. "I suppose if the goal is to best the Lion of Nemea, you can't quite accomplish that without provoking the lion to anger. I gather, then, I have earned a point?"

"Without a doubt." She heaved a sigh of satisfaction. "I will never forget this evening."

"I'll give you that," he said wryly.

"I never dreamed it would be quite so enjoyable to bash a man over the head with a bottle. I daresay that opportunity doesn't come along too often.

"I daresay."

"And you Max, you were so . . . so . . ." She brushed her lips across his.

He pulled her tighter against him. "So?"

"Brave and dashing and, oh I don't know what else but you were with your fists flying and men dropping right and left."

"Yes, well . . ." He had landed a few good punches. If he was with Laurie, they'd be slapping each other on the back and congratulating themselves on a job well done. He could have used Laurie tonight, although Pandora did manage to fell a few ruffians herself. Actually, upon further consideration, he did acquit himself rather well. "I suppose I did take care of a few of those rascals."

"Nine altogether."

"You counted?"

"Of course. It was fascinating. I may have missed one or two." She thought for a moment. "No, it was definitely nine."

"Pandora," he said slowly, "according to my research, a hydra is a snake—"

"A water snake, I believe."

"And Hercules defeated one with nine heads, did he not?"

"Indeed. I don't quite remember which test—" She pushed out of his arms and disappointment stabbed him. Excitement rang in her voice. "Max, the name of that establishment was—"

"The Lion and Serpent."

"Congratulations, Max." She laughed with delight. "You've earned another point."

"I thought two at the same time would be against your rules?"

"I thought you weren't following my rules. Besides, tonight's activity was not like buying a brooch or procuring a chemise; this was really quite difficult, and even a touch dangerous."

He snorted. "A touch?"

"Perhaps more than a touch. Given that, I shall certainly allow this to count as besting the lion and defeating the hydra."

"That's surprisingly gracious of you."

"On one condition."

He groaned. "I should have known. What is it?"

"That you take me there again."

# Chapter 11
## *Strategies Reconsidered*

**"I** cannot believe I could have been such a fool." Pandora reclined on the chaise in her bedchamber holding a cool, damp cloth to her forehead. "I gave him the second point."

"From your description of the night's events, I'd say he more than earned it," Cynthia said mildly.

"Hah!" Pandora lifted the cloth from her head and glared. "He could not have done it without my help."

Once again, Pandora considered the events of last night. Max had taken her home at once in a ride filled with excited chatter and a great deal of laughter culminating in yet another rule-breaking kiss. The experience at the tavern, not to mention the pleasure she found in his arms, had left her with a delightful euphoria, not unlike the drinking of one glass of champagne too many. This morning, however, she'd returned to earth with a thud and the realization she was one step closer to becoming the Countess of Trent.

"I don't know why you insist on being so stubborn about this. I have said it before and I shall say it again." Cynthia perched on the edge of a chair and leaned forward. "You *want* him to win."

"I do not." Pandora's voice was far sharper than she'd anticipated, and Cynthia smirked in response. More and more she wondered if Cynthia was right. Oh, not about winning. Pandora didn't doubt for a moment her desire to beat Max. It would not do to start a marriage with defeat.

*A marriage?*

Did she truly wish to marry him? She certainly found him exciting, and he did trigger the most remarkable feelings whenever he so much as gazed into her eyes. He was clever and kind, and regardless of whatever she might say aloud, Max was far and away the only man she'd ever met that she could even consider marrying. And she absolutely refused to dwell on what his touch did to her. Still, she would not marry without love.

*Did she love him?*

No, of course not. She dashed the silly thought from her mind. He intrigued her. Amused her. Nothing more than that. Besides, even if she did love him, which she didn't, but if she did, she was fairly certain he could never love her. The Earl of Trent was not the type of man to fall in love. Love played little role in the life of a man like Max. She was a prize for him to win, a reward for his efforts, nothing more.

She had given her word to marry him if she lost their game but how could she wed without love? The very thought lit a fire of fear deep within her.

She had no choice. She could not allow him to win.

"I simply do not understand you, Pandora." Cynthia punctuated her words with a long-suffering sigh.

"Precisely *what* don't you understand now?"

"Lord Trent is handsome and wealthy. His breeding is impeccable, his title unblemished. In addition, any man willing to do what you have asked is either a saint—"

Pandora snorted in disdain. "Saint Max? I hardly think so. Saints rarely frequent establishments such as the one we were at last night, unless they are looking for sinners to save. I daresay Max's previous visits to places like that have more to do with his sampling of the various ways to earn a place in hell rather than a desire to save others from that fate."

Cynthia cast her a pointed glance. "As I was saying, such a man is either a saint or a fool. And the earl is no fool."

"No." In point of fact, the man was far cleverer than she'd anticipated. She wondered if she'd taken their game as seriously as she should have up to now. His victory was a very real possibility.

"Or," Cynthia paused dramatically, "he is indeed a wonderful man and you would be the fool to let him slip away."

"I believed we have already established that

I am a fool," she snapped. "I gave him two points."

"He *earned* two points."

"Nonetheless, he is doing extremely well, and he still has a great deal of time remaining. At least with Grandmother's party in the country this week, I will be rid of him for a while. And since he is insisting on my witnessing his attempts to pass my tests, my absence should slow him down and even out the playing field a bit."

"Pandora." Admonishment colored Cynthia's voice. "That's not at all fair."

"Of course it's fair. Max told me himself everything was fair. Besides, this sojourn in the country is not my idea. Grandmother has this event every year right in the midst of the season, and I would not presume to ask her to change her plans. It's always been terribly inconvenient, although I must admit for once I am rather pleased with her timing. It will give me a chance to think without the distraction of wondering what Max is up to and how he's progressing." *And the opportunity to come up with a feasible plan to defeat him.* "You are coming, aren't you?"

"Of course, if you still wish me to." Cynthia stood and stared down at Pandora. "Because I will admit you are right about one thing: you, my dearest friend, are indeed a fool."

Pandora rose to her feet. "How can you say that to me?"

"Because it's true. You are the one who has long encouraged me to assert myself and speak my mind. Very well." She drew a deep breath. "As fond as I am of you, I see it quite clearly. The earl is an unequaled catch and will make you a perfect match."

"If he's so perfect, *you* marry him." She hated the petty note in her voice, but the very last thing she needed was her closest friend telling her what she preferred to ignore.

"I would without a moment's hesitation, given the chance."

"Fine. If—when—I win, I shall select you for his bride."

"Excellent. I can assure you I will appreciate him and all that he has to offer." Cynthia grabbed her pelisse and gloves and headed toward the door.

"What about love?" Pandora shot the words like an arrow. "I know you wish for love as much as I do."

Cynthia swiveled back sharply. "Of course I do. But Trent is a good man and it would take little for any sane, rational woman to love him with her whole heart and soul."

"And I'm not sane and rational?"

"Not when it comes to this," Cynthia snapped. "Furthermore, I cannot imagine, with time, Lord Trent would not love her back."

"Well I, for one, do not care to risk my future on that questionable premise."

Cynthia shook her head. "You are the most intelligent woman I know. I admire your strength, your courage, and your willingness to do exactly as you please. But here and now I must say I have never heard you say anything so—well, stupid."

"Stupid?" Pandora gasped.

"Stupid." Cynthia squared her shoulders.

"You've told me a hundred times: life is not worth living without a certain amount of risk. Were you wrong?"

"No, but—"

"Then how on earth can you stand there and say you are unwilling to risk your future?"

Whether it was the heretofore unnoticed strength in Cynthia's manner or the underlying truth of her comment, for once, words failed Pandora.

"Just as I suspected, you can't." Cynthia nodded crisply, turned, and strode from the room.

Pandora sank down on the chaise and stared in stunned disbelief. Cynthia had never spoken to her quite like this before. Why, Pandora was always the one to take the lead, to speak her mind, and yes, to encourage a certain amount of risk.

What had happened to her?

In spite of her protests, was she falling in love with Max? And was it the most terrifying feeling she'd ever known?

What was she going to do?

Abruptly a thought popped to the surface. Surely Cynthia wasn't serious about her willingness to marry Max? Certainly her declaration carried no more weight than that of any comment tossed off in the heat of anger? Still . . .

Pandora sighed and fell back on the chaise, slapping the cloth back on her forehead. Cynthia had finally become all that Pandora had wished her to be. She had taught her too well. What was she going to do with the girl now?

More to the point: what was she going to do about Max? How was she going to keep him from winning the game and stealing her heart in the process?

And how long could she continue to ignore the nagging thought that perhaps on both counts, it was already too late.

"I daresay, Max, I do apologize." Laurie poured healthy portions of Max's best brandy into a pair of crystal snifters.

Bloody hell. Last night had not gone at all as he had planned. He'd assumed the Hellion would be furious with Max and use the incident as an excuse to dissolve their bargain. Instead, Max was somewhat battered and two steps closer to marriage.

"I never would have sent Jacobs to drive you had I suspected he would make such an error." He put the stopper back into the decanter and turned to face his friend, holding out the second snifter in an age-old offer of peace. "Imagine, confusing the Lion's Lair with the Lion and Serpent."

"It is hard to believe," Max said dryly, and accepted the drink.

"Be assured, Max, I shall take him to task for this."

"Oh, don't be too hard on him, he is getting on in years. It is a bit of a surprise, though. Aside from his hearing, I understood Jacobs to be most reliable."

"Yes, well . . ." Laurie drew a long swallow of the liquor, savoring the satisfying sting burning his throat. He knew from the tone in Max's voice as well as the look in his eye he didn't for a moment believe Jacobs was responsible. "Decent of you to be so understanding, given that you do look rather the worse for the experience."

Max tenderly fingered a bruise on the side of his jaw. "I must admit, at first, I did plan to demonstrate to you precisely what you missed, but all things considered, there was no real harm done. The evening was successful." He sank into one of two leather wing chairs flanking the fireplace, cupped his hands around his glass and grinned. "Quite successful."

"Somehow, I cannot bring myself to congratulate you." Laurie settled into the remaining chair and took another long sip. "So, old man, how many times do you suppose we have sat in these very spots and contemplated the nature of the world?"

"Hundreds, maybe more."

"And how many times have we vowed never to allow any chit to trap us into the unrelenting bonds of matrimony?"

"I can't recall one."

"Very well." Laurie rolled his gaze toward the ceiling. "How many times have *I* vowed never to be trapped into wedded bliss?"

"You? Once again, hundreds at least. But it's not precisely a trap if one is heading into it willingly," Max said mildly.

"Call it what you will, a trap is still a trap." He rested his elbows on his knees and leaned forward. "Rhetoric aside, Max, if a wife is what you want, there are plenty of others to choose from. Miss Weatherly is an excellent example, although she's probably been ruined by her proximity to the Hellion."

Max laughed. "She was something of a surprise, wasn't she?"

"Indeed she was." An unexpectedly pleasant surprise. She'd appeared so quiet and proper at first until the moment she'd exploded in defense of the Hellion. He was hard pressed not to admire the way she'd stood her ground on behalf of her friend. He smiled to himself every time the memory surfaced and it did so with surprising frequency. Her eyes—green, if he remembered right—had flashed with indignant fire. A charming blush had spread up her lovely neck and the interesting way her lips pursed when she called him a prig . . . now, *there* was a woman who could warm a man's bed for a lifetime.

*For a lifetime?*

The thought jolted him back to his senses. Obviously all this talk of marriage had played havoc with his mind.

Max watched him with a raised brow, as if he knew the turn Laurie's thoughts had taken.

"However, Miss Weatherly is not the issue," Laurie said firmly.

"Not for me."

Laurie ignored the implication in Max's comment. "No, you're determined to wed the most willful, opinionated female ever to walk the face of the earth." He slumped back in the chair. "You are beyond hope. Next, you'll be declaring your undying love."

Max silently swirled the brandy in his glass, studying it as if he'd never seen such a fascinating sight. A moment passed. Then another.

"Max?" Laurie's voice rose. "You're not in love, are you?"

"I'm not certain I would recognize love if I saw it. Let me ask you something." Max's gaze met his. "Why are you so set against my marrying Pandora?"

Laurie blew out a long breath. He knew it would come to this. He should have confided in Max years ago.

He and Max had shared confidences since their friendship began in boyhood. They'd attended school together. Played pranks, discovered girls, and grew up side by side. They were as close as brothers—indeed, closer than many. Each trusted the other with his dreams and desires, hopes and fears.

They'd gone their separate ways briefly when Max had stubbornly insisted on purchasing a commission in the army. He rarely spoke of his military days, and from what little he had said, Laurie suspected that the grim reality of war could not be shared with anyone who had not experienced it firsthand.

A scant year after his return, Max had retreated to his family's country estate and refused to come to town even for the season. In hindsight, Laurie recognized that he'd been too concerned with his own petty problems at the time to worry about his friend's state of mind. His vague recollections of his occasional visits during that odd period were shrouded in the mists of drink-induced oblivion. He had failed Max then. He would not fail him now.

And now was probably not the most opportune time for the complete truth.

"Even a casual observer will agree she has

broken any number of hearts through the years. I would hate to see yours lying bruised and battered in the street. There's nothing more to it than that." Laurie shrugged. "Besides, I am simply not up to the strain of helping you recover. You'd no doubt wish to spend every evening pursuing loose women, frequenting places like the Lion and Serpent, downing whiskey and gin and God knows what else, all in an effort to erase the painful memories."

Laurie drew a healthy swallow, then studied his friend over the rim of his glass. "On further consideration, it would be a sacrifice, but I would be more than willing to help you mend your broken heart."

Max laughed. "I knew I could depend upon you."

"Always." Laurie lifted his glass and nodded. The vow echoed in the room. Abruptly the lighthearted mood between them vanished.

"I want you to stop undermining my efforts," Max said, his voice level and cool, his manner resolute.

"I would if I could, my friend, but," Laurie drew a deep breath and braced himself for the worst, "I can't."

For a long moment silence hung between them, heavy and fraught with unspoken challenge. Max's gaze caught his own, unwavering and determined.

"We have always made a formidable team together."

"Indeed we have."

"It has been some time since you and I were on opposite sides of a contest."

"Indeed it has."

"Still . . ." A slow grin spread across Max's face. "I have always rather enjoyed matching wits with you."

Laurie mirrored Max's grin with his own. "As have I."

"If memory serves, the last time the dispute also centered around a woman. And I believe I was victorious."

"And the time before, I was the victor. And the time before that as well."

"Odd." Max shook his head. "I don't recall it that way."

"That is odd." Laurie pulled his brows together in feigned concern. "I remember it distinctly."

"Regardless, if you insist on carrying out your promise to frustrate my efforts, thereby helping Pandora—"

"I am not helping her. I am helping you."

"That too is debatable, but as I was saying," Max paused, obviously considering his words, "you are in essence becoming a minor player in our game. And as with any game, there are rewards for the winner and penalties for the loser. Do you agree?"

"I suppose." Laurie's voice was cautious.

"Therefore I propose a side wager. Up the stakes, as it were."

"Up the stakes?" Laurie raised a disbelieving brow. "They can scarce get any higher. You are already risking marriage with the Hellion if you win, and only the name of the bride changes if you lose."

Max sipped his drink and shook his head. "I seriously doubt Pandora would actually name a wife for me. The more I see of her, the more I think all she really wants is my defeat. I suspect she would be more gracious in victory than I planned to be. Besides, I am hard pressed to believe any suitable woman, and Pandora did agree to choose someone suitable—"

"I don't trust her." Laurie's voice was grim.

"I do. At any rate, no suitable woman would be willing to wed a man she did not know because of a bargain she had no part in. The stakes, should I lose, are really rather paltry."

A wager between the two of them would indeed make the entire endeavor a bit more interesting. "What did you have in mind?"

Max set his glass on the table beside him, leaned forward, and steepled his fingers, looking every bit like a card sharp with a trump in his hand. "There are aspects to these tests that are proving rather costly. I have already commissioned a jeweler to create a necklace strung with golden apples for the final point. However, it costs a small fortune. It would give me a great deal of pleasure to see you foot the bill."

"Very well."

"Excellent. And while I do not plan to lose, should I lose, what would you suggest as your prize?"

Laurie thought for a moment. At once the answer struck him. "Do you recall my plan for your escape?"

"I can scarcely forget it."

"I was quite looking forward to it. Should you lose, I propose we take the journey I had originally proposed. A long trip to somewhere amusing. And of course, women to help ease you through your defeat."

"You are nothing if not thoughtful," Max murmured.

"And you will pay all expenses."

"I would not have it any other way." Max raised his glass. "Are we agreed, then?"

Laurie lifted his snifter. "We are." He clinked Max's glass with his own.

"I give you fair warning, my friend." A smile remained on Max's face, but determination gleamed in his eye. Abruptly Laurie realized Max was not merely playing an amusing game or agreeing to an entertaining wager. "I do not intend to lose."

"Ah, but your loss is the only way to save your life."

Max laughed and downed the last of his brandy. Laurie followed suit and tried to ignore the conflicting thoughts tumbling through his head.

If indeed Max had already fallen in love with the Hellion, losing this contest of theirs would in truth break his heart. Could Laurie really play a role in that?

Yes. He pushed his doubts aside. Rescuing Max from a disastrous future was the one sure way to repay him for a lifetime of friendship. It would not be easy. Still, he wondered if he didn't have an ally in the Effington family itself. Why else would he be invited to the house party of the family matriarch, the Dowager Duchess of Roxborough?

Even so, Laurie might be able to save Max from himself, but could even the most dedicated friend deliver him from the power of love?

# Chapter 12
## *A New Field of Play*

**B**y the gods, she was restless.

Even the feel of the horse beneath her and the exhilaration of flying across the countryside with complete abandon didn't ease the turmoil that gnawed at her. She couldn't sleep and couldn't keep still.

Pandora slowed the horse to a canter, then to a walk. No need to push the poor creature because she was out of sorts. And even here, in the far reaches of her family's ancestral estate, peace eluded her.

Max was to blame for it. All of it. Lingering unwanted in her mind like a persistent melody. Of course, she had to admit he was also indirectly responsible for the taste of excitement she sought to find now on horseback. When they'd parted, she hadn't thought to return the boy's clothing he'd provided for her. Impulsively she'd stuffed them into her baggage and brought them to the country. This morning, it was barely dawn when she'd dressed quietly, taking care not to wake Cynthia asleep in the next bed, and slipped out of Effington Hall and down to the stables. She managed to avoid all but two of the stable boys, who paid her no heed, as if they were used to such goings-on when the entire Effington brood was in residence.

She spotted the small lake ahead, dotted with geese, and directed the horse toward the copse of trees hugging the southern bank and the treasure hidden there.

It was at once odd and wonderful to be sitting astride. She hadn't done anything like this since she'd traded in the schoolroom for the ballroom. She'd nearly forgotten the glorious sensation of freedom riding in this manner provided.

She reached the pathway that skirted the lake and the horse turned in the right direction, as if he sensed where she wished to go. No doubt other members of the family occasionally sought the same sanctuary she did.

She had no idea exactly which Effington relations were in attendance this year. She and her parents, accompanied by Cynthia, had arrived late last night and gone directly to bed.

At any other time, she would have been eager to greet cousins, aunts, uncles, and the assortment of various friends invited for the festivities. In spite of her complaints about the timing of her grandmother's annual party, she always loved coming to the country.

The huge, rambling hall had seemed like a castle when she was a child and the well manicured park a magical setting. Even as she grew up, the magic endured, never failing to give her a sense of serenity and connection. This was the ancestral home of her family and regardless of where she lived, it was here her heart belonged.

Pandora pulled the horse to a stop at the tree line and slipped from the saddle into ankle high grass still wet with dew. The pretty chestnut animal nuzzled the growth around the trunk of the oak that had sheltered horses and children and whoever else ventured here for as long as she could remember. She debated whether or not to tie the reins to keep the beast from straying, then decided he had no interest in anything save the tender green shoots he nibbled on. Besides, Effington horses were always well behaved and she would not be far.

With an eager step, she walked around the oak, trailing her fingers along the bark, passed an ash and another oak, and abruptly, as though by the wave of a sorcerer's wand, she saw it.

A small Greek temple nestled among the trees.

Her spirit lightened as it always did in this special place and she wanted to laugh aloud. She approached it with joy and a measure of reverence, as if it would disappear if she wasn't careful. It had been a very long time since her last visit.

The temple was small and perfectly round, with a domed roof held up by columns. There were no actual walls. One could walk up the two steps that encircled the structure, and if not for the placement of several curved benches inside, step into the building at any point.

In spite of the open design, the columns provided a sense of privacy. Pandora had more than once stumbled on relations or guests taking advantage of its secluded location for a clandestine rendezvous. The building was built of marble, although as a child she'd always believed it was created of spun sugar. It would have been blinding in the direct sun, but set here amid the trees, dappled sunlight painted it with dancing patterns of green and gold.

Pandora entered the temple, moving to the circle that marked the very center of the stone floor, just as she always had. The structure was no more than ten feet across, a measurement taken by children lying head to head. From here she could see through the trees to the lake beyond, even though the temple could not be seen from the lake itself. A fanciful child could well imagine the temple did not exist at all, unless one was directly upon it.

It was that very characteristic which prompted most of the family to refer to the structure with tolerant affection as the Duchess's Folly. After all, what good was a garden structure if no one could see it? But her grandfather had built it for his new bride nearly sixty years ago. The reasons why he'd placed it where he did and why it had been constructed as it had were known only to the two of them. To Pandora it was never a folly and always a temple.

Her gaze rose to the rotunda, its height giving a spacious feel to the enclosure. This was the only part of the building that wasn't white. Instead, it was painted a deep, perfect blue, with silver stars scattered across its surface like the night sky held captive here forever.

She tilted her head back to stare upward at the dome and without thinking raised her arms in a nearly forgotten ceremony of childhood. Long ago, she'd been certain if she reached far enough and stared long enough and wished as hard as she could, the magic here would sweep her off her feet and she'd fly up through the painted sky and on to a mystical world inhabited by Greek gods and fantastic creatures. And heroes.

"I should have suspected I would find a goddess within a temple." A familiar voice sounded behind her.

Her heart leapt. *Traitorous heart.*

She resisted the urge to jerk her arms to her side. "Pray that the goddesses themselves did not hear you. Foolish mortal, they could well strike us dead for your presumptuous comment. They are exceedingly jealous, you know."

"They have much to be jealous of," Max said softly.

Her face warmed at his words. She dropped her arms and turned. He leaned against a column, arms crossed over his chest, a slight smile on his lips, a pale bruise shadowing his jaw.

"What are you doing here?"

"Admiring the scenery." His gaze flicked over her. "Didn't you tell me you never wore men's clothing?"

She crossed her arms, mimicking his stance. "Did I?"

"You did. And in a rather indignant tone, if I recall. However." Once again his gaze traveled over her, slower, more like a touch than a mere look. Her stomach fluttered. "I do believe they suit you."

She lifted a shoulder in a casual shrug. "Well, then I shall have to change my entire wardrobe. Perhaps you could introduce me to your tailor?" A tailor who obviously knew what he was about judging by Max's attire. She'd never seen him so informally dressed. From his high boots to his fashionably snug breeches to his creamy white skirt, scandalously open at the neck, he looked every inch like a modern Apollo. Or a hero. "He seems to do an excellent job."

"As well he should given his bills."

"You haven't answered my question."

"Very well." His voice was serious but a light danced in his eyes. "I should be delighted to introduce you to my tailor."

She tried not to laugh and failed. "You know full well that's not what I meant. Now, what are you doing here?"

"How could I possibly stay in London if you are not there?" His tone teased, but there was a subtle undercurrent that gave her pause. Was there truth in his words, or were they simply well-practiced flattery?

"Do you always know the right thing to say?"

"Not with you." He grinned. "You, Hellion, are an enigma. A challenge."

"Am I? How delightful."

"Delightful for you, perhaps, but an ongoing quandary for me." He stepped farther into the temple, clasped his hands behind his back, and sauntered from one column to the next. "I find myself completely at a loss as to your true attitude toward me. One moment I am convinced you wish me to win this game of ours and the playing is a unique form of courtship. And the next moment I discover you have retreated from London without so much as a word."

He stopped and cast her a chastising look. "I daresay it wasn't entirely fair. Not in the spirit of the game, and all that. I am working with a limited amount of time, you know. How can I be expected to earn points if you are nowhere to be found?"

"It was no secret. My grandmother has this gathering at the same time every year. My visit here could be determined with a single question. Besides, you seemed to have found me with little effort. Even this morning." She frowned. "How did you know where I'd gone? There was no one about when I left the house."

"I was. I followed you."

"You followed me? From where?" She sucked in a breath. "You're staying at the hall?"

"Did I fail to mention that?" He continued to prowl the perimeter of the temple and she was forced to turn with his steps. "I arrived late yesterday, shortly before you did."

Indignation surged through her. "You simply cannot follow me all over the country and make yourself at home."

"On the contrary. I could do exactly that if I wished, but in this instance, I didn't." He leaned forward and peered closely at the striations in the marble of a column as if they were the most fascinating things in the world. "I was invited."

"Invited? By whom?"

"Your mother."

She gasped. "My mother? Why on earth would my mother do such a thing?"

"She no doubt feels I should meet the entire family." He straightened and resumed his circular stroll. "Since I shall soon join their number."

She bit back a sharp reply.

"Although I suspect the Effingtons might be better taken in small doses than all at once."

Her annoyance eased. Perhaps her mother had done her a favor after all. The poor man probably had no idea of exactly what he had gotten himself into. She couldn't resist a smug smile. "Indeed, Max, many of us are much easier to, oh, adjust to individually. Together we can be rather—"

"Terrifying?" He glanced at her, a resigned smile on his lips.

"I was going to say daunting but perhaps terrifying might be appropriate given the right circumstances."

"In sheer numbers alone, your family is," he blew a long breath, "overpowering."

"Don't tell me the Earl of Trent is actually nervous about a simple family gathering?" She studied him skeptically. "Surely your own family has similar—"

"My family is not extensive. My father died

when I was in the army. There remains only
my mother, a few distant cousins, and the odd
relation a dozen times removed." He ran his
hand down the side of a column as if their
discussion was of no consequence. Was it?
"So, you see, you will have little to worry
about in term of family interference once we're
wed."

"Apparently what you lack in relations you
more than make up for in arrogance." Still, she
had to admire his confident nature. And had
to admit his persistence was flattering. "Why
are you so determined to marry me?"

He turned toward her. "Why?" His brow
furrowed and his gray eyes darkened, like a
storm cloud before a rain. Her heart thudded
and she held her breath. What was he thinking? What would he say?

*Did he love her?*

*Could he love her?*

*Could she love him?*

*Or did she already love him?*

"You're everything I want in a wife. You
meet all—"

A hard pain stabbed through her and for a
moment she couldn't breathe. "Your requirements." Her voice was sharp. "Yes, yes, I
know. You keep reminding me."

"And I meet yours, remember?" He stepped
toward her, a questioning expression on his
face. "It's how this ridiculous bargain of ours
began."

"It's not ridiculous." Damn the man anyway. She pulled her gaze from his and stared
at the lake beyond the trees, wondering in the
back of her mind how it could appear so se-

rene when her entire world was engulfed in chaotic emotions she didn't care to examine. She was a prize to him. Nothing else. She should have expected as much. He had never promised anything more.

"Pandora?" Concern sounded in his voice.

She kept her gaze on the lake, afraid if she looked at him he'd see her feelings in her eyes. Feelings she didn't quite understand herself. Or perhaps, simply couldn't accept.

"And what of . . ." She couldn't bring herself to say the word. "What of affection, Max? Don't you wish for affection in a wife?"

"I thought we shared a certain amount of affection."

She looked at him then. "Do we?"

"I thought so." He ran his hand through his hair. "I thought, when we kissed . . ."

"That's what you call affection?" Surely the man didn't believe desire, for it was nothing more than that, was the same as love?

"Well . . ." He looked like a trapped fox desperately seeking a means of escape.

She drew a deep breath and forced herself to achieve a measure of calm. She could scarcely blame him for being as thick as one of the temple columns. It was as much her fault as it was his. She hadn't mentioned love before. Hadn't told him it was the most important thing she wanted in a match. It wasn't part of their bargain. A bargain she had agreed to. A bargain she had to live with. "It's of no consequence."

She turned away, but he grabbed her elbow and pulled her into his arms.

"Pandora." He stared down at her with a

look so intense she caught her breath. "Kiss me now."

For a moment she wanted nothing more than to melt against him. To meet his lips with hers and forget he wanted to share her body but not her soul. She steeled herself against the bittersweet temptation. "I think not." She pushed out of his embrace. "It's against the rules."

"We've broken it before."

"Nonetheless." She walked to the edge of the temple, leaned against a column and gazed out at the trees. "I hadn't anticipated seeing you here. It's rather disconcerting."

"I could leave."

She glanced at him over her shoulder and smiled. "You were invited and it would not be well received if you were to leave now. Besides, there will be any number of other guests including Miss Weatherly."

"You know, I believe I misjudged her the first time we spoke."

"Oh? What makes you think that?"

"Nothing really." The trapped animal look again flashed across his face replaced quickly by an expression of innocence. An expression not to be trusted. "I've just realized anyone you have as much fondness for as you do her, must surely have more to her than one can see at first glance." He smiled as if his words actually made sense.

"What are you planning now?" The answer struck her and she turned and moved toward him, wagging a threatening finger in his direction. "If you have any ideas about using her again to attract my attention—"

His mouth dropped open and his eyes widened. "I am wounded to the quick, Pandora. I would never do such a thing."

She raised a brow.

"Again." He grinned.

Why was that blasted grin so compelling? Coupled with his eyes it was a weapon she couldn't counter. It dissolved her defenses and she was willing to forgive him practically anything.

"I must say, though, it will be nice to see a friendly face amid the legions of Effingtons watching my every move, no doubt looking for any social faux pas I may commit." His manner was casual, but at once she realized he was indeed nervous about her family. Good.

"Excellent way to approach it because you will be on display. Consider it another test."

"Will I earn extra points?" he said hopefully.

"It's a family, Max, not a nine-headed snake. And it shouldn't really be too bad." She wandered idly around the circumference of the temple, circling him. Now he had to turn to follow her progress. "It is only four days with one devoted to the ride and an entire evening to grandmother's ball. It's always a wonderful affair, extremely well attended and with so many people, no one will pay any notice to you at all."

"That's something anyway," he said under his breath.

"So, that leaves a mere three days and nights, that it will be just the family and whomever we've invited."

"Three days." He smiled weakly.

Pitiful creature. She could almost sympathize with him. Almost. "This is the first time my mother has issued an invitation to anyone who could potentially *join* the family."

"The first time?" Was that a touch of green in his complexion? She tried not to smile.

"The very first. Whether my grandmother or the present duchess or any of my other aunts, not to mention my uncles, cousins and assorted other relations will attach more significance to your presence because of that I can't say for certain." She frowned, crossed her arms and tapped her chin with her finger. "Although, I should warn you, most of my family disagrees with my parents. They feel I should have been wed long ago whether I wished it or not. Still, even at this point they are exceedingly particular about whom—"

He reached out and grabbed her arm. "Would you stop pacing round and round me like that!"

She tilted her head and looked at him with feigned concern. "Why, Max, are you feeling ill? You don't look at all well."

Something in her manner must have given her away. His eyes narrowed. "I'm quite fine, thank you."

"You really needn't worry about my family."

"I'm not worried," he snapped. "I intend to use everything at my disposal to charm each and every one of them from the dowager duchess all the way to the smallest child."

"Good luck, my lord." She glared up at him. "Pity, though, it shall be a wasted effort. You will never be a member of this family."

"Why are you so determined not to marry me?" His gaze bored into hers.

"I told you in the beginning: I am not seeking a husband. Any husband. Especially you."

"Why?" His brows drew together in frustration and his gaze searched her face. "We suit so well together. I meet all of your requirements—"

*Not all!*

"—And you can't deny there is more than that between us. Whether that is affection or . . . or . . . something else, I don't know. I do know, I will have you as my wife."

"Only if you win." She shook off his grip.

"Do not delude yourself, Hellion." He smirked and she wondered if bashing him with a bottle would be as satisfying as bashing a tavern ruffian. "Victory is inevitable."

"Indeed it is, but not yours." Possibly even more satisfying. "Your last point was a gift—"

"A gift?" He rubbed his jaw. "Thank God I don't receive many such gifts."

"If it wasn't for me you would never have gotten out of there alive and whole," she said loftily.

"If it wasn't for you, the melee wouldn't have begun in the first place."

"Regardless, up to now I have allowed you—"

"Allowed me? Hah!" Max glared as if he couldn't believe she would say such a thing.

"Yes, allowed you to play exactly as you've wished." No doubt whatsoever. Bashing him with a bottle would be infinitely more satisfying. "And I have given you a great deal of leniency in the process. But from this moment forward, I assure you, I will take an active role in your defeat."

"Excellent." Sarcasm rang in his voice. "The game was proving to be far less a challenge than I had originally anticipated."

She fisted her hands on her hips and raised her voice. "Then I shall consider it my responsibility to do all I can to ensure you are not plagued by boredom!"

"How thoughtful of you. I'll remember to add 'gracious in the face of certain defeat' to my list of requirements for a wife." The level of his voice matched hers. "Although I daresay boredom is not something I anticipate with you for a wife!"

"Hah! I would rather be torn apart by wild camels in the deserts of Egypt before I would even consider keeping you entertained as your wife or anything else!" Her breath was ragged and heat flamed her face. Had she ever been so angry with anyone?

Max stared at her, his ire obviously as great as hers. His eyes smoldered hot and fiery and she wouldn't have been at all surprised to see smoke rise from him toward the dome and soot encircle him on the floor.

What was going on in that obstinate head of his? If he wanted to call their bargain off right now, that was just fine with her. But she would claim her right to pick his bride. And she'd name a suitable bride, all right. The ugliest suitable bride she could find. And fat, too. Someone the size of a small government building. And old. If he thought she was on the shelf she'd show just how crowded that shelf really was. Ugly and fat and—

An odd sort of strangled snort erupted from him. "Camels?"

She jerked her chin up. "Camels!"

"Wild camels?" He pressed his lips together as if he was trying not to . . .

"Yes, wild camels," she said slowly. Surely the beast was not amused?

"In . . . Egypt did you say?" He bit his lip and his eyes seemed to shimmer. The very way they would look if he was desperately trying to restrain himself.

She stepped closer and stared up at him suspiciously. "Max?"

"Pandora." He could barely choke out her name.

"You think this is all very humorous, do you not?"

"Not at all." Again, he emitted that strange muffled sound and his eyes filled with tears. "It's quite serious."

She studied him carefully. Why, the man was about to explode with laughter and obviously realized she would not take it at all well. Still—she bit back a wicked smile—what would it take to shatter his control?

"Indeed it is, Max. Just the other day, I was speaking to an older, unmarried woman, the size of a small government building, by the way, although that's of no importance at the moment. She mentioned that wild camels are becoming an increasing problem in the desert."

"Imagine that." He swallowed hard.

"And even invading the streets of Cairo. Running amuck, as it were."

"Really?" He didn't look at all comfortable. How long could he last? She was hard pressed not to laugh herself.

"Why yes, there are even rumors," she glanced from side to side as if to make sure they were alone, "purporting that they have commandeered a ship and are on their way to England at this very moment. Of course, it is spring, and I daresay storms may slow their progress."

"Indee—" His brow furrowed and he stared at her. "What did you say?"

"That I was speaking with someone the size of a small government building?" she said innocently.

"After that."

"About spring storms?"

"Previously."

"Oh, about the wild camels invading England?"

For a moment he looked at her as if he questioned her sanity, then a grin broke across his face and he laughed. "Nicely done, Hellion."

"It was entirely my pleasure." She returned his grin.

"I'm certain it was." He shook his head, his expression sheepish. "I probably deserved it and I do apologize. The absurdity of your wild camels struck me and . . ."

"The straw that broke the camels back as it were?"

He laughed. "Exactly."

She joined him and nearly forgot the anger of a moment ago and the unexpected ache preceding it. She promised herself to examine that later. It was enough right now to simply savor the pleasure of his presence, and, even if they had nothing else between them, she did enjoy his company.

"It's still early, Max. No one ever rises before ten, and I suspect my horse has become rather restless waiting for me." She started toward the edge of the temple and glanced back at him. "Would you care to race to the stables?"

"Will I get an additional point if I win?"

"Don't be absurd. Besides, I haven't raced on a horse riding astride and dressed like this in years. I'll be shocked if you don't win." She turned and headed out of the temple.

"Do I get a point if I let you win then?" His voice trailed behind her.

"No!" She laughed and strode through the wooded area to her horse. Quickly she swung herself up and into the saddle. The last thing she wanted was help from Max. There was a truce between them now, and she wasn't at all certain she was prepared for, or could resist, even his most casual touch.

Within moments Max eased a large black beast beside her and patted the animal's powerful neck. "Prime bit of cattle here, Pandora, and the other horses in the stable are all equally impressive."

"My family has always prided itself on the quality of its mounts. If you're satisfied with this horse, I'm sure you can have him for tomorrow's Ride."

"Excellent. But what exactly is the Ride?"

"The Roxborough Ride is something of a fox hunt without the fox."

"Without the fox?"

"It sounds a bit odd, I know, but it's a family tradition and began long before I was born." She grinned. "You'll see tomorrow. It's great fun."

"I look forward to it. Now." He gestured in a grand manner. "After you, my dear. Given your lack of recent experience, it seems only fair I should allow you to go first."

"Don't think I won't take the advantage offered." She looked in the direction of the house, far too distant to be seen from this point. "I'll start from the other side of the lake and signal to you when I'm ready." She glanced at him. "Agreed?"

"Agreed," he said with a smile and a look in his eye that warmed her deep inside.

"Then I'll be waiting for you at the stables." She cast him a flirtatious smile, reined the horse toward the lake, and nudged him to a brisk walk. Max's laughter rang behind her.

The man was insufferable and God help her she . . . what? Liked him? Of course. Was fond of him? No doubt. Had some affection for him? Possibly. Cared for him? Perhaps. Loved him?

She didn't know. Not really. It certainly felt suspiciously like everything she'd ever heard about love. There was no question he had a strange effect on her. Since she'd met him she'd been moody and restless and not at all her normal self. She thought about him constantly and seemed to be truly alive only when he was by her side.

And what except love would have given such pain when he more or less admitted he didn't love her?

Still, if she had difficulties recognizing love, perhaps he did as well? The idea lifted her spirits.

Not that it mattered at the moment. She'd meant what she said about taking an active role in defeating him. After all, she could always name herself as his bride. If, in fact, she did love him. And if he loved her in return.

It was rather a pity she'd never been in love before. If she had she'd surely recognize the symptoms now.

For one thing, was it love to want to thrash him nearly as much as you wanted to kiss him?

She was infuriating. And delightful. Lord, with every moment spent in her presence he wanted her more. Pity he didn't understand her for so much as a single second.

He watched her horse canter away from him, her back held straight and regal, her legs straddling the animal. *Lucky beast.* He shifted in his saddle, abruptly uncomfortable and conscious of the snug fit of his breeches.

He frowned and reviewed the last few minutes. What on earth had he said to overset her so? She was as sharp and biting as ever during most of their conversation, but he'd always assumed she'd relished those verbal battles as much as he had. Oh, certainly they'd lost their tempers toward the end. The woman was so incredibly stubborn, it was something of a miracle he'd been able to put up with her for long as he had.

Her dark hair hung halfway down her back and it swayed with the rhythm of her hips and the gait of the horse. He blew a long breath. Could he wait until the end of the game for her? He didn't question his success. Not since the moment he'd realized passing her tests had more to do with a creative mind and a clever twist of words and phrases coupled with a broad dose of symbolism than any overt act of mythic heroism.

Still, he did rather relish the idea of being her hero. Of having her look at him with admiration and . . .

He groaned aloud. That's what had fouled her mood. She'd asked why he wanted to marry her and he'd once again responded with a list of requirements. She'd asked about affection and he'd responded with lust. God help him, how could he be so blind? So stupid? Even a total fool should have realized she was asking about love.

Did she want love from him? Or did she simply want the victory of his loving her? It was never part of their bargain. Not on his list of requirements or hers.

Did he love her?

She was always in his thoughts. And indeed, it seemed these days he simply existed in an empty void when he wasn't with her. That his heart beat and his blood surged and his mind quickened only in her presence. And he wanted her with a need unlike anything he'd ever known. No. He sighed and pushed the thought away. He was confusing lust with love again.

Did she love him? He was confident that she liked him. It was possible she was even somewhat fond of him. Why, hadn't her reaction to Muriel, the serving girl, been suspiciously like jealousy?

He had already decided winning her hand was not enough without winning her heart as well. Why? Why did he care? What did it matter? Why was it so very important it had become his ultimate goal in this game of theirs?

She reached the far side of the lake, glanced in his direction, and waved.

Was this, then, love? This need to have her by his side. To touch her hand and look into her eyes and hear her voice, her laugh. To challenge her wits and have her challenge his. To do battle with her and win. Or lose. To take her in his arms and forget the rest of the world.

He returned her wave, surprised to note the steadiness of his hand when his heart and his stomach and his mind seemed caught in a turbulence born of uncertainty or perhaps perception.

Had love crept upon him unnoticed in the night? Slipped into his life unannounced? Caught him unawares in a secluded parlor or a moonlit graveyard or in the midst of a tavern brawl? Or was it long before they'd ever spoken? When a pretty hellion who waltzed too close to the edge of scandal had caught his eye had she caught his heart as well?

He stared at her figure in the distance and wondered how the Earl of Trent, a man who prided himself on knowing the answers, now had only questions.

Her horse shot forward and at once he realized the race was on. He spurred his mount and took off after her, putting his thoughts aside for now.

But not before he noted, perhaps, he did indeed already know the answers.

# Chapter 13
## *Interference*

Laurie paced the width of the magnificent library at Effington Hall and tried to ignore generations of Effingtons glowering down at him. At least they had the decency to remain silent.

Where was Lord Harold, anyway? Laurie wasn't especially eager for this meeting, but he preferred to put it behind him before he encountered Max or the Hellion. It was well past noon, and as much as he'd managed to avoid them since he'd arrived this morning, confrontation was inevitable. Max would, no doubt, be annoyed by his presence initially, then, with luck, amused at his arrogance in coming here.

He stopped below a painting of a dour-faced Effington matriarch and wondered if Max realized the Hellion could look like this some day. He glared back at the portrait. No. Pandora Effington would never resemble this imposing creature. One only had to look at her mother to know that.

How would the Hellion react to his presence? The blasted chit hadn't seemed to recognize him when he'd attempted to rescue Max. Of course, he'd gone out of his way to avoid her in the last five years. Certainly he had spotted her at various balls or assemblies, but the crush was always such that it was easy to escape her notice.

Not that the Hellion would have paid him any heed even if he'd had the temerity to cross her path. She'd been far too busy charming the latest lovestruck suitor vying for her favors in any given season and dancing along the edge of society's dictates to give him a single thought.

She'd survived the scandal of her second season and the race to Gretna Green, and as far as he had observed, never done anything quite as untoward since. In spite of that her reputation as a hellion had grown.

Well, what did she expect? A woman, especially a woman who looked like she did, with an exuberant charm and an outspoken manner to match, simply could not go on year after year without attracting notice. Add to that the outrageous number of duels, wagers, and gossip that accompanied her, plus her refusal to consider marriage to even the most eligible of men up to now, and the blame for her reputation could be placed on no one's head but her own. Certainly not his.

Still, he was not at all sure Max or the Hellion, or her father, would see it that way.

Perhaps this was not such a good idea. Perhaps there was a far more intelligent way to save Max than venturing directly into the Hellion's family stronghold. Perhaps he would be well advised—

"Lord Bolton."

Laurie started and turned.

Lord Harold stepped into the room and closed the door behind him with a firm snap. He was a few inches shorter than Laurie, still a handsome figure of a man, even though he was surely in his fifties. In the back of his mind, Laurie wondered if all the Effingtons retained their fine looks well into old age. He glanced back at the portrait. Well, not all of them.

"Good day, Lord Harold."

"That's yet to be determined." The older man strode the long length of the room to a large, imposing mahogany desk and seated himself behind it in an equally imposing matching chair, obviously where the Duke of Roxborough conducted estate business.

Laurie understood the duke was unable to attend his mother's party this year and was grateful he not did have to face him as the head of the family. Or, for that matter, the dowager duchess, a woman with a formidable reputation.

"Sit down." Lord Harold gestured to a chair before the desk. Laurie quickly took the seat, noting it placed him an inch or two below Lord Harold's eye level.

"Now then, how long has it been, Bolton?" he said crisply. Pandora's father was the youngest of the duchess's four sons and as such would never inherit the title. Even so, he had an air of no nonsense authority that would well serve any duke.

Abruptly Laurie realized he might be better off facing a duke or a duchess rather than a father. He swallowed hard. "Five years, sir."

"That long, eh? Given that, I must say I was surprised at your presence here and your request for a meeting. Nearly as surprised as I was to learn Lady Harold had issued you an invitation." Lord Harold narrowed his eyes. "Why do you suppose she did that?"

"I don't know, sir." Laurie had been trying to determine the answer to that question himself.

"I assume you wish to discuss my daughter?"

"Yes, sir."

"Well, I will tell you that nothing has changed between then and now. I made a promise long ago never to force Pandora to marry any man she did not wish to."

"Yes, sir, I remember, but—"

"I have to admire your persistence, though." He leaned back in his chair and studied Laurie as if he was an intriguing bit of ancient pottery. "I've got to hand it to any man who refuses to accept defeat even when it's inevitable."

"Thank you, sir, but—"

"Especially since I could easily lay the blame for my daughter's current unmarried state directly at your door."

"Sir, I—" Would he ever get a word in?

"You did bestow the title of Hellion of Grosvenor Square on her, did you not?"

Laurie swallowed hard. "Yes, sir, but—"

Lord Harold held up a hand. "No need to explain, my boy, I can well understand how the heat of the moment can lead to an ill-advised comment. Pity it has continued to cling to her."

"It doesn't seem to have bothered her unduly," Laurie said without thinking.

Lord Harold chuckled. "No, indeed it hasn't. My daughter has not only relished the title, but done her best to live up to it."

Laurie snorted.

Lord Harold raised a brow. "Nonetheless, it's my belief it's that very attitude that has prevented her marriage to this point. She's been far too busy being independent and outspoken and free of spirit to allow any man close enough to recognize a suitable husband when she saw one."

"Sir, I—"

"Pity." Lord Harold shook his head. "There have been any number of young men I would have been happy to welcome into the family." His assessing gaze flickered over Laurie. "I confess, I did not disagree with her refusal to marry you at the time. Felt you were too flighty. Too young. Not at all ready to settle down. It appears you've matured since then."

"Thank you, sir. I—"

"And it seems Pandora may finally have found a man to her liking. It's about time." He rose to his feet. "Damn tricky business, marrying off daughters."

Laurie jumped up. "Sir, I—"

"Let me give you a piece of advice, my boy." Lord Harold pinned him with a firm gaze. "Don't ever have daughters. Sons are what you want. Heirs and minor problems at best. Wish I had had sons." He breathed a heartfelt sigh. "I love the girl with my heart and soul, but you throw a son into the world and wash your hands of him. A daughter is trouble forever."

"Thank you for the advice, sir. But I—"

"Glad we had this little chat." Lord Harold started for the door. "Good to clear the air after all these years."

Laurie stepped after him. "Sir—"

"Forget all about Pandora, Bolton. Find yourself a nice girl. Someone biddable, but with a bit of spirit. Wouldn't want to live your days in a constant state of boredom." He reached the door and turned back. "And take into account her family, especially her parents. If you run across any fools that allow her to call them by their given names or give her the funding to live her life as she pleases—run as if your life depended on it. It well might." He nodded and reached for the door handle.

"Lord Harold, sir, wait." Frustration sharpened his voice.

Lord Harold's brows pulled together impatiently. "What is it now?"

"I haven't said what I came to say, sir."

"I thought you wanted to talk about marriage to Pandora."

"I did but—"

"And we did. And now we're finished." He turned to leave.

Damnable man was as difficult to deal with as his daughter.

"No sir, I haven't yet begun." Lord Harold turned with a frown. "I didn't come here to speak about my marriage to your daughter."

He drew a deep breath. "I wanted to talk about her marriage to the Earl of Trent."

Lord Harold considered him for a moment, then heaved a long-suffering sigh and headed for the other end of the room. "Brandy?"

"Thank you, sir." Laurie brightened. A good drink would certainly make this discussion a lot easier. He followed Lord Harold to a cabinet and watched him pull open a door and rummage inside.

"What is it you wanted to say?" The cabinet door hid his head and muffled his voice.

"I don't think Lord Trent is an appropriate match for the Hel—Miss Effington." Laurie summoned his courage and plunged ahead. "And I think you should forbid it."

"What?" Lord Harold straightened, decanter in hand, and glared. "Dash it all, why should I do that?"

"Well, sir." Laurie cleared his throat nervously. "It's this game they're playing."

"Yes, what of it?"

"I fear each of them is so determined to win," he eyed the decanter in Lord Harold's hands, "they are abandoning all sense of propriety and indeed have already found themselves in mortal danger at least once."

The older man's brow furrowed. "I was afraid these tests of hers would kill him."

"Not Trent, sir, Miss Effington." Was Lord Harold planning on pouring a glass, or would he just hold the blasted decanter all day?

"Spit it out, man, what are you trying to say?"

"Yes, sir." This would certainly be easier with a glass in his hand. "Trent disguised her as a boy and took her to a rather disreputable, no, a distinctly unsavory tavern, where they were involved in a nasty brawl. Trent suffered more than a few injuries."

Concern lit Lord Harold's eyes. "And my daughter?"

"Oh, she's fine, but I understand she was forced to protect herself by breaking bottles over the heads of ruffians."

"Good God!" Lord Harold's jaw dropped.

"Indeed, sir." Laurie couldn't resist a smug smile. "Three times. Knocked them unconscious."

"Three times?" Pandora's father shook his head, obviously shocked. "Felled them, you say?"

"Yes, sir." Perhaps this called for a drink?

"By Jove." A slow grin spread across Lord Harold's face and pride shone in his eyes. "The girl's an Effington, all right. Most spirited family in all of England."

Laurie stared, stunned.

"Always loved a good fight. Would pit anyone of us against any miscreant or villain anywhere in the world. Been in that spot myself more than once in my younger days, too. Never thought it would be up to my daughter to carry on the family tradition. She's an Effington through and through." He winked slyly. "But gets a lot of it from her mother."

Laurie's shoulders slumped. "So you're not going to put an end to this? Forbid her to marry Trent?"

"Are you daft?" Lord Harold scoffed. "Lord Trent's the one who suffered in the incident.

He can obviously protect her or she can protect herself."

"But the scandal if this comes out."

"Does anyone else know about it?"

"I don't think so."

"And they won't will they?" There was an unmistakable threat in Lord Harold's voice. "We wouldn't want a repeat of that Hellion of Grosvenor Square business, would we?"

Laurie nodded reluctantly. "No sir."

Lord Harold's gaze assessed him. "You look like hell, man. Did you want that brandy or not?"

"Yes sir." He might as well accept defeat graciously. At least on this front.

Lord Harold pulled two glasses from the cabinet and handed him one.

"But, I am curious, sir." He held out his glass and Lord Harold obligingly filled it. He took a quick sip. "Good brandy, sir." He paused to choose his words. "Given what I've told you, why are you willing to allow this game, and more than likely a marriage as well?"

"First of all, as you no doubt realize, if this is what she wants, I probably couldn't stop her." He poured a glass for himself and replaced the decanter. "Secondly, from all I've been able to determine, the earl is an excellent match."

He led Laurie to a sofa and they each settled at opposite ends. "Good family, fine fortune, unblemished title and his war record is outstanding. He's a man of honor and means. No father could ask for more."

He caught Laurie's gaze with his own.

"Don't take my previous comments about my daughter incorrectly. I would not hand Pandora over to any man who was not worthy of her. Lord Trent is a good man."

He raised his glass and drew a long swallow. "In addition, I suspect the incident you related was, if not instigated, then at least exacerbated by my daughter. Am I right?"

Laurie nodded.

"I can't hold him completely responsible for that." He absently swirled the brandy in his glass and studied Laurie. "Let me ask you a question. If you don't want Pandora for yourself—"

"I can assure you, I don't, sir," Laurie said quickly.

Lord Harold raised a brow. "Very well. If you don't want her, why are you so obviously against her marriage to Lord Trent?"

"He's my oldest friend." A glum note sounded in his voice.

"I see." Lord Harold laughed then sobered. "I'll give you one more reason why I won't forbid this match." He stared at his brandy for a minute then met Laurie's gaze. "I think she likes him. Maybe even more than likes him."

"How can you tell?" Laurie said dryly. "She's not making it easy for him."

"But she has agreed to this bargain. She's never really risked marriage before. That nonsense with you was more youthful foolishness than anything else. I suspect her feelings for him are stronger than even she expects." He shrugged. "Even Peters agrees."

"Peters?" Laurie pulled his brows together. "Who is Pe—"

A sharp knock sounded at the door and it swung open.

"Harry, I must talk to you. When you and Grace first met, how did you know—" the Hellion stepped into the room and stopped. "Oh dear, I am sorry, Harry, I thought you were alone."

*Harry?*

They set their glasses down on their respective side tables and rose to their feet. She smiled pleasantly and walked toward them. Laurie had to admit she was indeed a beauty.

Recognition lit her eyes and she held out her hand. "You're Lord Trent's friend, aren't you?"

He took her hand and brought it to his lips, never taking his gaze from hers. The blasted woman still didn't remember him. "Indeed I am."

"Please forgive me. You look familiar, but," she shook her head and bit her bottom lip, "I can't seem to place you."

An odd sort of muffled snort came from Lord Harold. Laurie dropped her hand.

"Pandora, my dear," Lord Harold said with a note of amusement in his voice. "Surely you remember Lawrence, Viscount Bolton?"

For a moment nothing happened. Then her eyes widened and she gasped. "Dear Lord, you're the twit!"

Where on earth was the man?

Cynthia stood on the steps of the wide terrace. A servant had suggested she might find Lord Trent out of doors, but so far she was having little luck. Now she stood debating whether or not to look in the garden or venture into the mazes, daunting as they were, for him. If she weren't already encumbered by the large paper-wrapped package she clutched tightly in her arms, she wouldn't have hesitated to search further. Her burden was uncomfortably heavy, its weight growing with every step since she'd retrieved it from its hiding place amid her packed clothing.

Cynthia had absolutely no qualms about speaking to Lord Trent. The confidence she'd garnered at their last meeting had, if anything, grown stronger. It was quite pleasant to realize she could indeed take a hand in shaping the events of the world, rather than waiting for them to shape her.

There were perhaps a dozen people out and about. Some strolled the grounds. Quite a few sat in chairs on the terrace enjoying the fresh air and the fine spring day.

"Miss Weatherly."

She glanced over her shoulder. Lord Trent strode across the terrace toward her. "Good day."

He smiled in greeting. "A footman said you wished to speak to me." His gaze slid to her package. "May I take that for you?"

"Please," she said with relief, and handed it to him.

He hefted it in his hands and raised a brow. "What is this?"

"I'll show you in a moment." She cast her gaze over the terrace and then scanned the park to make certain Pandora was nowhere to be found. "If you would be so kind as to accompany me to the garden?"

He smiled. "It would be my pleasure."

They walked down the steps toward the formal plantings laid out in a manner best to be seen from the terrace and Effington Hall itself. She stopped.

"No, this will never do. The garden is far too open." She nodded at the high boxwood hedge that marked the square maze to the right of the garden. "That maze will serve much better." She started toward it with a determined step. "It would be best if we were not seen."

"Whatever are you up to, Miss Weatherly?" An amused tone sounded in his voice.

She slanted him a quick glance. "I am doing precisely what I said I would. I am lending you my assistance."

"You are?" He laughed. "How?"

"I'll explain when we're out of sight of the hall. There are too many people about here."

"It does seem rather crowded."

"Oh, it's not at all bad yet," she said lightly. "The gathering grows larger every day with those who couldn't stay for the entire length of the duchess's party but come for only a day or two. Most of those here now are Effingtons. It is an exceedingly large family."

"So I've heard," he said in a dry manner.

She smiled. "It is rather overwhelming if one isn't used to it. I've been invited here for the past two years and I can assure you, for the most part, they are all quite charming."

"No doubt," he said, as if he didn't believe her. "So I gather there is no one I should be particularly concerned about."

"You, Lord Trent, should be concerned

about them all." She took a few steps before she realized he was no longer with her. She stopped and looked behind her.

Trent stood stock still with a look of unease on his face. "What exactly do you mean?"

Good Lord, the man was truly concerned. She laughed. "You really have nothing to worry about. It won't be that bad. Now, are you coming with me?"

"Of course." He nodded and stepped forward, and again they started toward the maze.

"The Effingtons are very nice. Oh, the dowager duchess can be a bit formidable but that's probably more a result of age and her position as family matriarch. And the duke, Lord Harold's oldest brother, is charming, but he carries this, well, air of authority that can be a touch intimidating. I gather he is not here this year, but his wife the duchess is. Her Grace is quite lovely and very nice although she does have a habit of studying you as if she was trying to determine exactly what you're made of and whether or not you measure up to Effington standards.

"And then there are Lord Harold's two middle brothers, the lords Edward and William, and their wives and children—although Pandora's very favorite cousins haven't arrived yet. Add to that various distant relations and—" She glanced beside her. Lord Trent had disappeared. She sighed and turned. Once again he looked as if he was rooted to the ground.

"Are you certain I have nothing to be worried about?"

"My lord, you are being ridiculous." She planted her hands on her hips. "From what

Pandora has said, from what I myself have observed, you are everything any family could wish for. As I've told you before, you are a perfect match for Pandora."

"But will they think that?"

"Any fool can see that, and I doubt there is a single fool among this entire family. Besides." She heaved an exasperated sigh. "Each and every one of them feels Pandora should have been wed long ago. Why, you could probably be hunchbacked, with two heads and drool coming out of both mouths, and as long as you were still moderately respectable they'd tie a ribbon around her waist and hand her over to you with a wink and a healthy dowry."

He chuckled and walked toward her. "I hardly think they would accept drool. Two heads, perhaps."

"Perhaps." She laughed and he fell into step beside her. "Still, I am serious when I say you needn't worry."

"We shall see," he murmured.

They approached the maze and stopped at the entrance. The height of the hedge was nearly eight feet. Pandora had told her once both mazes had been planted more than a century ago, although the gardens they flanked were routinely dug up and redesigned with every new Duchess of Roxborough.

"So." Lord Trent studied the entrance with an air of skepticism. "Which way do we go?"

"Pandora told me the secret of both mazes once, but I must admit, I really don't remember. Besides, we only need to go around one corner to get the privacy we require." She stepped into the maze, confident he would follow.

"Privacy? I must confess, you have piqued my interest, Miss Weatherly."

She turned to the right and followed the maze around one turn. "This will do. Now." She clasped her hand together in anticipation. "Open the package."

He studied her curiously for a moment, then untied the string around the wrapping and pulled off the paper.

"It's a drinking cup," she said quickly. "I know it looks far too big to be a cup, but that's what she—that's what it is."

"It's Greek, isn't it?" He examined the cup. It was about the size of bowl, nearly a full foot across, with handles on each side and a stem that flared to a circular base. It was black in color overall, banded by a wide strip of an earth red shade embellished with stylized figures rendered in black. "And very old."

"Oh, it's ancient. Look at the design." A note of eagerness rang in her voice.

"Interesting," he murmured.

"Goodness, my lord, it's more than interesting." She stepped closer and traced the design with her finger. "See here? This gentlemen—I can't remember his name, Thes-something, it doesn't matter—but look at what he's fighting."

"It looks like a bull." Trent's brows drew together in concentration.

"It is a bull. And not just any bull. I'll tell you the complete story later, but this is a bull from Crete," she said with a note of triumph.

"A bull from Crete," he said slowly, then

met her gaze and grinned. "A bull from Crete."

"Congratulations." She beamed. "I believe you have another point."

His grin faded. "I can't accept this."

"Why on earth not?" She stared in astonishment.

"It doesn't seem quite sporting." He shook his head. "Not in the spirit of the game, and all that."

"Not in the spirit of the game?" She snorted in a distinctly unladylike manner. "And I suppose purchasing a gold horn or procuring a chemise from a woman who has apparently been an acquaintance for years is in the spirit of the game?"

"That was different." His brow furrowed as if he was trying to determine exactly how they were different.

She scoffed. "Nonsense. Besides, Cretan bulls are exceedingly difficult to find."

"Where did you get this?"

She thought for a moment. Lady Harold had given her the cup knowing full well she'd give it to Trent. Pandora would not be at all pleased. The less he knew, the less he could reveal. "It was a gift. It was given to me, and now I'm giving it to you."

"It would give me five points," he said under his breath turning the cup over in his hands. "Still . . ."

My, but the man was stubborn. "If you truly feel you can't accept the blasted thing as a gift in the spirit of the ridiculous game—"

She snatched the cup from his hands, walked a few paces, placed it on the ground, then turned to him and clapped her hands to her cheeks. "Oh no. Look!" She pointed dramatically to the cup. "A bull! No doubt from Crete! Oh, I do hope someone can capture the beast!"

Lord Trent stared at her with a mild look of alarm. The very same look one might give a relation whose bottle was not completely corked.

She huffed and fisted her hands on her hips. "I say again, can't someone capture this beast?" Her voice rose. "This bull? From Crete?"

"Capture . . ." His eyes widened and he laughed. He stepped to the cup and picked it up with a flourish.

"Well done, my lord!" Cynthia applauded. "I have never seen the capture of a bull, especially a bull from Crete, accomplished with such skill."

"Thank you, Miss Weatherly. I do appreciate the compliment, but have you ever considered, perhaps"—a wry smile quirked his lips—"you spend entirely too much time with Miss Effington?"

# Chapter 14
## *An Uneasy Alliance*

**F**or a moment Pandora could only stare in horror.

It had been years since she'd so much as given the twit a second thought. And even then it had only been to hope he'd somehow vanished from the surface of the earth.

Lord Bolton swept a low exaggerated bow. "At your service, Miss Effington."

"I don't want you to be at my service. I don't want you to be anything. And most of all, I don't want you to be here. What are you doing here?"

"I was invited," he said.

"Invited? Hah! Who would have invited you?"

"Your mother."

"My mother?" Indignation swept through her. "First Trent, now you? How could she?"

Lord Bolton shrugged.

The last thing she expected when she walked in to speak to her father was a confrontation with her past. Didn't she have enough on her mind with Max present? Wasn't her life far too complicated already? She certainly didn't need an awkward, and nearly forgotten, incident from years ago rearing its irritating head in the form of Viscount Bolton.

Her father cleared his throat. "I suspect you two have any number of things to discuss, and while I dare not leave you alone, the servants complain whenever there is blood on the carpet; this is an exceedingly large room." He nodded toward the far end of the library. "I'm certain I have something I can attend to at the desk."

He stepped to a table beside the crimson sofa, picked up a glass of brandy, cast her an encouraging smile, and strode off.

She crossed her arms over her chest and studied Lord Bolton. Now that she saw him again she remembered how handsome she'd once thought him. Grudgingly she admitted the last five years had served him well. He was perhaps more attractive now than he'd been then, with an air of confidence brought on by maturity. Of course, he was still a twit.

"Why are you here?

"I told you, I was invit—"

"No. I understand how you came to be here, although I do not understand *why* the invitation was issued. What I want to know is why you accepted."

"I had nothing better to do." He swaggered to one of the tables flanking the sofa and picked up a glass that matched her father's. "I thought it might be amusing."

"Amusing?"

"Indeed." He took a thoughtful sip. "I am well aware of the bargain you have made with Trent. As he is here, well, I did think it would be entertaining to watch him attempt to pass your tests."

"I doubt he'll be doing any such thing while he's here." Would he? Why hadn't she considered that possibility? This might in truth be the best place for Max. Had he realized that?

"Then perhaps I should leave."

"Excellent." She stalked to the still open door and gestured for him to go ahead. "I'd be delighted to have someone see you to the gates."

He shook his head in feigned regret. "But I can't. It would be the height of impolite behavior. I am nothing if not polite."

"You, my lord, are a twit!"

"Perhaps." He raised his glass in a toast. "But an extremely well-mannered twit."

"I doubt that," she said sharply. "A well mannered twit wouldn't have come here in the first place."

He chuckled. "I did not say I was intelligent, merely polite."

"And are you honest as well?"

He frowned as if trying to decide. By the gods, if she had a bottle in her hand right now she'd certainly put it to good use. "When it can't be avoided, I suppose."

"Then don't avoid it now. Tell me the truth." She trapped his gaze with hers. "Why are you really here?"

He stared at her silently, as if choosing his

words. "How much do you wish to win this game with Trent?"

"I never play a game I don't want to win." Caution edged her voice.

"Neither does Trent. However"—he drew another swallow—"I want him to *lose*."

She pulled her brows together in confusion. "Surely you can't think you and I—"

He laughed shortly. "Not in my worst nightmare."

"Excellent. On that, then, we agree." She studied him carefully. "But I thought you were his friend."

"I am. His oldest and dearest friend. That is precisely why I want him to lose."

She shook her head. "I still don't understand."

"It's really quite simple, my dear. I don't wish to see you break his heart." He met her gaze directly. "As you did mine."

"Good Lord!" She sucked in a sharp breath. Shock swept through her, and without thinking, she advanced toward him. "I don't believe you."

"Be that as it may." He lifted a shoulder in a casual manner, as if to say it was of no consequence, but his eyes held a different story. "It's one unavoidable truth."

For a moment she could only stare. Guilt and shame welled up inside her. Pandora wrapped her arms around herself and pulled her gaze from his. Her mind whirled with questions and accusations and memories. She stepped to the tall windows that overlooked the gardens and the flanking boxwood mazes, one square, the other round, and gazed unseeing through the glass.

What on earth could she say to this man? As far as she knew, she'd never broken anyone's heart before. Oh, certainly there had been scores of suitors who had pledged their undying love, but she'd never quite believed any of them. Still, she'd always tried to be gentle in her rejection, and most, if not all, had recovered sufficiently to wed someone else within a year of declaring she alone held his heart.

With Lord Bolton, she'd been anything but gentle. She'd never suspected his feelings. "I didn't know. I—"

Incredulity rang in his voice. "How could you not know?"

She stared out the window, barely noticing the spring blossoms coloring the garden, seeing only the events of what seemed like a lifetime ago.

"It was a lark. We went to Gretna Green as a diversion. To see the others marry. Nothing more. I never dreamed your intentions were serious."

"Perhaps they weren't at first," he admitted in a grudging manner. "But then everything in that little escapade went wrong. The accident with the carriage, and—"

"That horrible inn." She shuddered at the memory of a dark, dank place filled with miscreants who'd leered at her as if she was a woman of the streets. "I still thank the gods we lingered only a few minutes."

"Not to mention the trio of fathers hot on our trail." She could hear a smile in his voice.

"And those two gentlemen, each of them swearing—oh, what was her name now?"

He chuckled. "I can't recall."

"Neither can I, but I distinctly remember both claimed Miss Whoever-she-was had promised to marry each of them." She shook her head. "What a night that was!"

His voice sobered. "Then, when the families involved insisted the only way to avoid scandal was for all of us to wed, well, I thought: why not? But you declared, how did you put it?"

She cringed. "I don't remember."

"Oh yes, it was something to the effect of preferring to be devoured by hungry lions in the coliseum at Rome rather than marry me. I was devastated. You see," he hesitated, and a knot settled in her stomach, "I was in love with you."

"I am truly sorry." She turned to face him. "I had no idea."

He stared at her, his gaze intense. "Would you have married me had you known?"

"Of course not," she said without thinking, and immediately regretted her quick response. He lifted a brow. "What I mean is that we scarcely knew each other. We'd shared a few dances and a couple of rather inane conversations."

"Nonetheless." He raised his chin staunchly. "I was in love."

"I really did not..." A thought struck her and she paused. "You certainly did give up quickly for a man in love."

"I spoke to your father," he said loftily.

"And," she prompted.

"And . . ." For the first time he looked ill at ease. "And that was it."

"That was it?" Irritation wiped away her guilt. "You claim you were in love with me and further charge I broke your heart, yet all you did to win me back was talk to my father?"

"Well . . ." Bolton looked as if he wished he were anywhere but here. "It seemed the thing to do at the time."

"I was right all along. You are a twit."

"You made a fool out of me." He aimed his glass at her. "You humiliated me in front of all of London. Held me up to ridicule. I am still trying to live down the scandal."

"Hah!" She scoffed with disbelief. "Some scandal! It's barely remembered. And even when it is," she narrowed her eyes and pointed an accusing finger, "your name is not the one connected with the incident. It's the Hellion of Grosvenor Square who bears the brunt of that business. The Hellion of Grosvenor Square whose every move is watched with an eye toward propriety. The Hellion of Grosvenor Square whose entire life has been overshadowed not so much by that incident, which as I've already noted, is nearly forgotten, but by the title a twit bestowed on her!"

She poked him hard in the chest.

"Ouch." He drew back with a look of apprehension in his eye, as if he feared for his life.

*As well he should!*

"And who is responsible for that?" She poked him again. He stepped back. "Who is that twit?" She poked him once more.

"Stop that." He rubbed his chest with his free hand.

"Well?" Her voice threatened far more damage than her finger.

"Let me think—"

"Bolton!"

"Very well." He had the grace to look chagrined. "I'm the twit."

"And tell me one more thing." She glared up at him. "Just how long did it take you to get over your broken heart? To fall in love with someone else to the same degree you did with me?"

"I'm not sure I can remember. It was a long—"

She clenched her teeth. "Bolton."

"Very well. If I recall, I recovered in a rather miraculous manner after I named you the hel—" He shrugged apologetically. "It did take much of the sting out of it."

"Bolton!"

"The memories are so dim . . ." He sighed in defeat. "I'm not certain. At least a month."

"A month?" She could barely choke out the word.

"I think so." He smiled weakly.

"A *month*." She spun on her heel and stalked across the room.

"That should take some of the guilt out of it for you." Hope colored his voice.

She whirled toward him. "Guilt? I feel absolutely no guilt whatsoever. For the barest moment, I did experience something akin to the mild regret one feels at having selected the cod over the haddock at dinner. But guilt?

Hah! Besides, what I broke wasn't your heart.
It was your pride."

"Nonetheless, it hurt," he muttered.

She wasn't sure if she wanted to smack him
or throw something at him or laugh hysteri-
cally or break down and weep. Perhaps she
should ask Harry to shoot him. His aim was
probably better than hers. That's what fathers
were for, wasn't it?

A nasty thought flitted through her mind.
Given the rancor the viscount had obviously
retained against her all these years . . . "Does
Trent know about, for lack of a better word,
us?"

"No." Bolton downed the rest of his brandy
and cast her an uneasy glance. "He was not,
well, himself that season, and he stayed in the
country much of the year. I was far too embarrassed initially to mention it all, and then
simply never got around to it."

"That's something, anyway," she murmured.

"You know." Bolton glanced at the cabinet
where the brandy was kept, but was apparently far too polite a twit to ask for a refill. Or
perhaps he was concerned she wouldn't be
able to resist the lure of a bottle as a weapon.
"I haven't spoken of all this in years. Whenever I thought of it, or you, my memories
might have been a bit, well, slanted, shall we
say."

She raised a brow. "A bit?"

"More than a bit. Now, for the first time, I
realize you may be right. It may well have
been my pride you injured. I am willing to
forgive you."

"You are willing to forgive me?" she said with amazement.

"Absolutely." He smiled magnanimously. "And in addition, admit, perhaps, all things taken into account, you have indeed borne the brunt of the past. And that, perhaps, is my fault."

She studied him through narrowed eyes. "Perhaps?"

"Perhaps." His smile widened to a grin.

Given the long-lasting repercussion of his actions on her life, she certainly wasn't willing to forgive him so much as the use of the wrong fork at dinner. Still, her irritation with him dimmed. Blast it all, the man's grin was as irrepressibly charming as his friend's. "I'm not sure I entirely trust you."

"Then we agree." He beamed. "I don't entirely trust you, either."

"So, now that you have forgiven me and accepted blame—"

"Perhaps."

"Perhaps," she chose her words carefully, "where does this leave my game with Trent?"

"Oh, nothing has changed in that regard," he said matter-of-factly. "I still want him to lose."

"Because you fear I'll break his heart?"

He gazed at the glass in his hand, turning it this way and that in an obvious effort to ensure no drop of liquor had escaped his thirst. "In the midst of your ranting about lions and raving about the coliseum, do you recall what else you said?"

"No." Unease twinged through her.

He met her gaze. "You said you would never wed without love."

"Did I?"

"You did indeed." He nodded. "So regardless of any newfound revelations I've reached regarding the past, I still believe this bargain of yours carries the distinct possibility of heartbreak."

Her breath caught. "Does Max love me?"

"I don't know. I don't know that he knows. Do you love him?"

"I don't know."

"Well, in that, at least, you are well matched."

So Max had discussed the possibility of love. How very interesting. Thoughtfully, she stepped to the cabinet, selected a decanter of brandy, and returned. Bolton held out his glass and she obligingly filled it.

"Feeling as strongly as you do about love playing a role in marriage," he paused, "and I assume you still feel that way, unless with your advancing years you have decided marriage for any reason at all is better than no marriage whatso—"

"I haven't," she said sharply.

"Very well. Given that, I seriously doubt you will hold Trent to his agreement to wed a bride of your choosing, should you win. However, if he wins, both of you would be obligated to abide by your word and you will marry." He lifted his glass. "Regardless of how either of you feels." He threw back a rather impressive swallow of the liquor.

"I see," she said slowly. "My victory ensures that a choice remains. Trent's leaves no room for anything but marriage."

"Exactly. Therefore I have a proposition to offer you."

"Oh?"

"I propose we join forces."

A snort of disbelief sounded from the other side of the room.

"Together, victory is assured."

"I do want to win," she murmured. Besides, hadn't she already realized as the winner, she could still wed Max, if that was what she wanted? And what she thought he wanted? But an alliance with the twit? It was at best an uneasy truce. "I still do not trust you."

"The best allies are those who do not completely trust each other. So, do you accept my proposal?"

"I assume we would keep this between us. Not mention it to Lord Trent. He might not think it was quite—"

"In the spirit of the game?"

"Exactly."

"On that point, I agree completely. Good God. Max would never—"

Laughter sounded at the open door. Cynthia stepped into the library, followed by Max, carrying what appeared to be an ancient Greek drinking cup.

"Pandora, we were look—" Cynthia caught sight of the viscount and stopped short. "Oh dear, it's the prig."

"Twit, actually," Pandora said under her breath.

"Laurie?" Max's brow furrowed. "What on earth are you doing here?"

"He was invited," Pandora and Cynthia said in unison. Cynthia's eyes widened and Pandora slanted her a questioning glance. "How did you know?"

"I simply assumed he wouldn't be here unless he was invited." Cynthia appeared distinctly uncomfortable.

Pandora narrowed her eyes. "Do you know him?"

"Well, I . . ." Cynthia floundered.

"I know I would never have forgotten such a charming face," Lord Bolton said smoothly. Cynthia blushed.

"Laurie, what are you doing here?" Max said.

"As they said, I was invited."

Pandora sighed. "Apparently, my mother's doing, although her reasoning escapes me. But I do intend to find out."

"I often receive invitations," Lord Bolton said immodestly. "I am considered quite an excellent addition to any gathering. I am unmarried, wealthy, titled, and unfailingly polite."

Max studied him. "I didn't know you even knew the Effingtons."

"Did I fail to mention that?" Lord Bolton took a sip of his brandy. His gaze slipped to Pandora and a wicked spark shone in his eye. "My acquaintance goes back years."

Cynthia cast Pandora a puzzled look.

"Yes, he's a very old, and nearly forgotten, acquaintance," Pandora said, with a dismissive wave of her hand. "It's of no consequence."

Max's gaze slid from Pandora to Lord Bolton and back and he appeared to be trying to figure out a vexing problem.

"I still do not—" Max started.

"What is that?" Pandora said quickly, nodding at the cup Max held. If Max were to learn of her long past relationship with his friend, she would prefer it be revealed at a time of her choosing. And this was definitely not the right moment.

"This, my dear, is my fifth point." He stepped toward her and presented the cup with a flourish. "A bull from Crete."

She accepted the cup and studied it. It appeared vaguely familiar. Annoyance surged through her. She frowned and glanced at him. "Where did you get this?"

"It was a gift." His grin widened.

"A gift? Grace has a piece exactly—" She glared. "Did my mother give you this?"

"Absolutely not," he said staunchly.

"Then where—"

"I gave it to him." Cynthia's chin rose and she stepped forward. "It was given to me and I in turn gave it to him."

"But why would . . ." The answer struck her like a bolt from above. By the gods, it wasn't enough that Cynthia was thoroughly behind Max's efforts; now she was obviously doing what she could to assist him. How could she? Consorting with the enemy. Her dearest friend. Pandora shot Lord Bolton a grim look. "I accept."

He lifted his glass in a salute.

"Accept what?" A note of suspicion sounded in Max's voice.

"Your point, obviously," Lord Bolton said.

"Although I daresay, it seems a little weak to me, Miss Effington. I'm not at all certain you should award him a point for this. After all, it's not as if this was a real bull. No, this is really not at all—"

"Lord Bolton," Cynthia said, with a slight quiver in her voice but determination in her eye. "Have you seen the gardens? Perhaps you would care to accompany me?"

He raised a curious brow. "Why, Miss Weatherly—it *is* Miss Weatherly, isn't it?"

She nodded.

"I should like nothing better." He handed his glass to Pandora, stepped toward Cynthia, and offered her his arm. Regardless of whether she was actively helping Max or not, Pandora simply couldn't allow her go off with the twit without at least a warning. If Max was a scoundrel, no doubt he'd learned much of what he knew from the twit.

"Cynthia, I really don't—"

"It's a lovely day, Pandora." Cynthia shot her a quick smile and took the viscount's arm. "We shall be just fine."

"Indeed we shall," Lord Bolton murmured, looking down at her, and the couple strolled out of the room.

For a moment, Pandora could only stare after them. What had gotten into Cynthia? Usually, Pandora had to stand behind her and push to get her to so much as exchange polite pleasantries with a gentleman. And a man like the twit was a man to be avoided. Perhaps Pandora should go after them.

Max chuckled. "That is an interesting combination."

"Hardly. His reputation is no better than yours." Pandora glanced at him, abruptly aware of the weight of the cup in her hands. "However, he is right. This—" she held the pottery up, "—scarcely counts as a Cretan bull."

"Of course it counts." He moved closer and ran his fingers over the black on red design. "You see, here is the bull battling with, I believe it's Thes—"

"Theseus."

The ancient utensil was much larger than a modern cup, but even so, his hand nearly obscured the pattern. "When Hercules captured the Cretan bull he brought it back to Greece."

His fingers trailed over the figures in a slow caress and her stomach fluttered. Was the room warmer than a minute ago? "There, it was released to wreak havoc on the countryside."

"Was it?" She knew the myth of course. Knew well the tale depicted on the piece, yet she couldn't tear her gaze from the sight of his touch on the cup.

"It was up to Theseus to recapture it." The timbre of his voice held her spellbound, the movement of his hands mesmerized her, and she wanted . . . what?

"Still," her voice was uneven and she glanced up at him. He stared with an intensity in his gray eyes that stole her breath. "I'm not sure this is at all fair."

"Fair?" he said softly. "I told you all is fair."

"Is it?" She raised her head and her gaze drifted to his lips and back to his eyes, darker now, an approaching storm.

"It is." The odd yearning she'd noted before in his presence swept through her and she wondered how she could endure this sweet ache without his touch. She waited for the brush of his lips on hers fearing even the beat of her heart would break the moment between them. He bent closer.

"I think it counts as a point." Harry's voice sounded from across the room.

Pandora and Max jerked apart, as if caught doing something they shouldn't, which perhaps they had been. She struggled to recover her senses. What was wrong with her? She'd completely forgotten her father was still present.

"Lord Trent." Harry strode toward them.

Max leaned close to her, his voice low in her ear. "I had no idea your father was here. Not precisely the way I'd intended to meet him for the first time."

She shrugged in helpless apology.

"Lord Harold." Max stepped toward. "It is a pleasure to finally meet you, sir. I had planned on speaking to you during my stay here."

"Excellent." Harry's gaze traveled over him in an assessing manner, taking the measure of the man no doubt. "I had planned exactly the same thing.

"Now then, Dora." Harry turned his attention to her. "There's no way the poor man could actually capture a living breathing Cretan bull. I think the cup should suffice for your test."

Max flashed her a triumphant grin.

"But Harry," she said in annoyance. "It's

not at all fair. Why, this was a gift."

"The chemise was a gift and you accepted that," Max said under his breath.

"This is scarcely different from purchasing a point."

"Ah, but you accepted the horn," Max murmured.

"Precedent, my dear," Harry said with a chuckle. "It's been set."

"Even so, it's not in the—"

"Spirit of the game?" Max shook his head. "I disagree. The difficulty inherent in this game dictates I take whatever advantage comes my way. The true spirit of our match requires me to be prepared to seize whatever opportunity might present itself. What do you say, sir?"

"Quite right, my boy." Harry cast her a quelling glance. "He gets the point, Dora, and I'll hear no more arguments about it. What does that make now, Trent?"

"Five so far, sir."

"Nearly halfway. Damn fine job you're doing." Harry chuckled and shook his head. "Never thought you'd make it this far, not alive anyway."

"That is subject to change," she muttered.

"Now then, Trent, have you had a chance to look around?" Harry's eyes lit up. "You don't by any chance play billiards do you?"

"I have on occasion, sir." Max nodded. "I quite enjoy it."

Harry's brow raised. "Are you any good?"

Pandora groaned to herself. If there was anything her father liked more than exploring ancient ruins, it was a good game of billiards.

"Splendid. We have an exceptional billiard room here. Dora, we shall see you at dinner." He started toward the door. "I find billiards an excellent way to get a good sense of a man. He paused and glanced back. "Are you coming, Trent?"

"Yes, sir." Max leaned toward Pandora. "I shall look forward to dinner," he paused, "Dora." Max joined her father before she could so much as utter a single protest and the two disappeared down the hall.

"Now then, Trent, I rarely play for more than a few shillings a . . ." Her father's voice faded in the distance.

Pandora stared after them, the urge to throw the cup at Max almost irresistible. Was the man truly put on this earth to annoy her, or was that just an unavoidable aspect of his nature and hers? When they were married . . .

*When they were married?*

She gasped. When had it changed from *if* to *when?* Was Cynthia right? Did she indeed wish to marry him? To spend her days and nights for the rest of her life with him and him alone? To bear his children and grow old with her hand in his?

And if she did, did that mean as well that she loved him? Had love blossomed when she wasn't looking? Had it slipped into her life, into her heart, when she'd been distracted by her efforts to best him? Had it dawned unnoticed with a stormy-eyed gaze or the quirk of a grin or the passion of a kiss?

Without warning the answer struck her and she clutched the cup tighter to her and acknowledged the truth.

A life without Max would be no life at all.

# Chapter 15
## *Advantage is Gained*

**P**andora smiled and made the appropriate conversation, but her thoughts were far from the gentleman seated beside her at dinner. Lord Wiltshire was a distant relation, and the more he droned on endlessly about subjects of interest only to himself, the more distant she wished him. Lord and she thought Bolton was a twit.

Even though there were nearly forty people present, in her grandmother's eyes, this was an informal family dinner. In the duke's absence, her grandmother, as the dowager duchess, sat at the head of the table with the duchess, Pandora's Aunt Katherine, to her right and Trent, surprisingly in a place reserved for an honored guest, to her left.

It might not have been correct according to society's endless rules of precedence, but the Effingtons had always done exactly as they'd pleased in their own home. Her uncles, Lord Edward and Lord William, together with their wives, Abigail and Georgina, and her parents sat at the head of the table. Everyone else was arranged with an eye toward interesting conversation and the ever-present possibility of a marriage match.

Pandora mentally noted the need to discuss this evening's seating with whichever aunt had seen fit to place her between Lord Wiltshire and a very young man with a rather bad complexion and the annoying habit of trying to peer down her bodice whenever the opportunity arose.

"It was of course entirely the fault of the lady in question, although to my mind . . ."

Pandora nodded with feigned interest, knowing full well her skill at this type of deception was such that the gentleman would leave the table completely confident he had held her enthralled throughout the meal. Out of the corner of her eye she kept a close watch on Cynthia and Lord Bolton, who were seated directly across the table.

She was hard pressed not to stop and stare openmouthed. Cynthia was positively charming the twit. From what she could see, he hung on every word. And why not? This was certainly not the Cynthia she knew. This Cynthia's eyes sparkled, and high color stained her cheeks. This Cynthia cast flirtatious glances, and her laugh sounded over the table like the ring of crystal bells. This Cynthia was the beautiful, confident creature Pandora had always suspected she could be.

*How fortunate she was sitting beside Lord Bolton and not Max.*

How could she think such a shocking thing?

Cynthia was her dearest friend, and in spite of her comment about her willingness to marry Max, Pandora didn't have the slightest doubt Cynthia wanted him to win Pandora's hand. No indeed, she pushed the disturbing idea aside. It was jealousy, nothing more.

*Jealousy?*

She had never been jealous of anyone. She was Pandora Effington, the granddaughter of a duke. Whether it was deserved or not, she was known as the Hellion of Grosvenor Square. She had never had reason to be jealous. Was this what love did to you?

"Don't you agree, Miss Effington?"

Pandora stared at Lord Wiltshire. What on earth had he said? She nodded with a noncommittal smile. "Indeed."

"My thoughts exactly." He bobbed his head emphatically. "I said that very same thing the next . . ."

*Love.*

She might as well admit defeat right now. She did indeed love him. She loved the way his dark brow rose in disbelief and the way his laugh wrapped around her and warmed her soul. She loved his confidence and his arrogance, his strength and his intelligence. She loved his genuine interest in her parents' studies and his willingness to play their game. She even loved his calling her Dora, or, better yet, Hellion. On his lips it was a term of endearment.

*But did he love her?*

She cast a quick glance around the long table. He was doing exactly as he had promised: charming her family, especially its female members. They were obviously falling under his spell. And who could blame them? The man was indeed a rake, a rogue, a scoundrel, and a beast. No woman in her right mind could resist that combination. Why had it taken her so long to realize it?

But Lord Bolton was correct. She may well love Max but it wasn't enough. She wouldn't be able to bear it if he didn't love her in return, and she could never marry him without his love. There was no question: she couldn't let him win.

Lord Bolton was right on another count as well: there was a strong possibility of heartbreak in her bargain with Max.

And she very much feared it would be hers.

"Tell me, Lord Trent, has your apprehension eased somewhat?" The dowager duchess leaned toward him, a twinkle in her blue eyes. "We are extreme in number, but not nearly as daunting as you no doubt have been led to believe."

Max laughed. "Indeed, Your Grace, the anticipation was far worse than the fact. Still, no man wishes to hear his concerns are so easily noted."

"Not noted so much as expected. Only a fool would not have some trepidation upon meeting so extensive a family. Especially one with means, ability, and ambition. Add to that the odd fact that for the most part we care very much for one another, and . . ." A slight smile played on her lips. "Upon further consideration, I was mistaken. We *are* rather daunting."

"An attribute matched only by your charm."

"You are a scoundrel, Lord Trent. I have always quite enjoyed scoundrels. My husband was a scoundrel in his day, and I rather suspect all four of my sons, before their marriages of course, were scoundrels as well." She studied him thoughtfully. "No man makes a better husband than a reformed rake. I have great expectations for you."

The dowager rose to her feet, Max barely a beat behind her, signaling the end of dinner. She stood about Pandora's height and was approaching eighty, but appeared a good ten years younger. She possessed a relaxed manner Max rarely encountered in anyone of her years and station.

"Now then, the gentlemen shall retire to the billiard room, the ladies may go on to the music room." She glanced down the table. "Miss Weatherly, I do hope you will play for us later? You do play so beautifully."

Miss Weatherly blushed. "I would be honored, Your Grace."

"We shall all look forward to it." She inclined her head toward Max, her voice for his ears alone. "She is a lovely young woman and quite accomplished on the pianoforte. It has long been my regret that none of my granddaughters has even the tiniest bit of musical ability."

"Yet I'm certain they are proficient in other skills."

The dowager sighed. "They are Effington women, my lord. They are one and all stubborn and independent. I have no one to blame but myself, although one's attitudes on such things does tend to change with the years."

"I can well imagine," he murmured.

The dowager turned toward the door. "I should like a word with you. Would you accompany me to the drawing room?"

"I should be delighted, ma'am." He held out his arm and she rested her hand on it lightly. He glanced at Pandora. She stared back, eyes wide with astonishment. He cast her a satisfied smile, then escorted the dowager through the door and down a short distance to a large drawing room, stylish yet obviously designed with the comfort of a family in mind.

Only then did he realize they were not alone. Pandora's aunts and her mother trailed behind them. In spite of his success with the Effington women at dinner, unease trickled through him.

The dowager seated herself on one end of a damask sofa and indicated he should join her. The other ladies settled elsewhere about the room. They were all unique in appearance and coloring, but shared a common beauty. He could well see why the dowager's sons had been attracted to any one of them. At once he realized he was encircled and wondered exactly what form his attractive inquisition would take. He didn't doubt for a moment an inquisition was precisely the purpose of this gathering.

The dowager's gaze met his. "Lord Trent, we are all well aware of your bargain with Pandora."

"I hadn't realized news traveled that quickly," he said wryly.

"News of this nature has a life of its own." She chuckled and nodded at the duchess. "Katherine."

"My mother maintains her primary residence here, but the rest of us spend most of our time in town." The duchess smiled slightly and amusement lit her eyes. "This game you and my niece play is the talk of London. Abigail and Georgina have both heard about it."

"Indeed we have, my lord." Lady William laughed. "It is fascinating and delightful."

"I, for one, am holding my breath to see which of you wins," Lady Edward said.

"And holding your purse as well." The dowager waved her arm in a sweeping gesture to encompass the room. "My daughters enjoy nothing more than a good game. I believe Katherine has wagered a substantial amount on the outcome, as have Abigail and Georgina. Grace is the only one among us who does not have a financial stake in your match."

"I simply couldn't. Should Pandora hear of such a thing . . ." Lady Harold lifted a shoulder in an apologetic shrug.

"Quite right, my dear." The dowager nodded in approval. "I myself have risked a few pounds with a neighbor. While financial considerations are not the issue, I will confess most of the money is on you. However, my first concern is for Pandora's future. She should have been married long ago."

"We were married at her age," Lady Edward added, Lady William bobbing her head in assent.

"In spite of that, not one of us here would have forced her to wed." A chorus of nods echoed the dowager's words. "We have never seen Pandora risk marriage before."

"Well, there was that incident—" Lady William started.

Lady Edward interrupted her. "I cannot believe that dreadful man has the nerve to come—"

"Abigail," Lady Harold snapped, and cast a sharp look at Max.

"Oh, dear." Lady Edward clapped her hand to her throat. "It's of no consequence."

"As I was saying," the dowager continued. "She has never deliberately risked marriage before. It's an encouraging sign. We have discussed this and we are agreed." She directed him a no-nonsense look. "Pandora has made an excellent choice."

He wasn't entirely sure exactly what he expected, but he knew this wasn't it. "I'm delighted you think so, ma'am."

"We do, but do not for a moment think our approval is based on nothing more than Pandora's attitude and your admittedly charming presence. We would never allow her to marry on that basis alone. We have made inquiries regarding your finances—"

"Not that wealth is a great consideration," Lady Edward said quickly. "We are not so shallow as that. It is simply something to keep in mind."

"—Your family—"

"You bear an old and respected title." Approval sounded in Lady William's voice. "Your mother is a bit of a snob and may not ultimately care for us but that's of no consequence."

"—Your reputation—"

"You have a sizable reputation when it comes to women, my lord." Lady Harold smiled with tolerant amusement. "However, your behavior has not been marked by scandal or more than the usual gossip."

"—Your history—"

"The Dukes of Roxborough and the Effington family have a long tradition of service to King and country. My daughter's husband died fighting Napoleon." The duchess sighed and shook her head. "We have only admiration for those who stake their lives in service to the crown."

"I'm not sure what to say." His immediate reaction was irritation at this obviously thorough invasion of his life. Of his privacy. "I have never been dissected in quite so complete a manner."

"Please, don't be annoyed with us." The dowager's brows pulled together. "Do understand, Pandora is her father's only heir, and also currently possesses a tidy fortune of her own." The older woman cast a disapproving look at Lady Harold, who seemed rather intent on studying a fascinating aspect of the ceiling. "It is to be expected that she would attract men who might well wish to marry her for financial gain alone. We act only in her best interests. Someday, should you have daughters—"

Heads shook and gazes rolled toward the ceiling.

"—You will understand."

"I believe I understand completely right now," Max said slowly. "I cannot fault you for wishing to protect Pandora. Rather, I should applaud you."

A communal sigh of relief filled the room.

The dowager studied him for a long moment. "You do have a way with you. What a charming scoundrel you are." A satisfied smile spread across her face and she leaned toward him. "I would play a game with you myself if I were a year or two younger."

Max grinned, reached for her hand, and brushed his lips across it. "I can think of nothing more delightful."

The dowager laughed. "You have our wholehearted approval."

"Which does little good if you do not win," Lady Edward said pointedly.

"However," the duchess said, "we don't know if you are aware of it, but there are untold opportunities here to pass the remainder of your tests."

At once the room erupted into a flurry of feminine chatter.

"There are those nasty geese on the pond."

"The stables are always in need of cleaning."

"Don't we have cattle? Somewhere?"

"And an occasional boar."

"Or Cousin Percival."

Laughter and talk filled the air and he was hard pressed to separate one comment from another. At last the room quieted.

"As for the man-eating mares." The dowager folded her hands primly in her lap. "You may consider us tamed."

\* \* \*

"She does play wonderfully well," Lord Bolton murmured in Pandora's ear.

"Doesn't she, though?" Pandora said with a touch of pride. She had always enjoyed listening to Cynthia play the pianoforte. It was as if her heart and soul flowed through her fingers.

But now, in spite of the beauty of the piece, Pandora's head was filled with far too many thoughts of Max to concentrate.

He stood next to her grandmother doing his best to win her favor. The beast could well charm the birds in the trees. The sweet, frail aged lady didn't stand a chance against him. The absurdity of the thought struck her and she bit back a grin. No one had ever referred to the Dowager Duchess of Roxborough as a sweet, frail aged lady. Perhaps it was Max who didn't stand a chance.

What on earth had transpired in the drawing room? Immediately after dinner, Max had flashed her that triumphant smile of his that made her long to throw something, then escorted her grandmother out of the room, followed by her aunts and her mother. Initially, she'd felt a bit apprehensive for him. But when they reappeared, Max was alive, whole, and rather pleased with himself. Cynthia's recital had started a few minutes later and Pandora had had no chance to speak to him.

On one hand she was pleased he'd survived. Why, the Effington women were not biddable, fragile flowers. Pride surged through Pandora. She was an Effington, but more, she was an Effington woman. And weren't Effington women the most stubborn, most determined, most—

She gasped softly and her spine stiffened.

Lord Bolton glanced at her suspiciously, his voice for her ears alone. "Whatever is the matter?"

"Man-eating mares," she said under her breath. "He's tamed man-eating mares."

"How do you know?" he whispered.

She nudged him with her elbow and nodded in the direction of Max and her grandmother. He bent down and the dowager duchess leaned toward him and said something in his ear. Max responded and straightened, an amused smile on his face.

"She does look rather tamed." Lord Bolton's low reply was thoughtful.

"Indeed she does." Pandora clenched her teeth. Max obviously had another point. It wasn't enough he had Cynthia and her parents on his side, now he apparently had the support of all the Effington women.

Cynthia finished and the assembly broke into enthusiastic applause. Certainly this group well appreciated Cynthia's skills. The Effingtons, Pandora included, had no musical ability whatsoever, something no one was particularly proud of ... although on occasion, one of their number had had the mistaken belief he could play or, God help them all, sing, and more than one family gathering had been forced to politely endure their efforts.

Talk resumed with the end of the entertainment and the gathering broke into small groups. Pandora was not inclined toward idle chatter. She wanted to confront Max, still standing beside her grandmother's chair.

Lord Bolton appeared trapped in a conversation with a lady every bit as deadly as Pandora's dinner companion. He caught her gaze and shot her a silent plea for rescue. She shrugged in a helpless manner as if there was nothing she could do, and ducked her head to hide the grin she couldn't quite stifle. As she headed in Max's direction she was halted twice by people wishing to exchange pleasantries, and in spite of her impatience, managed to leave each with the impression of a mutually satisfying chat.

Max and Cynthia stood talking beside the pianoforte. He said something and she laughed. She started toward them, then stopped short, struck by the image they presented. Both were tall—one fair, the other dark, one complementing the other. A perfect picture. Her heart stilled.

Lord Bolton joined them and Max's gaze traveled the room until it met hers. Warmth glowed in his eyes and he smiled. She forced an answering smile to her face, but a cold fear burned in the pit of her stomach.

"Miss Effington?" Lord Wiltshire's voice sounded to her right and gratefully she turned toward him. Conversation with the man was as mindless now as it had been at dinner. She stayed long enough to be polite, then excused herself and slipped through the door leading into the conservatory and out onto the terrace.

An urgent need to escape drove her on. She crossed the terrace and continued blindly down the walkway leading to the gardens and the mazes. She ignored the branching paths that would take her to either maze; in spite of the star-filled sky and her knowledge of their solutions, she had no desire to be trapped inside a boxwood cage in the night. All she wanted was to keep walking. All she wished was to escape.

*Escape?*

It was as foreign a concept to her as jealousy, yet tonight she'd known both. Pandora Effington had never run from anything in her life. She knew her reactions were absurd. Cynthia had no interest in Max, other than her desire to see him wed Pandora.

Her steps slowed. Of course, Cynthia had no idea Pandora loved Max. Certainly she was convinced Pandora never would have agreed to their bargain if she truly didn't want to marry him. Still, hadn't Pandora declared long and loud that she had no desire to be Max's wife? What if Cynthia had finally believed her?

And what of Max? From the moment she'd first spoken to him until now, Pandora had done absolutely nothing to indicate she cared for him or ever could. She'd set him a series of tests designed for his failure. She'd gotten him involved in a game she had no doubt was the talk of London. She was directly responsible for his bruised and battered body. Could she blame him if he now turned his attention and his affection toward Cynthia? And if he had, was it too late?

The thought stopped her in her tracks.

No! She had no proof Max cared for Cynthia or she for him. She was leaping to farfetched assumptions based on nothing of true significance. Cynthia's assistance with the game. Max's obvious enjoyment of her musical skills. The striking couple the two of them made. If she hadn't been so caught up in the throes of her own turbulent emotions, she would never have entertained the idea in the first place.

She swiveled on her heel and started back to the house. Pandora had always considered herself a fighter, but she'd never really had to fight for anything.

If a fight was what it took, whether with Cynthia or Max or simply herself, by the gods, she was an Effington, and Effingtons did not know the meaning of the word "defeat." Why, hadn't she already won a victory of sorts merely by admitting her love for Max?

And that upped the stakes of their match. It was no longer enough to win the game, she had to win his love as well.

*Love.* She snorted in disdain. It certainly was not at all the rapturous emotion portrayed by poets. So far it had brought her only jealously, doubt, fear, and pain. No, it was much more like a dire illness complete with unpleasant aches in the pit of her stomach and the hot flush of fever. Spots would probably break out on her face at any moment.

No, love was not at all as it was represented. A falsehood no doubt perpetuated by others in love who knew the true nature of this plague and wanted the rest of the world to be as miserable as they were. Unfortunately, discovering the truth meant you were already beyond hope. Pity, it was such a simple truth.

Love reeked.

# Chapter 16
## *Momentum Shifts*

"**S**he doesn't seem at all herself today."
Max steadied his horse, keeping the beast beside Miss Weatherly's far gentler gray mare. "Is something amiss?"

"I don't know," Miss Weatherly said thoughtfully. "She is uncommonly quiet. I must admit, I've never seen her so reserved. She loves the Ride and is usually quite animated."

Max studied Pandora across the milling crowd of riders and horses. She sat perched upon a sidesaddle, with an air of complete confidence. He suspected she'd much rather be riding astride, although she was far too aware of society's rules to flout them publicly. He chuckled to himself. How many of those restraints would she disregard once they were married?

Her gaze met his through the crowd and he tipped his hat and grinned. She smiled in a

232

manner cool, yet cordial, as if they were no more than polite acquaintances.

What in the name of all that was holy had he done now? He reviewed the events of last night.

He'd done nothing she could fault him for, unless it was for charming her grandmother. But that was not only in the spirit of the game, it was in the best interest of their future. Besides, he quite liked the Dowager and liked as well the knowledge that her spirit would flow in the veins of his children.

Still, there must be something. He'd last seen Pandora right after Miss Weatherly's recital. He was talking to her, and Laurie joined them, and . . .

"Miss Weatherly, do you think she could possibly be, well, jealous?"

Miss Weatherly's brow furrowed. "Jealous of what?"

"You and me."

Her eyes widened. "That's absurd. There's no reason for Pandora to . . ." She paused. "Oh, dear."

"Yes?" he said, trying not to sound eager.

"Well, I did mention, once, that if she wasn't willing to marry you," a blush spread up her face, "I would be."

He grinned. "I'm flattered."

She sighed. "You needn't be. It was one of those things one says in anger, without thinking, but certainly doesn't mean."

He raised a brow.

"I am sorry. I do hope I haven't offended you."

"Only my pride," he said wryly.

"Whatever are we going to do to relieve Pandora's mind?"

Max returned his attention to Pandora. She sat straight and tall in the sidesaddle, every inch the perfect daughter of nobility.

"We can't allow her to think there is anything between us."

A perfect Effington.

"We have to make certain she understands that."

A perfect Countess of Trent.

"My lord," impatience rang in Miss Weatherly's voice, "are you listening to me?"

"Indeed I am."

"Well then, what are we going to do?"

"Do, Miss Weatherly?" He couldn't prevent a wide grin that grew from an odd exhilaration deep inside him. Jealousy came from only one source. "Why, nothing at all."

"Excellent morning, don't you think?" Max sidled his horse up to Pandora's.

"It's lovely," she said with a polite smile. Lord help her, she had no idea what to say. How to act. She hadn't had this feeling of complete awkwardness since she was very young and had discovered the rather intriguing differences between boys and girls. No. Now that she thought about it, she'd learned the equally intriguing power girls could wield over boys at approximately the same time and doubted she had ever experienced a single awkward moment. Until now.

"I daresay, I didn't expect so large a crowd." Max glanced from side to side, assessing the gathering. "About a hundred, I would think."

"At least. Effingtons, assorted guests, and neighbors." Her perfect smile stayed on her face but she cringed to herself. Did she sound as insipid to his ears as she did to her own? Now that she understood her feelings, she wanted nothing more than to be with Max every minute—and nothing more than to keep him at arm's length. "It's become rather a significant event."

"Really?" His eyes gleamed with amusement. What was so humorous? He couldn't possibly know her feelings. The beast. "Tell me about the Ride."

"The Roxborough Ride started when a long-ago duchess decided foxhunts were rather barbarous. At least for the foxes. So she decreed foxes would no longer be a part of the hunt on Effington land."

"I see. And as she was one of those extraordinary Effington women, no one saw fit to challenge her decision."

"I wouldn't think so." *Extraordinary?* Did he include her in that assessment? "Besides, she didn't forbid anyone not to take part in a hunt elsewhere, just here. Still, it seemed to those involved that the best part of the hunt wasn't really chasing the fox, but racing through the grounds, jumping hedges and walls, and splashing through streams."

Max smiled. "Rather tricky, though, a foxhunt with no fox."

"Rather. And somewhat confusing as well to go aimlessly about the countryside with no direction and no end in sight." With each word, the newfound tension of being in his presence eased. "So a circuit was laid out, and through the years, obstacles added and a scoring system developed. And the Roxborough Hunt became the Roxborough Ride."

She nodded at a man directing riders. "The stablemaster is in charge of the event. He arranges the courses in advance and with a gathering this large, divides us all into teams, usually about twenty riders each."

"I do hope we're able to ride together," he said. "We are both rather competitive, and as challenging as it is to play against each other, I suspect the two of us will make a formidable team."

"Oh, do you think so?" Pleasure washed through her at his words. Obviously, her concerns about Cynthia were groundless. "Perhaps *too* formidable a team."

"I can't wait to find out." His tone was light but there was an undercurrent to his words that sent a delightful shiver up her spine. Was he still talking about the Ride?

The stablemaster called for attention and the riders turned in his direction. Pandora leaned toward Max, her voice low. "In the past, I've asked him to put Cynthia on my team; however, I did not have the opportunity to speak to him this year." *I was far too busy imagining things that didn't exist.* Regret stabbed at her. "She is not nearly as confident on a horse as she is at the pianoforte. Should she be named to your team instead of mine, would you keep an eye on her?"

"It would be my pleasure," he said in a polite manner.

She glanced at Cynthia and noted Bolton on the horse next to hers. Pandora heaved a sigh of exasperation. "Your friend is constantly at Cynthia's side."

"So it seems."

"I don't trust him."

"Neither do I," he said thoughtfully. She slanted him a sharp glance and received an expression of utmost innocence in return. Was he worried about Cynthia? He hadn't seemed to be concerned about her skill on horseback. Was it Bolton's attention that troubled him?

She pushed the question out of her head. Once again, she was drawing a conclusion from nothing at all. She vowed silently not to waste another thought on this nonsense and turned her attention back to the stablemaster.

To her relief, she and Cynthia were both assigned to the third of five teams. Max and Bolton were on the fourth team.

Max wished her good luck and started toward his team, then paused and looked at her over his shoulder. "By the way, you *do* realize I have earned another point, don't you?"

"Man-eating mares?" she said with grim resignation.

"What else?" He grinned and directed his horse toward the area where his team was to gather. She stared after him, not quite certain if she wished to scream in frustration or laugh at his arrogant charm.

A few moments later she guided her horse to stand beside Cynthia's.

"Good morning." Cynthia greeted her with a hesitant smile. No doubt the poor dear was already anxious about the Ride.

"It's a beautiful day, isn't it?" Pandora said cheerfully, noting to herself that it had indeed become a much better morning since her chat with Max. *Extraordinary.* She grinned and reached over to pat Cynthia's hands, tightly gripping the reins. "Do try to relax. Horses seem to know when riders are nervous."

Surprise widened Cynthia's eyes. "But I'm not nervous."

Pandora raised a brow.

"Well, perhaps just a bit." She frowned and shifted uncomfortably in the saddle. "I always feel as if I am about to slip off on one of these things, and it's such a very long way to the ground."

Memories of the times Cynthia had done just that flashed through Pandora's mind. "Just try to relax and move with the horse instead of against it."

"I do try," Cynthia said, as if she wasn't entirely sure of the answer herself. What had happened to the self-assured creature she'd been last night?

Pandora studied her for a moment, then leaned closer. "You play the pianoforte like an angel. It's a true gift. I can't even hum in tune, no matter how much I try—not that I would, given the reaction my singing has drawn in the past—"

A genuine smile quirked Cynthia's lips.

"Regardless, I shall never do better." Pandora shrugged. "I ride well but that's a skill, not a true talent, and I've done it all my life. It's simply a matter of practice. The more you ride, the better you become, and perhaps someday—"

"I cannot possibly live that long." Her tone was dry, but it was apparent her apprehension had abated.

"Well, I shall never live long enough to be able to carry a tune."

"This is one of your 'I too have flaws' speeches, isn't it?"

"Of course." Pandora grinned. "But you've made it through two previous Rides, and you'll survive this one as well. Don't forget you can forgo any section you wish."

"The beginning, the middle, and the end sound like an excellent idea," Cynthia murmured.

Pandora laughed. Cynthia knew full well any rider with the slightest concern could choose to omit that particular series of obstacles.

The first team received the signal to start and surged forward in a wave of excited shouts and laughter. The start was staggered, in the interest of safety, and each team cleared one course and moved onto the next before a new group began. Pandora and Cynthia watched the first set of competitors, exchanging observations about the form of this rider or the best approach to that obstacle. In a mere thirty minutes or so it was their turn.

Pandora gave Cynthia a few last words of encouragement and they were off. The first course was always the easiest, with the lowest jumps and least difficult obstacles and even Cynthia had no problem.

But the Ride grew more difficult as it progressed.

The morning flew by in a blur of fleet-footed

horses racing over the countryside, jumping hedges and walls and temporary fences as if they were heirs to Pegasus himself. Midway through the Ride there'd been no major mishaps, simply a great deal of sheer fun. Even Cynthia had relaxed enough to enjoy herself.

Every now and then, Pandora would catch a glimpse of Max in the team behind hers. He rode as well as he did everything else. Of course, she would have been surprised if he hadn't. The blasted man probably was in truth a hero reborn. Although he needn't be so clever. He was halfway to victory. How would he try to twist his words the next time to claim a point? And how could she stop him?

As always, the competition between teams, while good-natured, was fierce, even though the winners received only token prizes: flowers and ribbons and two pounds each that were traditionally passed on to the stable boys and grooms. The Ride culminated in a grand picnic on the banks of the lake.

They approached the fifth course and Cynthia reined in her horse. "I know this is only as far as I made it last year, and I did so want to go on but," she nodded at the complex arrangement of natural obstacles and those placed by man, "this is somewhat beyond my ability."

Pandora knew better than to encourage anyone with the slightest doubts to continue. Success when it came to a competition like this had as much to do with the bond of trust between horse and rider as it did with the skills of either.

"You're certainly not alone." Fully half of the ladies on their team, and a few of the men, had already conceded defeat and now rode alongside the course observing those who continued. "You may not have gone farther than in the past but you seemed quite at ease this year. A little more time in the hands of my family and we will indeed make an excellent rider out of you yet."

Cynthia laughed. "There is not enough time in the world. I'll make you a bargain, Pandora."

Pandora raised a brow. "I'm not sure I need another bargain."

"I shall play my music and you will applaud for me. And you shall ride your horses and I will cheer your victory."

Pandora laughed. "Agreed."

Cynthia joined the other observers and Pandora caught up with her team.

By the time they reached the final course, Pandora had to admit even she was finding the Ride a bit more challenging than in the past. No doubt her skills were not as sharp as they once were. The sedate riding she was limited to in town did not serve to hone her abilities. Still, she had no doubt she would finish and took the fast jumps and quick, narrow turns laid out with an ease that restored her confidence. She joined the rest of her team to await the finish of their slower members with a delightful sense of satisfaction she hadn't really known since her game with Max began and accepted their compliments with a gracious smile.

The lake lay just past the last course. Tents offered welcome shade, tables were laid with food, and as always, she was surprised by just how hungry the Ride left her. Those who had completed the final course had already turned their horses over to stable boys and descended on the mid-afternoon feast as if they'd never seen food before. Pandora could scarcely wait to join them.

A cry sounded off to one side. She twisted in the saddle.

Those who had withdrawn from the competition battled to control their mounts. A rabbit darted under the cover of a low bush and she knew at once what had startled the animals. Confusion reigned amid the chaos of frantic beasts and distraught riders, and it was difficult to separate one figure from another. One horse reared, another took off across the course, a streak of gray.

Her heart lodged in her throat.

*Cynthia!*

Pandora struggled to break her horse free from the knot of milling riders and horses trapping her in their midst, but escape was impossible. There was scarcely room to turn, her every move blocked.

"Look! They'll catch her!" a gentleman to her left shouted.

Pandora's gaze shot to Cynthia's pale figure clinging to the horse, two riders from another team in hot pursuit, one slightly in front of the other.

Max? And Bolton?

Both men rode animals far superior in quality to Cynthia's gray mare, but her mount had a speed born of fear. The panicked creature headed straight for a wall. Pandora gasped and her fists clenched in terror. The beast dodged the obstacle and she couldn't believe Cynthia managed to hang on. Max was within a hair's breadth of her, Lord Bolton barely a stride or two behind. It took no more than a handful of seconds, but it was as though the scene before her slowed to the pace of a dream.

Max reached out to catch the reins flying unfettered behind the animal's neck but the leather strips eluded his grasp as if they had a life all their own.

"Come on, Max," Pandora said in a tense murmur and leaned forward in her saddle, urging him on through sheer power of will and prayer alone. She'd never felt so helpless.

Max fumbled for the reins. Lord Bolton gained ground. Good God, one false step, one stumble, and all three horses would fall in a tangled heap, taking their riders with them. She held her breath.

The next moment, Max had the reins in his hand and pulled the horse to a halt. A murmur of admiration swept through the crowd. Pandora heaved a sigh of relief.

Max slipped off his saddle and reached to help Cynthia dismount. Even from here she appeared overly pale and completely done in. He wrapped his arm around her waist, handed his reins and hers to Bolton, then started toward the tents and tables set up around the lake. A moment later, he scooped her into his arms and carried her.

"My word." Aunt Abigail trotted up on her right. "The earl certainly does have a fine hand with"—she emphasized the word—"*cattle.*"

No doubt, there was no other choice. Cynthia looked as though she was about to collapse.

Aunt Georgina rode up on her left. "Indeed he does. Quite impressive, the way he managed to," she paused for emphasis, "*capture* that cattle."

Certainly that would be the only reason for him to take her in his arms.

"Pandora, are you listening to us?"

"Of course," she murmured, and glanced from one aunt to the other. They bore no physical resemblance to each other, yet wore the identical smug smile. Pandora drew her brows together. "What did you say?"

"Oh, we simply think the earl is quite heroic," Georgina said lightly.

"Indeed." Abigail nodded. "Almost legendary. Why, he very much reminds me of—oh, Hercules comes to my mind."

"Mine too." Georgina's eyes widened. "Especially the way he captured the cattle."

"Captured the cattle?" Pandora said slowly. She glanced at her aunts' matching grins and at once understood their meaning. "Absolutely not." She shook her head firmly. "This is far and away too weak to count as a point."

"Nonsense." Georgina smirked. "Of course it counts."

"Without a doubt." Abigail's voice was smug. "And I'm sure the duchess will agree."

"And the dowager," Georgina added.

"Well, I don't," Pandora snapped.

"Nonetheless," Georgina's hand fluttered in a dismissive wave. "That's point number seven."

"Am I the only one not willing to surrender my future to Trent without a second thought?" Pandora glared at one aunt, then the next. "Does he have the support of all the women in this family?"

The older women traded glances. "All except your mother."

"She's neutral, I believe."

Pandora snorted in disbelief, the image of a Greek cup flashing through her mind. "Hardly."

"Well," Georgina shook her head, "she has not laid so much as a penny on it."

Abigail nodded. "That certainly seems neutral to me."

"Not to me," Pandora muttered, vowing to herself to have a long chat with her mother at the first possibility.

"Come along now, Pandora, I'm famished." Abigail turned her horse toward the lake.

"As am I. Besides, we do need to make certain Lord Trent realizes he has achieved another point." Georgina's eyes twinkled with delight and she reined her mount to follow her sister-in-law. "Just in case he hasn't noticed."

Pandora glanced at Max carrying Cynthia and narrowed her eyes. "Oh, I suspect he's noticed all manner of things."

She started after her aunts, keeping watch on Max out of the corner of her eye—not that there was anything to watch, of course. He was simply being a gentleman. A hero. His actions regarding Cynthia didn't bother her at all because they meant absolutely nothing.

Still, it was worthwhile to note, Max's seventh point was not nearly as disturbing as the sight of Cynthia in his arms.

"I say, Max, put her down. Or let me carry her." Laurie's voice behind Max rang with annoyance. "You can lead the blasted horses and I'll take Miss Weatherly."

"I do appreciate the offer." Max didn't break his stride. "But I'm doing fine, thank you."

"I really can walk, my lord," Miss Weatherly said with an exasperated sigh.

"I am sorry, Miss Weatherly, I would be remiss in my duty if I allowed you to walk. You could barely stand after your ordeal."

"Perhaps, but I'm much recovered now." She glared at him. "You and I both know the *real* reason why you refuse to put me down."

Max held his tongue, refusing to confirm or deny her charge.

"I wouldn't at all mind carrying her," Laurie called.

"Do you see her over there? Staring at us." Cynthia groaned. "You do know what she's thinking, don't you?"

"Why, Miss Weatherly, I have no idea what you're getting at."

"Why, Lord Trent," she mimicked, "I don't believe you for a moment."

He grinned.

"And I must confess, I don't understand." Miss Weatherly's brow furrowed. "Why do you want to encourage jealousy on Pandora's part?"

"It's not that I particularly wish to encourage it, simply take advantage of it. Think about it for a moment, Miss Weatherly, what triggers jealousy?"

"I imagine a sight like this might trigger jealousy," she snapped. "Your closest friend, wrapped in the arms of the man . . ." She paused and her eyes widened with realization. "Oh, I see. Jealousy, then, would be a good sign."

"A very good sign."

"Actually," Laurie's voice rose with annoyance, "I should rather enjoy carrying her."

A private smile lit Miss Weatherly's face. "My Lord, do you think there is even a hint of jealousy in his tone?"

So that was the way of it. He'd suspected as much. "I think there is much more than a hint."

Her smile grew. "What an interesting sign."

Max laughed and continued his trek toward the lake. It hadn't seemed so far at the beginning, but he had to admit, while not overly heavy, Miss Weatherly was becoming something of a burden. He wouldn't mind handing her over to Laurie one bit. Although that would do none of them any real good. No, far better to risk serious physical injury than pass up this opportunity to fuel Pandora's jealousy.

Of course, he could be completely wrong. The idea took him by surprise. Pandora's reactions could well have more to do with her position as the center of attention than any feeling she might have for him.

Exactly how far would he have to go to find out?

# Chapter 17
## *An Unfair Advantage*

**"Y**ou really have managed to tame them, haven't you?" Pandora said, nodding at the Effington ladies.

Most of those still lingering after the Ride sampled the mouth-watering myriad of delights spread on the long cloth-covered tables. Others engaged in animated analysis of the competition. And a fair number, including Pandora and Max, strolled along the pathway that encircled the lake.

"I have to confess, it did not take a great deal of effort." Max chuckled.

"I'm so glad to know you were not overly fatigued by the ordeal," she said wryly.

He laughed. "Not at all. But I will admit when I walked into the drawing room and discovered your aunts and your mother one step behind, I did wonder if I'd met my fate."

"Apparently they are all more than willing to help me meet mine," she muttered and glanced toward the picnic area. Her aunts and her mother had migrated together, and given the surreptitious looks cast in her direction, Pandora was certain she and Max were the main topic of conversation.

"I should have known it was no mere co-incidence that saw two of my aunts on my team and the duchess and my mother on yours. What better way to keep an eye on us both and twist your most insignificant action into a point?"

He tried to hold back a grin and failed.

"I suspected as much," she said grimly. "They have not only given you their blessing, but they are now actively lending their assistance. Capturing cattle." She scoffed. "Will they be flushing a boar from the woods for you, too?"

"One can only hope," he murmured with a wicked twinkle in his eye.

"It's not fair, you know, to receive so much help from those outside of the game."

"I disagree. Everything is fair. And I did warn you I intended to take every advantage offered me. If that includes the assistance of your family, well, it would be impolite to refuse."

"I'm certain they'd forgive you."

"Perhaps, but it's a chance I'm not willing to take. However," he paused, "in the interest of fairness, I will grant you this: you too may accept help wherever you may find it."

"How very gracious of you."

He could well afford to be gracious. He had the entire female contingent of her family behind him. She might as well have her calling cards engraved with Max's crest and *The*

*Countess of Trent* right now and save herself the trouble later.

She sighed. "At any rate, I gather you liked them."

"There was nothing to dislike. But I was under the impression all that mattered was whether they liked me."

"I believe we have ascertained that."

"They are one and all quite charming and rather clever. They remind me very much of you."

"Do they?"

"Except they are not opposed to my marrying you," he said pointedly.

"They do not know you as I do," she said primly.

"I rather thought I improved upon further acquaintance. The more one knows me, the more one loves me."

"Love?" She tried to laugh, but it came out as an awkward strangled sound. "I don't believe love was part of our bargain."

"Should it be?"

"I really haven't given it much thought," she lied. How odd. She was willing to admit to Bolton she wouldn't marry without love, yet she could barely utter the word in Max's presence.

A goose waddled across the path in front of them.

"Should we think about it?"

"To what end?" She held her breath.

His brow furrowed and he appeared deep in thought. Finally he released a long sigh. "I have no idea."

Her heart fell. Still, what did she expect? A

fervent declaration of his affections? A pronouncement of undying devotion? Given the tasks she'd set before him, she could scarcely blame him if he detested her. Still, she hadn't managed to dissuade him thus far and he did continue the game with a fair amount of enthusiasm. For whatever reason, he remained intent upon marrying her. And he did appear to enjoy her company.

Unless, of course, he simply wanted to win and the prize itself no longer mattered.

"When we first met, you said you did not want a husband. Why are you so determined to avoid marriage?"

"I see nothing wrong with marriage when entered into willingly and with . . . affection by both parties."

"And will that be the case with us when I win?"

"*If* you win."

"*When* I win."

"I agreed to the terms of our bargain."

"That takes care of the question of willingness. What of affection?"

Affection? Like that seen on the faces of elderly ladies when gazing at their pug dogs? Or were they back to love? Unending, eternal, and forever?

For a moment she wanted to confess her feelings—abandon caution and throw herself headlong into the terrifying bliss that was apparently love. Is that what he wished to hear? Why? Because he too was caught in this dire illness? Or did he simply want the victory of having won her heart while he continued his effort to win her hand? Fear and pride held her in check.

"Why, Max, you have tamed man-eating mares," she said lightly. "What woman alive would not be fond of you?"

He studied her for a long moment, as if trying to read whatever thoughts lay beyond her comment. He pulled his gaze from hers and they walked on in an uncomfortable silence.

"Does Miss Weatherly feel the way you do about marriage?"

Cynthia? Why was he concerned with Cynthia's feelings about marriage?

"Cynthia has always been more interested in marriage than I have."

"I see," he murmured.

Exactly what did he see? Not that his question bothered her in any way. Why, she'd have to be jealous for it to bother her and she absolutely refused to allow that.

Three more geese waddled past.

She glanced toward her mother. Grace still chatted with Abigail, but the duchess and Georgina were no longer with them. Good. Hopefully they had found something to discuss other than she and Max.

"Given your lack of interest in marriage, or your lack of interest in marriage with me," a wry smile quirked his lips, "should I lose, which I won't—"

"Which you *will*."

"Which I *won't*, how do you foresee spending the remainder of your life?"

"My life?" The question caught her by surprise. She had always known she didn't want a marriage without love, but had never particularly considered what she would do if she failed to find that.

She was well aware she could not blithely continue to go through season after season. She was already one of the oldest unmarried women at any social gathering. Another year or two and the appeal of her independent nature would fade. Gentlemen who had sought her for her beauty and her spirit would express interest only for her fortune. The possibility of love would vanish altogether.

She could see herself the object of tolerant affection but still the subject of whispered comments. *"I hear she was a diamond of the first water once. What a shame she has come to such an end."*

Was there anything more pathetic than an aging hellion?

There were few opportunities for anything else. She could never find a position as a governess. Even if she was inclined in that direction, she had no particular skills. And while the life of a cyprian or courtesan or other ladies of a disreputable nature certainly had a bit more appeal, she was unskilled in that area as well. She suspected one had to have developed the talents needed for such positions at a much earlier age.

She knew enough about her parents' studies to join in their work and did not doubt she would excel; still, it was not particularly what she wanted.

*What did she want?*

She wanted a hero. She wanted Max. But she wanted him on her terms. She'd rather become a withered old crone, a lonely, wretched creature to be pointed out to young women as an example of the dire fate that could befall them should they be too independent or high spirited and fail to wed than have a husband who did not love her.

"Pandora?"

Her gaze met his and she gave him a half-hearted smile. "I don't know."

"Well, you needn't worry about it." He grinned down at her. "When I win—"

She laughed, her pensive mood disappearing with the slight breeze. "If you win."

"Did you enjoy the Ride, Lord Trent?"

Pandora and Max turned to greet the duchess and Georgina.

"I did indeed, Your Grace." Max nodded. "I only regret my team did not win."

"Oh, but your rescue of Miss Weatherly was far more impressive," the duchess said. "Besides, there is always next year."

"Next year?" Pandora raised a brow.

Georgina ignored her. "May we join you?"

"Of course," Max said gallantly.

"It is such a lovely day and I do so enjoy strolling beside the lake. Pity," the duchess waved toward the water, "they seem intent on spoiling it."

"Who?" Pandora furrowed her brow.

"Why, the geese, of course," the duchess said.

"There do seem to be an inordinate number this year." Pandora hadn't really noticed just how many before now. They covered a good portion of the lake, their squawking a constant background noise. Obviously, her mind was too full of other matters to pay them much heed.

Georgina crossed her arms over her chest. "Someone should do something about them."

The duchess nodded. "They are scaring the horses and terrorizing the dogs."

Pandora glanced at the area where the horses from the Ride grazed in complete serenity. "The horses don't seem particularly overset to me. And there isn't a dog in sight."

"Nonetheless," the duchess said firmly, "they are a hazard."

"Indeed they are." Georgina bobbed her head in enthusiastic agreement. "Why, they are positively Stym . . . Stemp . . ."

"Stymphalian," the Duchess supplied.

"Stymphalian?" Pandora laughed. "I daresay . . ." At once she understood. "Oh, I don't think—"

"Stymphalian. That's exactly what they are." Georgina paused for emphasis. "And *someone* should do something."

"Indeed, *someone should.*" The duchess gazed pointedly at Max. "Don't you agree?"

"I don't," Pandora snapped.

"Indeed I do," Max said slowly, then realization dawned on his face and he grinned. "Do you have any idea how *someone* would do that?"

Her aunts exchanged helpless glances.

The duchess shrugged. "Run at them, I suppose."

"Yelling, perhaps, and waving one's arms?" Georgina added.

"This isn't in any way—" Pandora started.

"Would it be enough to do it from the

banks, do you think," Max said thoughtfully, "or would *someone* have to actually get in the lake itself?"

"I wouldn't think so," Georgina said.

"Not at all," the duchess agreed.

"Oh, but if these are truly *Stymphalian* birds . . ." Pandora's voice rang with annoyance. She could see any protest on her part was futile. But if he was going to gain a point in so ridiculous a manner, she very much wanted him to earn it. "It would be virtually impossible for *someone* to get rid of them without getting wet."

"Very well." Max's gaze meshed with hers and laughter shone in his eyes. The beast. He took off his coat and started to hand it to her, then apparently thought better of it. "Lady William?"

Georgina took the garment. "I'd be honored."

Pandora folded her arms over her chest and glared.

Max leaned closer and spoke softly in her ear. "I believe this will be my eighth point."

"If you don't drown," she said through clenched teeth.

"A distinct possibility." He sighed dramatically.

"Hah!" She scoffed. "It's a very shallow lake. You'd have to stand on your head to drown."

"Don't you want to wish me well before I go off to do battle with Stymphalian birds?"

"They're geese," she hissed. "I should wish them well."

He straightened and shook his head in a

manner of exaggerated regret. "Geese can be very difficult."

"Then you shall have much in common!"

"If I do not return," he grabbed her hand and pulled it to his lips, "your face shall linger always in my memory. Your voice shall accompany me to heaven, but even the angels will pale in comparison. And your name shall be the last thing on my lips."

"Stop that!" She snatched her hand away and stifled a laugh. Blasted man. How could he make her laugh when she was so annoyed with him? If she did end up as his wife, if nothing else, it would be an amusing fate.

He grinned and turned toward her aunts, sweeping an exaggerated bow. "Ladies."

They nodded in a regal manner, as if he was going off to do battle with a fire-eating dragon and not mere geese, but it was apparent they were just as close to laughter as she was.

Max walked along the path for several yards until he reached a point where the fowl were thick on the bank and in the water. He flashed a grin at her, then squared his shoulders, raised his arms, and ran toward the birds, yelling in an unintelligible manner.

He flapped his arms and dodged this way and that. Some geese took to wing at once, others seemed stunned at the sight of him. He waded into the water, still shouting and waving as if he was about to take flight himself.

"I wonder that they don't think he's simply a very large featherless goose," Georgina murmured.

"He looks like a complete fool." Pandora huffed.

"Really," the duchess said thoughtfully. "I think he looks more like a man in love."

"Hardly," Pandora said. "He's a man determined to win. Love has nothing to do with it."

The duchess slanted her an amused glance. "There's little difference between the actions of a man in love and a fool."

Max splashed about in hip-deep water, keeping up a steady stream of loud shouts and wild gestures.

Within minutes, most of the geese had abandoned the lake, probably off somewhere, laughing to themselves at the absurd creature that had invaded their domain. All the human observers had gathered on the banks to watch the spectacle and there was no question as to their laughter.

Max turned in her direction, spread his arms in a wide questioning gesture, and called out, "Well?"

The duchess raised her hands and clapped. Georgina joined her, and soon everyone was applauding except Pandora. Max bowed in an overdone theatrical manner.

"The geese will be back. Probably the moment he leaves," Pandora said pointedly.

"It's my understanding he simply had to get rid of them," the duchess said lightly. "I don't believe there's any stipulation about keeping them away. Is there?"

Pandora shook her head, her voice resigned. "Not at all."

"Very well, then." The duchess nodded at Georgina and they started toward the spot where Max was emerging into a crowd of laughing congratulants.

"I quite like him, you know," Georgina said, her voice fading with every step. "Do you think she does?"

Pandora couldn't make out the answer. Of course she liked him. She more than liked him. The question was whether he more than liked her.

"Even wet, he is a remarkably attractive man." A voice sounded behind her.

Pandora turned. "Gillian." She embraced her favorite cousin. "When did you arrive?"

"Late last night. I was on the Ride this morning." Gillian glanced at Max with an approving smile. "Not that I'm at all surprised you didn't notice."

Pandora followed her gaze. "I've been rather busy."

"So I hear." Lady Gillian was the duke's daughter, and five years older than Pandora. A classic fair-haired blue-eyed English beauty, Gillian, now a widow, was well known in London's influential circles as a hostess for gatherings that attracted intellectuals, politicians, artists and writers.

"I suppose you know all about it?"

"My dear cousin, everyone in London knows about your bargain with Trent. It's the talk of the season. I gather the betting books at White's and elsewhere are full of wagers on both sides."

"Not to mention those made among members of my own family," Pandora said dryly. "And most of the money is on Max."

"Max?" Gillian raised a brow.

"That's his name." Pandora had the good

grace to be chagrined over the improper and too familiar usage.

"Of course it is." Gillian's gaze returned to Max, still surrounded by well-wishers. "How is he progressing?"

"He just earned his eighth point."

"I see. Only what? Four left?"

Pandora nodded. London gossip was often erroneous, but in this case its accuracy was impressive.

"Do you love him?"

She started to tell her but even with Gillian, found she couldn't say the words aloud. Gillian would understand. She had married for love. Still . . . She shrugged. "Is it a completely unpleasant emotion?"

Gillian laughed. "It gets better." She paused for a moment. "And what of the earl?"

Someone had handed Max a glass of wine and a blanket was wrapped around his shoulders. She studied his tall figure for a long moment and that now familiar yearning welled up inside her. "I wish I knew."

"You don't think this is an indication? After all, the man has put on a rather ridiculous, although vastly entertaining, public display. For you."

"He's very competitive. He wants to win."

"What he wants is you."

"That much I know," she said shortly. "What I don't know is why. Am I a reward for winning? Or does he truly care for me?"

"You could always ask him," Gillian said casually, as if she was suggesting nothing more significant than which way he preferred to tie his cravat.

"I've tried."

"Have you?"

"Well, I've never actually said, 'Do you love me?' But I have given him more than ample opportunity to tell me of his feelings. Whatever they may be."

"Pandora," Gillian said in a knowing tone, "men are truly charming creatures, relatively intelligent on occasion, and more than competent to choose a good horse or a fine brandy, but when it comes to things like love, they rarely seem to know what's in their own hearts." She laid a hand on Pandora's arm. "Ask him. Trent will give you an honest answer, and honesty between a man and a woman is as important as trust. And love."

"I can't." Pandora shook her head emphatically.

"Because you're afraid of the answer?"

Was she? Her stomach twisted. "Perhaps. Besides, I don't want to force him into some kind of half-hearted admission. I want him to tell me how he feels."

"Poor Trent. Effington stubbornness is always a force to be reckoned with."

Pandora raised a brow. "You are scarcely one to point fingers."

Her cousin laughed. "I'll grant you that."

Pandora turned her gaze back to Max. "So what do I do? How am I to know how he feels?"

Gillian's brow pulled together and she was silent for a long moment. "It's always seemed to me, the relationship between men and women is very much like that of hounds and foxes."

Pandora groaned. "So I've been told."

"A very good hound will chase a fox until he drops from exhaustion. A lazy hound, a hound whose heart isn't in the hunt, will lose interest. But a hound who truly wants the fox will let nothing stop him. He'll follow the fox anywhere and follow him forever." Gillian stared at Max thoughtfully. "That seems to be a rather determined hound."

Pandora followed her gaze to a sodden, laughing Max. "As of today, the possibility of his winning our game are excellent, and I will not marry him unless he loves me."

Gillian's gaze snapped to hers. "How will you avoid it?"

"I have no idea. But it does appear I have now become the fox, and the hound is gaining fast. I have to find a way both to elude the beast . . ." Max turned toward her direction, grinned, and raised his glass.

"And determine if his heart is truly in the hunt."

# Chapter 18
## *A Break in the Play*

"**W**hat are you doing here?" Pandora planted her hands on her hips and glared.

Max lounged against a stall with a nonchalant air.

"Waiting for you. I must say, though, I am surprised." His gaze traveled over her in an altogether too familiar manner that was at once annoying and exciting. "Here you are again in men's clothing. Twice in three days is rather impressive for something you 'never' do."

"And I have you to thank. It was you who provided the clothes, you who encouraged me to wear them, you who failed to request their return."

"How could I have been so thoughtless? I have led you to wreck and ruin. Is there any way I can make amends? Of course." A wicked light shone in his eyes. He stepped toward her and reached out. "Give me my clothes. Now. At once. Don't bother to protest, it would be best if you just do it."

She slapped his hand away and tried not to laugh. "Do all those Effington women who have become so fond of you know what a true beast you are?"

His brow furrowed. "Let me think. Why yes, I'm certain they do. In fact, they insist a reformed rake makes the best husband, and I suspect they believe me ripe for reforming."

"Not that they plan on taking on the task themselves."

"They are giving you that honor."

"How very thoughtful. I shall have to remember to thank them. How did you know I'd be here this morning?" She hadn't known herself until a long, restless night filled with disturbing dreams of heroes and searing embraces and the occasional goose forced her to abandon any hope of peaceful sleep and decide she might as well greet the dawn on horseback.

"Where else would you be?" he said, as if the answer was obvious. "After being forced to comply with society's edicts and endure a sidesaddle throughout the Ride yesterday—"

"I have used a sidesaddle since my first Ride," she said in a lofty tone.

"Pity. I don't know how women manage to stay on the things. They look damned awkward."

"They are rather. One does have to get used to them."

"Still, a skilled rider such as yourself must be frustrated by its limitations, especially during anything as challenging as yesterday's competition."

"I suppose, a bit . . ." Odd, it hadn't particularly bothered her before. It was only since she'd tasted the exhilaration of riding astride again for the first time since childhood that she'd given the restrictions of sidesaddles a second thought. And today it was that quest for freedom that had brought her here.

Exactly as Max had expected. Did he know her that well? And was that disquieting, or somehow pleasurable?

"Well, I am here to ride this morning." She straightened and started down the aisle, glancing in one stall, then another, and yet another. "Max," she said slowly, still moving from stall to stall. "Why are there no horses here?"

"Why?" An innocent note sounded in his voice.

"Max." Suspicion underlay her words. "Where are the stable servants? I know it's early, but even the other day there were a few boys here. Where are they, Max?"

"I suspect they may be with the horses. Or perhaps in the kitchens. Or possibly the village. Or in all likelihood at—"

"Max." She clenched her teeth. She didn't like the sound of this at all. "What have you done with them?"

A dark brow arched upward. "You sound as though you suspect I have slit their throats, dismembered their bodies and tossed the pieces to—"

"The geese?" she said sharply.

He stared at her with an indignant expression. "I can't believe you would suggest such a thing. Even in fun."

"I didn't really mean to sug—"

"Of course," he said thoughtfully, "if there were extra points involved . . ."

Shock held her for a moment, then she laughed and shook her head. "No extra points. You don't need any additional points. You're already up to seven."

"Eight."

"Seven, eight," she waved a dismissive hand. "It will hardly matter when you lose."

"*If* I lose."

"*When* you lose," she said without thinking, and glanced around once again. "Where are the stable hands and where are the horses? I would like to ride while it is still early enough to avoid being discovered dressed like a street urchin."

"I thought it would be best if they were elsewhere for the next few hours. They'll return before anyone is up and about."

"I'm not asking the right questions, am I?" She studied him closely. "The question isn't where they are, but why they've gone . . . isn't it?"

"Excellent, Pandora." Max grinned. "I knew you'd figure it out eventually."

"I'm so happy you're pleased." She heaved a frustrated sigh. "Now, answer the question. Any question."

"Very well." He sauntered into a stall and called over his shoulder. "The horses are in a pasture somewhere on the estate. I'm not certain exactly where. The stable hands have scattered for the moment but will return by late morning."

"Why?" She was hard pressed not to scream the word.

"I thought it would be easier without them." He retraced his steps, emerging from the stall with a pitchfork in each hand.

At once she understood. "Oh, no, Max." She backed up and held her hands out to ward him off. "I absolutely refuse to participate in this."

He stepped toward her and offered a pitchfork. "You don't have a choice."

"I most certainly do." She hid her hands behind her back and took another step away from him. "Don't think for a moment I'm going to take that. I never said I'd help you."

"That's true. However, you did agree to accompany me on the tests."

"Very well. I'll be happy to stand right here and watch."

"No." He shook his head in mock regret. "I simply cannot allow that."

"I have no difficulty with it at all," she snapped.

"Your father would say precedent has been set."

"Precedent?" She glared at him suspiciously. "How?"

"Well, you did help me at the Lion and Serpent."

"That was different."

"I doubt your grandmother would agree. I suspect she would consider your unwillingness to assist me a violation of the spirit—"

"The spirit?" she practically sputtered.

"—If not the actual terms of the game, and declare *you* to be disqualified and *me* to be the winner. I further suspect your aunts, the duchess and Ladies William and Edward, would procure a special license with remarkable speed and have us married before the week is out."

"They would never do that," she said staunchly.

"Would you care to find out?"

Visions of Cynthia's rescue and Max flailing at geese flashed through her head. "This isn't at all fair." She snatched a pitchfork from his hand. "And you couldn't get away with it if you hadn't charmed your way into the affections of my family."

"True. But once you have tamed man-eating mares, it appears all else falls into place." He cast his gaze over their surroundings. "Including cleaning the Augean Stables."

"If we're going to do this, let's get to it." She took a few steps, then stopped. "Exactly what are we supposed to do? I've never cleaned a stables before."

"That is a surprise," he said wryly.

"And I suppose the Earl of Trent is quite experienced at stable cleaning?"

"Not exactly, but I did receive instructions. The bulk of the work involves replacing dirty straw with fresh straw."

"Dirty straw?" Pandora stared at the floor of the nearest stall. Plain inoffensive dirt was not the worst of what soiled the straw.

"You could go ahead and simply award me the point," he said hopefully. "If for no other reason than my willingness to tackle such a task."

"You've been given far too many points already. This one you'll have to earn."

"As you wish, but I do think I earned it with the geese," he murmured.

She wrinkled her nose in disgust. "Pity I have to earn it with you."

He grinned and explained exactly how they were to proceed. It wasn't especially difficult to understand. It was, however, as hard as she'd suspected. Initially, Max would turn over and replace four forkfuls of straw to every one of hers. Within the first quarter hour, she had slowed to the point where he was doing nearly twice that for every one of hers. After a while she fell into a steady, if not overly productive, rhythm. Pandora certainly saw no reason to exhaust herself, and in spite of his argument, no good reason to assist him.

She and Max each worked in separate areas, exchanging only a few words here and there, although she was acutely aware of his presence.

It didn't appear to Pandora they'd made much progress. She'd always thought the stables here rather small, but today they looked the size of Windsor Castle. She straightened and stretched and exhaled a long, loud breath. "So, Max, are we finished yet?"

He glanced around but continued to fork over straw. "I wouldn't think so, but I suppose, ultimately, it is up to you." He flashed her a quick grin. "We can stop whenever you feel I have earned my point."

She sighed, leaned on the handle of her

pitchfork, and watched him work. With each stroke, his shirt pulled tight across his back, outlining the hard lines of his body. His sleeves were rolled up over his elbow and the muscles of his arms strained against the fabric. She wondered when he'd wrap those arms around her again. They were indeed the arms of a hero. *Her* hero.

"Why did you join the army?" she said abruptly, surprised she had actually voiced the query she'd had in her mind since their first meeting.

"Curious question, but not an inappropriate place to ask it." He continued to work and spoke without looking at her. "Life in the British army, notwithstanding its grand uniforms and glorious history, makes this job look like a soiree in paradise. One of the many reasons why firstborn sons of noble heritage are not expected to join."

"Then why did you?"

"Misplaced notions of duty and honor, I suppose. Passed on to me by my father."

"He didn't try to dissuade you?"

Max shook his head. "Oddly enough, he had the same opinions about what a man, any man, owes his king and his country. The least of which is a willingness to give his own life."

A knot settled in her stomach at the thought of Max risking his life.

"My mother, however, did not share his view." He chuckled. "My mother does not share many of my views, either."

"Oh?" The knot tightened. Pandora forced a light note to her voice. "I suppose I shall meet her at some point."

"I daresay you won't be able to avoid it."

He fell silent and she studied him for a few moments.

"Was it truly awful?" she said, fearing the answer, yet curious all the same.

He shrugged. "She got over it eventually."

"Not your mother." She laughed. "The war."

He stopped and turned his gaze to hers. "Do you really want to know?"

She nodded. She very much wanted to know what made this man who and what he was.

"Very well." He returned to his work but was obviously considering his words. "My regiment joined Wellington's troops just before Talavera."

"Wasn't that a great victory?"

"As one views such things, I suppose, but it's not always easy to see the broader picture from the front lines." He paused for a moment. "We lost more than five thousand men, including two generals. There is a world of difference between common recruits and officers, and often it was they who did not command who had the greater skill in battle. Still, it is hard for men to lose those who lead them, no matter how incompetent they may be."

"Incompetent?"

"For the most part, officers purchase their commissions. It was not uncommon to see officers directing men in combat who had no concept of what they were about." His jaw tightened. "To fail in battle, to fail the men who depend on you, is often fatal."

"Is that why winning is so important to you?" she said slowly.

He frowned, his brows together thoughtfully. "Probably. It was a hard lesson to learn. Regardless of whether you're a brilliant battlefield tactician or an unqualified fool, the men you lead look to you for their survival. The end result of your failure may well be their deaths. For any man with a conscience, that alone makes failure unacceptable."

"Did you fail?" Her voice was quiet.

He trapped her gaze with his, his gray eyes dark with memories. "No, and I thank God every day for that. I was smart enough to realize I was not infallible and to take advantage of the experience that was available to me. Regardless of where it came from."

"But you earned a commendation. You were a hero."

He smiled in an offhanded manner, as if it was of no real consequence, but she suspected it was. "Hero is a relative term. I did little more than what was expected of me. I managed to keep men alive, including more than a few officers. Generals tend to look kindly upon that."

She gathered she would get no specifics from him and wasn't certain she wished to hear them at any rate. Still, they had never spoken of anything so serious as life and death.

"Does it bother you, talking about this?"

He shook his head. "It was a very long time ago. It feels like another lifetime." He hesitated, as if he debated whether or not to go on. "When my father died and I inherited his title, the attitude of the army, and Wellington, permitted men in my position to resign their commissions. So I did.

"My responsibility to my family dictated the decision. There was no one else to tend to the estate and other holdings. Still, it was . . ." his brow furrowed, "difficult to leave my men and not feel I was abandoning them. Failing them, in a way. Knowing the dangers they faced, the wretched conditions. There was never enough food or medical supplies, pay was always in arrears, the heat was often unbearable, disease was widespread . . ."

He blew a long breath. "At any rate, I returned home and tried to put it all out of my head. Laurie did what he could to help." He chuckled. "No doubt you can imagine what form his assistance took."

"No doubt," she murmured. That was her first season and she dimly remembered Max: a dark, handsome figure with a reckless, arrogant air.

"It worked for a while, but eventually the memories of death and dying, shattered bodies and equally shattered souls, overcame me. I retreated to my house in the country and spent nearly a year secluded with only Laurie's occasional visits and a great deal of liquor for company. So much for tending to my responsibilities.

"It took me a long while to accept and understand what I'd seen and experienced and played a role in. I suppose some might have thought me rather mad for a time." His gaze bored into hers. "Does that concern you?"

Her heart ached for him and she forced a

teasing note to her voice. "I suppose that depends on whether you are mad now."

"Oh, there is no question about that." He grinned. "I have taken on the Hellion of Grosvenor Square and her impossible tests. What man in his right mind would do such a thing?"

"None that I would have." She'd intended the comment to be of no significance, but it hung in the air between them with a meaning far deeper than mere words. Their gazes locked.

"And would you have me?" His smile remained, but his voice was as intense as his eyes.

She swallowed hard. "If you win, I have no choice."

"And if I lose?"

*Yes, if you love me.*

"But you do not intend to lose."

"No," he said firmly. "I do not intend to lose." He turned away and resumed his work.

She stared at him for a long time and wondered what would have happened between them if they'd never made this ridiculous bargain. Would his courtship have progressed along a more typical road? Would she still have fallen in love with him?

Possibly. But it would not have been nearly as exciting.

Pandora returned her attention to the job at hand, pushing the straw around in a perfunctory and totally ineffective manner, her thoughts absorbed with the lone question that tortured her mind and her heart.

*Did he love her?*

*   *   *

Max lifted a forkful of straw and tossed it to one side; the physical demands of his labor engaged his body but left his mind free to ponder their conversation.

He hadn't spoken of his military days to anyone. Ever. Distance and the intervention of the years no doubt leant perspective. He had come to terms with the devastation he'd witnessed long ago. Still, it was a surprise to realize he could discuss those days now without the agony that had once haunted him. He had healed himself and survived stronger for the torturous journey of heart and mind.

And she seemed to understand. Her eyes had mirrored the horror of his words but not a horror of him. Even when he'd recounted his escape from the rest of the world, a period when in fact he might have been truly mad, he read only sympathy and concern in her eyes. She was far more extraordinary than he'd ever expected.

Odd, that he would share the darkest moments of his life with this woman who had never known fear or want. Or perhaps not strange at all. He did intend to spend the rest of his days with her. The woman he loved.

*The woman he loved?*

He might as well admit it, if only to himself.

The realization changed everything. Could he really force her to marry him simply as the price of defeat? Bargain or no bargain, did he want her to marry him without love? Was love on his side alone enough?

No. A cold hand gripped his heart. Accepting his own feelings drove the stakes of their bargain to unforeseen heights. The inability to win her love would be the ultimate failure.

Could she love him? Perhaps she already did. Certainly jealously was an excellent sign, but he could not be entirely certain it was triggered by love. He could simply declare himself to her in hopes she would respond in kind.

But what if she didn't? Would he be able to bear the knowledge and continue on with the game? No, it was far better to try to determine her feelings before letting her know his.

"I've had quite enough." Pandora tossed her pitchfork aside and dropped on to a pile of clean straw, flinging herself backwards. She closed her eyes and folded her arms over her head. "Grandmother's ball is tonight and I'm already exhausted."

"You don't look exhausted." He leaned his pitchfork in a corner and moved to drop down in the straw at her side. "You look quite appealing."

"I feel anything but appealing. This is your fault entirely, you know." She smiled but didn't open her eyes. "I never should have allowed it."

"Ah, then it is in truth your fault." A strand of pale straw lay across her neck at the opening of her shirt. He flicked it away, noting the pulse at the base of her throat, yielding to the impulse to bend forward and brush a light kiss on the tempting spot.

She sucked in her breath. "What are you doing?"

"I simply removed a piece of straw," he said absently, allowing his lips to continue their ex-

ploration of the warm flesh of her throat and
knowing full well it was a mistake but unable
to resist.

"Max," she tensed beside him.

"Yes?" He trailed a line of kisses along the
side of her neck. Just one more moment and
he would stop.

"This is against the rules."

"Sorry." He pulled a deep breath. "It
slipped my mind for a moment." He shifted
to get to his feet.

"Max." She grabbed the sleeve of his shirt
and her gaze caught his. "You've broken it before."

His stomach tightened. "At the moment, it
seems—"

"Max. Break it again." She pulled him toward her, her blue eyes darkening. "Kiss me."

He gazed down at her. Her cheeks were
flushed, her hair tangled in straw, her delectable body laid out before him like an offering
to the gods. "One kiss could well lead to another."

"Could it?" she said lightly, drawing him
closer. "Perhaps we should see."

He stretched out beside her, gathering her
into his arms, and met her lips with his, her
mouth warm and pliant. He kissed her gently,
holding himself in check, resisting the urgent
need swelling up inside him, brushing his lips
across hers. She sighed and her mouth opened
slightly. He ran his tongue across the inner
edge of her lips and deeper into her mouth.
Her tongue met his tentatively and shock
coursed through him. He pulled her tighter to
him, the heat of her body searing his.

She wrapped her arms around his neck and his hands caressed her back in lazy circles, then drifted lower, to her buttocks. She shuddered and pressed her mouth hard against his. He ran his hand along her side, slipping under the hem of her shirt and up to touch her bare skin and skim the bottom of her breast. She gasped then stilled beside him but didn't pull her mouth from his. He cupped her breast, its firm fullness in his hand increasing his arousal. The pad of his thumb brushed her already hard nipple, tightening even more under his touch. Vaguely he noticed her tugging at his shirt and felt the cool morning air on his back.

He slipped his mouth from hers and sat up, yanking his shirt over his head and tossing it aside. Her eyes were glazed with desire.

"We should stop, Hellion. Now." His voice was a dry and raspy whisper.

"Should we?" She drew a ragged breath and smiled. "Why?"

"Because I won't be able to in another moment."

"Good," she murmured.

He closed his eyes willing a semblance of control to his rebellious body. She laid a hand on his stomach and trailed her fingertips in a wide circle. His eyes shot open and he sucked in a sharp breath. Her hand drifted lower to the top of his breeches and he knew he was lost.

He moved over her, his knees straddling her legs. Her chest rose and fell with short hard breaths. He lowered himself, stretching his legs along either side of hers, entrapping them.

He slid her shirt up to reveal smooth, creamy flesh and he wondered how long his restraint would last. His lips brushed across her breast and he traced it with his tongue. She started and arched upward beneath him, then fell back. He held the hard nipple gently between his teeth and flicked it until she moaned and her hands grabbed at his back. Slowly he whispered kisses from one breast to the other, then took it in his mouth.

"Max, oh, Max." She moaned and he rolled to lay beside her and meet her lips with his, her mouth now demanding and insistent. He responded in kind, caressing her breasts with a rough hunger, and she pressed closer against him. Her mouth was everywhere at once, tasting his neck, his shoulders. Her fingers explored his chest and drifted tentatively over his stomach. He held his breath. Her hand moved lower and her fingers brushed against his hard arousal and hesitated, as if she was unsure of what he wanted or what she wanted.

He mirrored her movements, running his hand over the plane of her stomach covered by the fabric of her breeches and down to the juncture between her thighs. Her legs pressed tightly together and he eased his fingers between them to feel her damp heat, stroking her until she groaned and her legs fell open. His fingers grazed the material, now wet and molded against her like a protective skin, and her hips moved to meet the pressure of his hand.

"Pandora." He gasped and pulled away, struggling to regain his composure. She gazed up at him, her lips slightly swollen, her hair disheveled and wild, her eyes sparked with passion. He wanted her as he'd never wanted any woman before. Bloody hell. This business of being her hero was damned difficult. Doing the heroic thing took more effort than he ever dreamed possible. Still, a hero would not take unfair advantage of the woman he loved.

"It's not too late to stop."

# Chapter 19
## *A Tactical Error*

**"S**top? You've suggested that once." She propped herself up on her elbows and stared at him in disbelief. "Why would you want to stop?"

He exhaled a hard breath. "I don't particularly want to stop. I simply realized—"

"Are you going to win this game?"

"Without a doubt."

"Then I shall be your wife?"

He nodded slowly. "That's my intention."

She studied him for a long moment. His hair was rumpled and his bare chest heaved with every breath. His eyes were dark with desire, molten lead, smoldering with promise. Could simple lust make a man's eyes look like that? Her pulse pounded. No. There was much more in his gaze than physical need. Her heart soared. "Would you like to know my intention, Max?"

"Your intention?"

"Um-hum." She wanted him, wanted this,

regardless of the consequences, the future. Win or lose, she knew there would never be anyone in her life she'd love the way she loved him if she ever loved again at all. And any man who looked at her the way he did was surely in love as well. She leaned forward and pulled off one of her half boots, then the other. "My heartfelt intention?"

"Heartfelt?"

She scrambled to stand and held her hand out to him. He grabbed it and pulled himself to his feet. She pressed herself against him and splayed her hands across his chest and he wrapped his arms around her. "You remember when I thought you were going to ravish me and you didn't?"

He nodded.

"Well." She leaned forward and flicked her tongue across his flat nipple and he jumped beneath her touch. "I was rather disappointed." She struggled to keep her voice calm. How could she be so wanton?

He swallowed hard. "You were?"

"Weren't you?"

"Oh, yes." He drew a deep shuddering breath.

"Then..." She gazed into his eyes and knew there was no more need for words.

He pulled her shirt up and over her head, then skimmed his hands along her sides to her breeches and pushed them down over her hips and they fell to puddle around her feet. She resisted the urge to cover herself with her hands and kept her gaze locked on his. He bent and pulled off his boots, then swiftly removed his breeches. She wanted to look at him, all of him, but she couldn't bring herself to drop her gaze and instead stared into his eyes. He pulled her to him and she felt him hard and hot between her legs. Her knees weakened and she molded against him, tilting her head back to greet his lips with her own.

He kissed her with a greed that swept away her doubts and her fears and she met his hunger and returned it in kind. She wanted, no needed, to taste his lips, his throat, his arms. To feel the muscles of his chest, his back, his buttocks beneath her hands. Need building to a frenzy of taste and touch and desire.

He held her tight and lowered her to the straw, his flesh scorching hers. She ran her hands along his sides and over his stomach and lower still to grasp his arousal, at once as soft as velvet and hard as iron.

He groaned. "Good God, Hellion."

His hand slipped between her legs and his fingers, wet and slick with her own desire, caressed her lightly. She held her breath, tense with anticipation. The pressure of his hand increased and she bit her lip to keep from whimpering at the unimagined pleasure. Everything around her vanished and she existed only in the sensation spiraling from his caress, enveloped in an exquisite haze of yearning. She throbbed against his touch and wondered that she could survive such an awesome state of ever-tightening tension. Surely she would explode into a million pieces.

Abruptly he stopped and before she could protest, rolled over to hover above her. He reached down and guided himself to nudge, gently at first, then slowly he slid into her.

She gasped. "Max?"

He paused. "Yes?"

"You do know I have never done this before?"

He gazed into her eyes. "I know."

"Well, just as long as you know . . ."

He nuzzled her neck and feathered kisses along the line of her jaw. He pushed deeper into her, filling her, a feeling at once odd and amazing, and continued until he hit the barrier of her maidenhood. "Hellion, I'm afraid . . . I don't want to hurt you."

She knew what to expect, knew it was inevitable, but they'd come too far to stop. And stopping was the last thing she wanted. Her muscles tensed. "Go on, Max. Please."

He moved gently, sliding out then in again. His mouth covered hers, his tongue seeking, probing. Her excitement rose. Without warning he thrust hard and buried himself deep inside her. A sharp pain stabbed through her and she cried out. "Max, no! Stop. Now."

"Wait, Hellion," he murmured against her neck. "Patience. Just wait. The pain will pass."

He moved slowly, his thrusts smooth and deliberate, and she gritted her teeth against the sting. It probably wouldn't be in the spirit of the game to stop at this point, although for a moment she thought the enjoyment that had preceded this was quite enough. Still, it wasn't as bad as it had been before. Rather bittersweet, actually, mingled with lovely sensations. Her discomfort eased, replaced by a growing tension. Tentatively she moved her hips to match his. His rhythm increased. Her pleasure heightened.

She gripped his shoulders tightly and arched upward to meet him, losing herself in a rapture she'd never suspected. His heart pounded against hers. Her body throbbed against his. She was caught in an ever-faster whirlpool of ecstasy and sensual awareness, and once more she wondered if she would indeed live through the sheer joy that encompassed her, and knowing she no longer cared. Nothing mattered except here and now and Max.

Without warning, something inside her burst, and waves of extraordinary delight washed through her, stealing her breath and her mind and her soul. Max held her tight and his body shuddered against hers. And for an instant or an eternity it was as if they were suspended together in one glorious never ending moment that defied time and distance and substance.

She was his and he was hers and nothing would ever be the same again.

"I never imagined." She buried her head in his shoulder and giggled. "Oh, Max, that was . . ."

"Perfect?" he whispered, and drew her closer against him.

"Perfect." She sighed. His heart soared. She loved him. She had to. It was in every look, every kiss, every touch.

"So," he nibbled on her shoulder, "can we consider the stables cleaned?"

She lifted her head and grinned, the gleam in her eyes stopping his heart. "I believe you more than earned that point."

He brushed his lips across her forehead.

"Max," she snuggled against him. "What are you thinking?"

"I'm thinking this straw is damned uncomfortable."

She laughed. "What else?"

"I'm thinking what a lucky man I am," he said softly.

"What else?"

"I'm thinking I'm bloody grateful this game is at an end."

She drew back and a frown creased her forehead. "At an end?"

"It's pointless to continue."

"Pointless?" Her voice was even but there was an odd look in her eye.

"Of course. You have to marry me now."

"I have to marry you?" she said slowly.

"Certainly. There is no other choice."

She stared for a long moment. "And that's what you're thinking? That's *all* you're thinking?"

"Well," his mind raced. What else should he be thinking? Even as he spoke he knew his answer was wrong. "Yes?"

"I see." She struggled to sit upright, grabbed her shirt and held it against her, her manner reserved and cool. "Tell me, Max, why do I *have* to marry you now?"

"Because you're ruined." He couldn't hold back a grin. "I ruined you."

"I don't particularly feel ruined."

He pulled his brows together. Surely she understood the end result of their lovemaking? "Well, you are. The only way to salvage your honor is with marriage."

"My honor is just fine, thank you," she said sharply. "Now, if you would be so good as to turn around."

"Very well, but it's a bit late to be overly modest, don't you think?" He pulled himself to his feet and turned his back to her. What on earth had gotten into the woman?

"And do get dressed."

He collected his clothes and pulled on his breeches. He could hear her dressing behind him. "Pandora?" No response. "You do understand, marriage is inevitable now."

"I understand no such thing." Her voice was cool and hard. "If you think you are going to get what you want simply with a mere dalliance in the stables—"

"Dalliance?" He jerked his shirt on over his head and swiveled to face her. "Is that what you think this was?"

"What do you think it was?"

Anger and confusion battled within him. "Up until now I thought it was what you wanted. I know it was what I wanted."

"It's one thing to seduce—"

He snorted. "Seduce? I'd scarcely call you seduced."

Her blue eyes sparked with anger. "—To seduce the women in my family to support, no, conspire with you to earn points in the most absurd ways possible, but quite another to do"—she waved her arms in a wide, encompassing gesture—"to do—"

"To do what?" He narrowed his eyes.

"To do . . . *this* simply to circumvent the rest of the game and force me to marry you. It's beyond belief."

He stared, choosing his words with care.
"You think that's why I did, why we did,
*this?*"

"Do you deny it?"

Certainly the idea had dawned on him, but
not until afterward. He hesitated for the merest second but it was enough.

"I thought as much." She tossed her dark
hair back with an angry jerk of her head. She
was completely dressed now, and turned on
her heel and stalked toward the door. "You
have *this* point, my lord, but you still have
three more to go, and time is running out. Do
not expect the rest of them to be this easy."

"Easy? Hah!" He glared at her retreating
figure. "I'll be picking *straw* out of my backside for the rest of my life."

"It's the least you deserve!" She swiveled
back to face him. Her eyes glistened with tears.
"Bargain or no bargain, I should rather have
my still beating heart ripped out of my chest
by giant vultures before I would ever, ever
marry you! And one more thing. I was wrong
when I said you were a bloody fine kisser."

"You seemed to enjoy it a few minutes ago,"
he snapped.

"A few minutes ago I was an inexperienced
virgin. Now that I have the vantage point of a
ruined woman, it's easy to see I was mistaken." She whirled and strode out the door.

"I've never had a complaint before. That
was unworthy of you, Hellion," he yelled after
her. "And damned inaccurate, too!"

What a lunatic the woman was. Insulting, of
all things, his ability to kiss. She certainly
hadn't indicated she was not enjoying every

single kiss, every caress, everything. He freely admitted he had no humility whatsoever when it came to his skills with women. He knew what he was doing whether it was kissing or making love . . .

*Love?* He groaned aloud. That was it. He hadn't told her he loved her. This was the perfect opportunity and it had slipped right passed him.

She was hurt and how could he blame her? He really was an insensitive, arrogant beast. He would have to make it up to her. Tonight. Sweep her off her feet and declare his love once and for all. After this morning he needn't worry about her response. He was confident she shared his feelings.

He started toward the house and a sharp pain stabbed him right below his left buttocks. He stopped and shifted the fabric of his breeches but the jabbing discomfort remained. He'd have to endure it until he got back to his rooms.

Bloody hell. It was Pandora's parting curse, no doubt.

He probably *would* be picking straw out of his backside forever.

"And then of course, I mentioned what a total fool she'd been for ever . . ."

The correct responses tripped off Pandora's lips, her polite smile never wavering, but if anyone had asked her directly what the topic of conversation was in the group of guests she'd joined at her grandmother's ball, she would have had no idea. Her presence here was a protection of sorts. An excellent way to hide while still in plain sight.

She'd never hidden from anything, but she wanted to hide now. From the world, and most of all, from herself. Now that she was a ruined woman. Not that she felt like a ruined woman, although she had no idea what she was expected to feel like, but she definitely wasn't her usual self. Her thoughts were chaotic and her emotions raw. Still, that had little to do with the act itself, only its aftermath.

She still couldn't quite believe it. By the gods, she'd lost her virtue. No, not lost it as she'd misplace a glove or a fan. She'd tossed it away, thrown it as hard and as far as she could, and with a great deal of enthusiasm in the process.

It was perhaps the most wonderful experience she'd ever had or probably would ever have again. Never in her wildest dreams had she imagined what being in Max's arms would really mean.

"Miss Effington?"

Her attention jerked to the faces staring at her expectantly. Any other time she would have recovered her composure without hesitation, but tonight she couldn't seem to muster the effort such a deception required.

"Please excuse me," she said with an apologetic smile. *I've squandered my virtue on a man I thought loved me only to discover he simply wished to force me into marriage, and I have no desire at this moment to engage in pointless drivel with people I barely know.* "I've just remembered something I must attend to."

She nodded politely and stepped away,

pasting a purposeful expression on her face.

She made her way through the crush of guests and barely noted greetings directed to her. Even when Georgina's daughters, Cassandra and Philadelphia, her cousins closest to her own age, wanted to speak with her, she begged off. All they wished to talk about was Max, and she had no desire to discuss him, even if he was the only thing on her mind.

She should have known better. Max wanted to win. Nothing else mattered to him.

And dear Lord, how the realization hurt. She'd never imagined such pain, never suspected anyone could endure suffering like this and still live. It was as if her heart really had been ripped from her chest. The hot ache of tears stung her throat and she ruthlessly forced them away. Without thinking, she raised her chin. She would not shed a single tear. Not here. Not in public. Oh certainly, she had cried in the privacy of her bath, wept until she thought there was nothing left. Obviously, she was wrong.

Just how long would this anguish last? How long until she regained her usual mood and manner? Or would she ever be the same again?

She accepted a glass of champagne from a passing waiter and sipped at it thoughtfully. Tears too were a new experience for her. She had never cried because of a man before and could not remember the last time she had cried at all. Love was indeed accompanied by a vast variety of heretofore unknown and unpleasant emotions: awkwardness, panic, jealousy, and now pain.

Pandora cast her gaze over the crowded ballroom. She hadn't spotted Max yet and hoped he had done the honorable thing and returned to London. Of course he would never do that. His conquest of her was the ultimate victory in their game and he would not leave without claiming his prize.

She did not look forward to their next meeting but it was inevitable. What would he say? What would she say?

And what was everyone else saying? She was amazed that all present weren't whispering among themselves about her fall from grace. It wasn't unusual for her to be the topic of gossip and she was confident Max would never reveal what had occurred between them. Still, she couldn't ignore the uneasy sensation that each and every person here was well aware of the encounter in the stables. Did she somehow look different now? Was there something about her that screamed of her indiscretion?

Of course not. It was no more than her conscience and a far too active imagination. She'd never paid a great deal of attention to her conscience but then her crimes had never quite reached this magnitude before. She tossed back the rest of her champagne and wondered if now she could truly live up to her hellion title. After all, she'd lost her heart and her virtue and what else really mattered?

"Miss Effington, may I have the honor of this dance?" A tall, attractive gentleman with a sober expression but pleasant eyes stood before her. She vaguely remembered him from the Ride.

"Of course," she murmured, handing her glass to a footman and accompanying her new partner onto the floor. She breathed a prayer of gratitude it was not a waltz. Her grandmother loved the waltz and insisted it make up the majority of the dances. The last thing Pandora wanted right now was to be in the arms of a man. Any man.

She performed the steps of the quadrille without effort and with very little thought. Her gaze drifted over the gathering. Perhaps it wasn't her imagination, after all. Her grandmother, the duchess, and her mother were seated in one area, exchanging idle chatter. Nothing odd about that, but she caught more than one pointed glance in her direction.

She executed a turn and noted her aunts speaking to Cynthia. Cynthia glanced at her, then quickly pulled her gaze away, as if she was hiding something. Or was Cynthia embarrassed? Ashamed? Of her? Heat burned her cheeks. Cynthia nodded to her aunts and they took their leave. She appeared to study the dancers for a moment, then swiftly stepped to the doors leading to the terrace and slipped outside. What *was* she doing?

Pandora wanted to follow her, but the last thing she needed was to draw additional attention to herself by leaving in the middle of this dance. A dance that seemed endless. A turn took her out of sight of the terrace doors. A few steps later they were again in view. A door opened and Max stepped inside.

She sucked in a shocked breath. Her vision narrowed and an odd dizziness swept through her. For a moment, she thought she'd collapse in a heap on the floor. Max? On the terrace with Cynthia? This was not her imagination creating something where nothing existed. Those with no need to hide did not sneak off for clandestine meetings in secluded places.

The dance at last came to an end. She murmured her thanks to her partner and excused herself. She accepted another glass of champagne and forced herself to think. Logically. Rationally.

She needed a plan and she needed one now. She didn't know if Max still wished to marry her. And if he did it obviously had nothing to do with love.

She couldn't let him win, but he needed only three points and she didn't know how to stop him. It seemed there was little she did know at the moment. Frustration and helplessness surged through her and she struggled to ignore the sense of panic that threatened to overwhelm her.

"Do you realize you and I have never danced before?" Max's voice sounded behind her.

She drew a deep breath and turned. In the split second before her gaze met his, she knew one thing she could indeed do to salvage what was left of her pride and perhaps her heart as well.

She tilted her head and favored him with her most brilliant smile. The very one she'd practiced before her first season. The very one that was second nature to her now. The very one that deepened her dimples and was, by all accounts, irresistible.

His eyes widened and a smile of appreciation spread across his face.

She knew if she knew nothing else, she absolutely could not allow Max to know he'd broken her heart.

And she could not let him know she loved him.

# Chapter 20
## *A Point Well Played*

**S**he gazed up at him through lashes dark and thick and lush. Her voice was husky in a wonderfully exciting way. "Haven't we, my lord?"

"No." His mouth was abruptly dry and he could barely croak out the words. "We haven't."

"How on earth do you suppose we've avoided dancing? It quite seems to me we've done everything else together." The look in her eye was as suggestive as her voice, and he swallowed hard.

He stared down at her mesmerized. Desire, hot and unyielding, gripped him. "You look exquisite tonight."

"Oh, my lord, you do turn a pretty phrase." She took a sip of her champagne, her gaze never leaving his.

God help him, he would do anything for this woman. Or anything to have this woman. "I gather you are no longer angry with me?"

"Come now, my lord, how could any woman in her right mind stay angry at you?"

"Excellent." He breathed a sigh of relief. She actually appeared pleased to see him. "After the way we parted this morning, I was somewhat afraid, actually, that—"

"Afraid? The Earl of Trent?" She laughed lightly. "Why, you're a hero. I can scarce imagine you afraid of anything."

"Perhaps 'concerned' is a better word. I expected you . . ." He stared at her thoughtfully. "I expected you—"

"Expected me to what, my lord?" Her eyes widened in innocence. "Ignore you? Avoid you? Grab a champagne bottle and bash it over your head? Shoot you, perhaps?" She flashed him a dazzling smile. "I would never even consider anything so absurd."

"You wouldn't? Why not?"

She laughed again. "As you well know, my aim is atrocious." She finished her champagne, waved to a waiter and handed him her glass. "Fortunately for us both, I am much more skilled with a waltz than I am with a gun."

"That is fortunate," he murmured, offering her his arm. She rested her hand in the crook of his elbow and cast him a look that could only be described as adoring. Too adoring. She had never gazed at him like this. Not this morning. Not ever. It was artificial and too polished. And it did not suit her. Or him.

A heavy weight settled in the pit of his stomach. He escorted her to the floor and drew her into his arms, at once remembering how perfectly her body fit with his and resisting the urge to pull her closer. Not that he could have done so anyway. In spite of her overly flirtatious and affectionate manner, she kept him at a distance not even the most proper matron could fault. No, there was no doubt in his mind now. The Hellion was furious.

They whirled around the floor with a natural ease as if they'd danced together always. As if their bodies and souls were made for each other. Bloody hell. Why couldn't she see that?

"I have been giving a great deal of thought to your comments this morning," she said, as if the topic at hand was of no more importance than the weather.

"Oh?" Caution sounded in his tone. "Which comments were those?"

"Your declaration that marriage was inevitable. To salvage my honor."

"I see." He wasn't entirely certain he wished to hear her thoughts. His gaze shifted from hers and he scanned the room over her shoulder. "And?"

"And as much as I do appreciate your ever so generous offer, I must decline. It simply wouldn't be, oh," he glanced down at her and she beamed, "in the spirit of the game."

"Very well."

"Very well?" Her eyes widened. "I am surprised, my lord. I expected another detailed explanation of my ruined state."

He caught sight of Laurie dancing with Miss Weatherly and calculated the number of turns on the floor it would take to narrow the distance between the two couples. He smiled down at her. "I rather like you ruined."

Her expression never wavered, but her jaw

tightened slightly and a flash of defiance shone in her eyes. "Now that I have had time to think about it, so do I."

"What?" What was the blasted woman planning now?

There was more than a touch of satisfaction in her smile. "It appears a whole new world of opportunities is now opened to me."

"Opportunities?" Surely she wasn't suggesting what he thought she was suggesting?

"Indeed. And I have you to thank for it."

"Me?"

"Oh, not for this morning, although I do owe you my thanks for that. No, it was you who pointed out when we first met that I could never be a governess. And you who assumed I had chosen another option. Now, I am well trained for that particular option."

The thought of Pandora in the arms of anyone twisted his heart. Without thinking, he pulled her closer and pinned her rebellious gaze with his. "The only thing you are trained for is marriage with me."

"It will scarcely seem worth the effort when you lose."

"When I win."

He spotted Miss Weatherly out of the corner of his eye and stopped so quickly Pandora stumbled against him. Miss Weatherly had completely slipped his mind. He turned and saw her facing Laurie on the dance floor, directly in front of the Effington women, exactly where she was supposed to be.

"What is going on there?" Pandora murmured.

"Perhaps we should find out," he said and

they started toward the couple, skirting
around the outer edge of the dancers.

Miss Weatherly's gaze flicked to his and
back to Laurie's. She squared her shoulders,
raised her hand, and cracked it across Laurie's
face.

Pandora gasped. "By the gods!"

"Good Lord." Shock coursed through him.
He'd never expected this.

Laurie clapped his hand to his cheek, his
mouth dropped open in stunned silence.

The music stopped and the entire gathering
focused on the tense scene. The dowager
waved sharply to the musicians and the music
resumed, the dancers falling back into step
while obviously trying not to miss a single
moment of what might well prove to be a juicy
scandal.

"I cannot believe you would have the nerve
to suggest such a thing." Miss Weatherly's
voice quavered and Max couldn't suppress a
touch of admiration. The chit had far more
courage than even he suspected.

"What?" Laurie's eyes were wide. "What
did I say?"

"If he's done anything to hurt her," Pandora
said under her breath. She and Max reached a
spot near her grandmother and stopped.

"You know perfectly well what you said.
What you implied! You ... you ..." Miss
Weatherly glared. "Prig!"

"Twit," Pandora said under her breath.

"A bore is what he is," Lady Edward said.

Lady William nodded. "I've always said he
was a bore."

"Now wait just one moment," Laurie said

indignantly. "I am many things but I am most definitely not a bore. I am quite charming and most entertaining. Why, in many circles—"

"He's a bore." Lady William sighed.

"No question whatsoever." Lady Edward shook her head. "The man is indeed a bore."

"A bore?" Pandora leveled Max an outraged glare.

He ignored her and stepped toward Laurie. "Now then, Bolton, apologize to Miss Weatherly. At once."

"Why?" Laurie's gaze shot to Miss Weatherly's and she looked away pointedly. "I didn't do anything to apologize for."

"Nonetheless," Max said in a stern tone. "An apology is in order. Unless you would prefer to handle this matter outside."

Laurie narrowed his eyes and studied him carefully. It was apparent to Max he was moments away from saying or doing something none of them would ever recover from. Max needed to get him out of here without delay.

"Very well," Laurie said slowly. "Outside it is." He headed toward the doors to the terrace. Max started after him.

"Nicely done, Lord Trent," the dowager duchess said. He paused and nodded, trying not to grin. "Did you see that, Pandora? How he bested that bore?"

"I could scarce miss it, Grandmother." Her expression was pleasant, but one look in her eyes, and poor aim or not, Max sent a silent prayer heavenward in gratitude that she did not have her pistol.

"You do know what that means, dear?" The dowager's tone left no room for protest.

"Oh, indeed I do," Pandora said, in a soft tone that chilled his blood. She leaned close and laid her hand on his arm. "Congratulations on your point, my lord. Do enjoy it. Tomorrow we return to London, and without your man-eating mares, achieving the last two points may be more difficult than you imagine."

"I doubt that." His confident tone belied his concern about at least one of those points. "It has not been particularly difficult thus far."

"Ah, but doesn't any competition grow harder the closer one gets to the end?" Her smile did not quite reach her eyes and the challenge in her tone was unmistakable. "Good evening, my lord."

She nodded to her grandmother and the other ladies then turned and marched away. He stared after her for a moment, realizing what a mistake it would be to dismiss either her anger or her cleverness. For the first time since they sealed their bargain he wondered if there was indeed the possibility of defeat.

Max pushed the thought aside and hurried after Laurie. He pulled open one of the French doors lining the far wall, stepped outside, and paused to search the shadows. Ornate candelabras balanced on the stone balusters cast circles of light on the far side of the terrace, and rectangles of light lit the area closest to the doors, but the rest of the terrace was illuminated only by starlight.

"Laurie?"

"I didn't say anything to her, Max." Laurie stepped forward, a grim expression on his face.

"Laurie, I—"

"Nothing at all." He touched the side of his face tenderly. "At least nothing to deserve this."

"Laurie, it's—"

"And I warn you, Max, if you feel compelled to thrash me simply to acquire another point I shall be forced to retaliate."

"Laurie—" Would the man ever let him get a word in?

"Very well, I confess." Laurie crossed his arms over his chest. "I might have implied that she was trying to lead but, damnation, Max, the bit of baggage was pushing me all over the bloody ballroom."

Max tried not to laugh. "Laurie—"

"And even so, I don't think that merited all this. It wasn't as if I said she didn't dance well or cast aspersions on her character because of her annoying tendency to try to dominate on a dance floor. In point of fact, Max," a note of disbelief sounded in his voice, "I rather, somewhat, possibly . . ."

"Like her?"

"Perhaps," Laurie said reluctantly. "Perhaps more than like her."

"I see."

"Come now, Max, you needn't take that tone it's not at all as if—"

A door opened a few feet down from the one Max used and Miss Weatherly stepped into sight. She glanced at Max.

Max grinned.

Miss Weatherly laughed.

Laurie glowered. "I say, this is not at all funny. A moment ago, you were outraged and you were prepared to defend her hon . . ." His gaze shot from one to the other and his eyes narrowed. "Or it was all an act?"

"And an excellent one at that." Max swept an exaggerated bow in Miss Weatherly's direction. "I commend you on an outstanding job. You have my thanks and my gratitude."

She bobbed a curtsey. "It was my pleasure, my lord."

"No doubt," Laurie muttered.

Miss Weatherly stepped toward him. "I did warn you I would do everything I could to ensure Trent's victory. In fact, it was my idea to invite you here in the first place. I thought it best to keep an eye on you, Lawrence."

*Lawrence?*

"You humiliated me in front of everyone. You made a fool out of me." A wounded note sounded in Laurie's voice but Max wondered how much of what he alleged was truth and how much was a play for sympathy. "I should have known better than to come anywhere near an Effington. This kind of thing is to be expected when you have anything whatsoever to do with that family."

Max frowned. "What do you—"

"Come now, don't be absurd." Miss Weatherly fisted her hands on her hips and fixed Laurie with a firm gaze. "You should know, if you have not yet realized it, the Effingtons, at least the Effington ladies, are well aware that this was all a sham."

"Well, it didn't feel like a sham." Laurie rubbed the side of his face. "It hurt."

"I am sorry." Miss Weatherly placed her palm on his cheek and abruptly Max noted

what an attractive pair the two made. Laurie
was but a few inches taller than she. In the mix
of light from doors and stars, their fair hair
glowed gold and silver and their tall figures
appeared ethereal, like fairy royalty stepped
from the pages of Shakespeare.

"Are you?" Laurie said softly, pulling her
hand to his lips.

"Er, Laurie," Max said uneasily.

"I am." Her voice carried a meaning far beyond her words. "I never wished to hurt you."

Laurie's arms slipped around her waist and
he pulled her close. "Do you promise never to
injure me again, then?"

"Miss Weatherly?" Max's voice rose.

Her response was too low for Max to hear
and he was damned grateful. Laurie laughed.
Without adequate warning, her arms were
around his neck and Laurie's lips met hers in
an overly passionate kiss.

"Good God," Max said under his breath.
Heat flushed his face and he quickly turned
his back to them. There were some things even
your oldest friend was not meant to see. Oh,
certainly he had seen Laurie kiss women before but they were, well, they definitely
weren't anything like Miss Weatherly.

*Miss Weatherly?* He groaned. If Pandora ever
did forgive him for all his other transgressions,
and judging by her manner tonight, forgiveness might well be a long time in coming, how
would she react to this? For some reason,
she'd apparently taken an instant dislike to
Laurie. No doubt she would place the blame
for this new development squarely on Max's
shoulders.

He cleared his throat in an exaggerated manner.

The sounds of passion remained.

He tried it again.

Miss Weatherly giggled. Laurie murmured something and laughed.

"Laurie?" Max tried once more. "Miss Weatherly?"

"It's all right, Max," Laurie said with a grin in his voice. "You may look now."

Max turned. Laurie and Miss Weatherly still stood face to face, entirely too close, with their hands clasped, but at least no longer wrapped in each other's arms. And they shared the most ridiculous grins.

"I believe I should go inside," Miss Weatherly said, gazing at Laurie.

"May a humble prig call on you when we return to London?" Laurie's tone was light but a serious note underlaid his words. Max stared at his best friend dumbfounded.

"If you don't, I should be forced to call on you."

"Miss Weatherly!" Max said, shocked by her promise.

"You were right, my lord, I have spent entirely too much time with Pandora." She cast one last smile at Laurie, then turned and headed for the door.

Laurie's gaze stayed on her until she vanished into the ballroom. Max raised a curious brow. "Do you have anything you wish to tell me?"

"She kisses extremely well, for a woman with no experience." A note of wonder colored Laurie's voice. "I suspect it was the enthusiasm . . ."

"Laurie," Max snapped, and his friend's gaze jerked to his. "What game are you playing?"

"Game?" Laurie said in a bemused manner. "I'm not playing any game."

Max stepped closer and studied Laurie for a long moment. The expression on his face was an odd mix of confusion and awe. "Don't tell me you're in love with her?"

"In love?" Laurie laughed. "Oh, I scarcely think . . ." He heaved a heartfelt sigh and raked his fingers through his hair. "I don't know."

"I never thought I'd say this but welcome to the club."

"It's one club I never particularly planned on joining," he said wryly.

"No man does." Max grinned. "Membership sneaks up on you."

Laurie narrowed his eyes. "Does that mean . . . ?"

"I'm afraid it does." Max shrugged.

"I see."

"What? No protest? No lecture on how Pandora will break my heart? No speech on how my life will be ruined? On my ultimate doom?"

Laurie shook his head. "Not now. I can't fight love." He paused. "Have you told the Hel—Miss Effington?"

"I had planned to tell her tonight." Max sighed. "I thought she already knew but apparently not."

"Let me make sure I understand this," Laurie said slowly. "You love the woman. But you haven't told her. And you have done everything in your power to pass these tests of hers with her entire family, and much of society as well, looking on in a manner that can't help but injure her pride publicly as well as privately. Yet you have failed to tell her of your feelings."

"I hadn't quite thought of it that way." Max's heart sank, a leaden weight in the pit of his stomach. "It does sound rather unpleasant."

He certainly hadn't intended to make her look foolish. It was simply an unwanted result of their game. Coupled with this morning . . . he blew out a long breath. It was not surprising she thought his lovemaking was an underhanded way to win the game and force her into marriage.

"So tell her you love her."

"No," Max said without hesitation. "Not now."

"Why not?"

"Because I don't know her feelings. I thought I did, but—" He shook his head.

He'd always been able to coax a true smile from her before, but tonight he was unable to penetrate her overly pleasant, and obviously counterfeit, manner. Had his assault on her pride destroyed any affection she may have felt for him? Was it his own arrogance that now refused to allow him to admit his feelings?

"I would prefer if you did not mention this to Miss Weatherly."

"Of course." Laurie's voice was thoughtful. "I won't say a word to Cynthia."

"Cynthia?"

"That's her name." Laurie shrugged sheepishly. "I know it's quite improper but it is so deliciously wicked. And you're scarcely one to talk. You call the Hel—Miss Effington, Pandora. And she calls you—"

"Max."

*"Come now, my lord, how could any woman in her right mind stay angry at you?"*

The weight in his stomach increased.

Except tonight, when she hadn't called him Max once.

# Chapter 21
## *A Desperate Move*

"**W**ell?" Pandora folded her arms over her chest and studied Laurie with a gaze that was at once apprehensive and impatient. "Will you help me or not?"

"I'm not entirely certain," he said thoughtfully. He stood before the fireplace in the Effington parlor, picking up and setting down assorted odds and ends that crowded the overmantel. A wicked-looking parrot perched amid the ancient objects and eyed Laurie as if he was a guardian gargoyle and not a mere bird. Laurie suspected the feathered beast would like nothing better than to sink his beak into a nice, tasty hand.

Aside from the bird, this was a fascinating display for its chaotic variety alone and he wished he could pay it the proper attention. At the moment, it provided nothing more than a way to conceal his thoughts on her outrageous suggestion.

"There is more than enough time left for

Max to succeed, and I have to do something."
She wrung her hands in an absent, nervous
gesture. "The game ends six days from today.
Max still has two remaining tests. How he's
going to defeat a beast with three heads, let
alone find golden apples, is beyond me, but
the man is wickedly clever and I have no
doubt he will devise something."

"Probably." Especially since Laurie had
picked up Max's golden apples earlier in the
day. Exquisitely wrought, the bauble was
three charms in one, strung on a gold chain
and in his waistcoat pocket at this very minute. He did not doubt his friend would win
their game and was no longer certain that was
a bad idea. He had ceased to view Pandora as
a wicked man-eating vixen.

She drew a deep breath. "If I leave London
in the company of a gentleman—"

"Or a twit, as the case may be." He replaced
the pottery.

"Or a twit." She shook her head and smiled,
obviously amused in spite of herself. "I shall
make you another proposal, Bolton. I will not
call you a twit if you cease referring to me as
the Hellion."

"But it has such a amusing ring to it," he
murmured.

"I rather like twit, too. It has a nice feel
when you say it. Somewhat resounding and to
the point. I think it's the Ts." She paused to
give it extra emphasis. "Twit."

"That's enough, thank you. I agree." He
crossed his arms and studied her. "So, is it to
be Viscount Bolton and Miss Effington, then?
Although it does seem to me, given your pro-

posal to run off together, it should be Laurie
and Pandora."

"Fine. Whatever you want." She waved her
hand in a gesture of disregard. "As I was saying, if we leave London together and lead Max
to believe we have gone to Gretna Green—"

"Repeating the sins of the past," he said
slowly.

"Precisely why it will work." She nodded.
"Essentially, I'm defaulting, and he'll be the
winner. But if I'm married, there's no prize for
him to claim. Max will realize the game is
over. It will be pointless for him even to come
after us.

"I will leave a note with Peters and instructions to deliver it to Max the day after we
leave. That should provide us with more than
enough time. The note will say something
about the last time we attempted to," she
swallowed hard, "elope, and how now that
we've found each other again, all our previous
feelings . . ." She spread her hands out, flutter-
ing them in a helpless manner.

Laurie stared, stunned. He never imagined
he would use the word "helpless" in connection with the Hel—Pandora Effington.

"Do you think he'll believe that?"

"His pride might have a bit of trouble with
it, but regardless, we won't return until Max's
time has expired."

"And if he cannot find you, he cannot earn
his final points."

"Exactly. Well?"

He frowned. "I do hope you take this in the
spirit in which it is intended, Pandora. I don't
mean any offense and my attitude overall on

marriage seems to have undergone a complete change in recent days, but I have no desire to marry, well, *you*."

"That works out quite nicely, then," she said dryly. "I have no desire to marry you, either."

"You don't?" Not that he was truly surprised.

"Absolutely not."

"You needn't be so vehement about it," he said under his breath.

"Oh, come now, Laurie. Compared to the last time, what was it? A choice between you or man-eating lions, a mere 'absolutely not' is fairly mild." She laughed softly. "My plan doesn't involve marriage, simply the appearance of the intention of marriage."

"The appearance of the intention of marriage . . ." In an odd sort of way he understood what she meant. Odder still, it sounded as if it could indeed work. "I can agree to that in principle, but have you considered the consequences of all this? Everyone in London is watching the contest between you and Max. Our going off together won't remain a secret for long. And we won't be accompanied by two other couples, a factor I always thought helped save you from complete ruin the last time. This plan will irreparably shatter your reputation."

"No doubt." She shrugged in an offhanded manner as if it was of no consequence. "I daresay, there are many who have long expected me to come to this end. The very least I can do is live up to their expectations. It's a fitting fate for the Hellion of Grosvenor Square, don't you agree?''

He stared for a long moment. She certainly didn't look like a hellion now. She appeared fragile and delicate and infinitely sad. What in the hell had Max done to her? ''Much of the blame for that can be placed on me. It is too late, but I am sorry.''

''Thank you, Laurie, but you simply awarded me the title. I did my best to live up to it.'' She shook her head and wrapped her arms around herself as if to ward off a chill or a truth difficult to face. ''It's been rather a challenge, through the years, to walk the fine line between too far and not far enough, knowing full well everyone is watching your every move, certain you were going to plunge into scandal and probably hoping for that very thing.''

''I can imagine.''

''Can you? Can you imagine as well that regardless of what you said aloud, privately, deep down inside, you simply wanted what everyone else in the world wanted? And you were terrified at the idea you wouldn't end up with even that, because you were too busy living up to a reputation you hadn't completely earned?'' Her gaze caught his. ''Just punishment for your sins, I suppose.''

''Hardly just,'' he murmured, struck by a wave of recognition. She was so very much like someone he knew. Himself? Wasn't his public side far different from his private side? And the private self was buried so deep inside, even Max would be hard pressed to recognize it.

"So, will you help me?"

"I haven't decided. There are a number of details to discuss." He paused. "For one thing, Max will probably kill me. Literally. With pistols at dawn, or possibly his bare hands."

"I doubt that. He shall probably be quite relieved," she said, more to herself than to him.

What on earth had happened? This was definitely not the Hellion—or rather, the Pandora—he'd bantered with in the country. It was as if her spirit was broken. Or her heart.

He should have realized it sooner. It explained everything. Max had broken her heart just as Laurie had feared. He ignored the voice in his head that reminded him he'd been more afraid of heartbreak for Max than Pandora. But how? Max loved her. She obviously loved him. Of course, if neither had confessed their feelings . . . what a sorry mess this was.

And what of Cynthia? What would her reaction be to the false elopement? As much as he suspected he cared for her and hoped she returned his feelings, she certainly didn't hesitate to do whatever she deemed necessary to assist Max. He could still feel the sting of her slap on his face as well as the equally wicked sting of humiliation. He could send her a note of explanation, but she would tell Max the truth and he would move heaven and earth to find them.

*Which was exactly what Max should do.*

"I would like to leave tonight."

"Pandora." He stepped closer and stared into her lovely blue eyes, shadowed with emotion. "Are you in love with Max?"

She pulled her gaze from his, but not before

he saw a flash of pain so intense it stole his breath. "It scarcely matters at this point. You said it yourself. If Max wins our game, there are no choices. Therefore, I cannot allow him to win. Now." She drew a steadying breath. "We agreed to work together. Will you help me, or not?"

Helping her now would certainly erase any debt of honor forged by the past. He owed her as much. And Max more than deserved a taste of his own tricks, after using Laurie in such a publicly humiliating way to earn a point.

"I cannot leave tonight." He exhaled a long breath. "But we can be off tomorrow."

Her brows pulled together in concern. "That may be too late. He could earn the last two points, and . . ." She wrinkled her nose. "Forgive me. It's panic speaking, nothing more. It's a new sensation for me and I find it rather difficult to control. Very well. Tomorrow it is." She caught his gaze. "You do promise not to tell Max about this?"

"Of course," he lied. He had twenty-four hours to come up with his own plan. If she and Max would admit their feelings to each other, the peripheral players in this game of theirs could attend to their own lives. And Laurie very much wanted to attend to his own life, particularly where it concerned the tall, willowy, and quite delectable Miss Weatherly.

"I will arrange for a carriage then. One last thing." He had to know all the details of her plan in order to develop his own. "Do you really think Max won't come after us?"

"Oh, I don't think that at all. I just said it would be pointless. You see, I have no intention of traveling north to Scotland." She smiled, the first real smile he'd seen on her since his arrival.

"We're heading southwest. Bath is lovely this time of year."

". . . So I think the way to resolve whatever has happened between them is to get them to work together." Cynthia paced the width of the sitting room off Lady Harold's bedchamber. "It seems to me they've been pitted against each other for the most part except when they've been made to join forces. For example, in the tavern—"

"Yes, Harry mentioned that little venture," Lady Harold said grimly. "I do hope you're not thinking of anything as risky as that?"

"Not at all. But I do have an idea." Cynthia drew a deep breath, then plunged ahead. "I propose a kidnapping."

Lady Harold's eyebrows rose. "And who do you suggest we kidnap?"

"Oh no, we're not the kidnappers. We're the victims. If Pandora believes we're in danger, she'll stop at nothing to rescue us. And Lord Trent will never allow her to come after us on her own."

"It could work," Lady Harold said thoughtfully. "Obviously someone has to do something, and as soon as possible. There are only a few days left before their game ends."

"Tomorrow, then?"

"Excellent." A frown creased Lady Harold's forehead. "A few days ago, I would have wagered a great deal of money that Pandora cared very much for Lord Trent. Now I'm not entirely sure what she feels."

"I'm certain she loves him. Nothing else makes sense. Have you seen her act so oddly over anything before?"

"Never."

"She wouldn't even speak to me just now." Cynthia shook her head. "She simply called through the door, said she was ill, although she didn't sound at all sick, and told me to go away."

"Pandora is never ill."

"I know. Even the thought is rather unnerving."

"With a bit of luck, we may be able to set things right, although I never thought I would be forced to plan my own kidnapping to ensure my daughter's happiness." She lowered her voice in a confidential manner. "What a delightful adventure this should be. I haven't been on an adventure in years. I did have a rather adventurous period once. It was then I met Lord Harold."

"Really?" The revelation was not all that surprising. Cynthia would have expected this was a woman with adventures in her past. "Does Pandora know?"

"Good heavens, I hope not." Lady Harold laughed. "Pandora is far too adventurous as it is without believing she is destined to carry on a family tradition."

"It doesn't sound particularly wise," Cynthia murmured.

"Now then, as for tomorrow. I think first . . ."

Lady Harold discussed the particulars of

their plan, but Cynthia couldn't keep her mind from drifting back to the intriguing idea of adventures. This would be her first, but would it be her last as well? Would she have further adventures to keep secret from her own daughter? A daughter blond and tall and very much like her father? Warmth flooded her at the thought of precisely who she wanted that father to be.

And wondered if that would be her grandest adventure of all.

Running away might well be the stupidest idea she'd ever had.

Pandora threw another dress into the small portmanteau on her bed. Still, it was the only idea she had at the moment.

Would the terrible pain of knowing Max didn't love her ever go away? Probably not. It had eased somewhat from the sharp, stabbing sensation of a knife in the heart to a dull, constant ache, but she suspected it would remain with her always.

Resolve squared her shoulders. If live with it she must, live with it she would. She could bear it, for the rest of her life, if necessary.

The rest of her life? Hah. She stepped to her wardrobe and yanked free another dress. What life? Her reputation would be in shreds and her future bleak, any possibility of happiness destroyed. Without Max's love she couldn't possibly be happy anyway.

Not that she was happy now. When she thought about it, she realized she really hadn't been quite herself since the moment they'd first spoken. Her usual manner had vanished, replaced by some stranger with a melancholy, ill at ease, uncertain nature. And she didn't like this new Pandora one bit.

Anger washed through her, as it had periodically since Max had broken her heart. How could he do this to her? How could he use that glorious moment they'd shared to further his own selfish ends? He was indeed a rake, a rogue, a scoundrel, and a beast in the very worst sense of the words.

She shoved the dress into the bag with a vicious punch as if it was responsible for her troubles. In truth, the blame rested as much on her shoulders as on Max's. If only she hadn't been such a fool. If only she'd kept her head about her and paid no attention to her heart.

If only she hadn't fallen in love.

And now she was running away. Even at this moment she knew full well the sheer idiocy of it. There might be other ways to save herself from marriage to a man who didn't love her, but she certainly couldn't think of any right now. And there was not a great deal of time left. She had no doubt Max would pass the last tests and her destiny would be sealed.

No. She would not go meekly to that fate. If the rest of her life was meant to be miserable and forlorn, at least she could choose the path that would take her there. As truly stupid as it might be, in just a few hours she would take the first step on that road.

And there would be no turning back.

# Chapter 22
## *The Stakes are Raised*

**W**hat was Laurie up to now? Didn't Max have enough on his mind trying to find a way to pass the last test? If this was another one of Laurie's attempts to thwart his efforts, old friend or no old friend, he'd be forced to thrash him or worse.

Rain splattered against the window. Flashes of lightning lit the windows behind the drawn curtains, the night an apt reflection of his mood.

He leaned back in his desk chair and studied the note delivered by one of Laurie's servants. It had sat on a table near the door, overlooked for nearly an hour before the butler had brought it to him.

*My dear Max,*

*I have decided to take the trip we discussed, although I shall not be traveling to any foreign shores. Even Scotland holds no appeal. I do not know when I will return, perhaps five months, perhaps five days. Thus my interference in your game is at an end.*

*I have further decided you are right. Marriage is not a trap if planned correctly. My previous attitude was only a ruse, a trick played on myself, to avoid the inevitable.*

*Odd, how we seem doomed to repeat the mistakes of the past. Although I must confess I would prefer to be lying in my own bath, always nice this time of year, contemplating the desperate actions of hellions and others of a trying yet appealing nature and thus to escape questioning my own character.*

*Forgive me for abandoning you at this time but I have no choice. I find I must follow my own course although, of the two of us, I would have expected such a thing from you rather than me.*

*Yours,*
*Laurie*

Max drew his brows together in confusion. This made absolutely no sense. Why would Laurie be going anywhere at all? And why would he leave so cryptic a message? Plus, the handwriting itself was neater than Laurie's usual scrawl, and several of the words appeared bolder. Max tried to dismiss a nagging sense of unease.

Without warning the door to the library swung open sharply. Thunder cracked outside in accompaniment.

"Maximillian." The familiar voice echoed in the room. "I want to know what is going on."

Max groaned to himself. The thunder was

more than appropriate. "Good evening, Mother."

The Countess of Trent swept into the room, like a frigate under full sail, swathed in silk and feathers. Imposing at the most innocuous of times, when in the throes of outrage she was overwhelming. Max was well used to standing his ground against her, and had done so since the age of ten. Still, it had taken facing death at the hands of Napoleon's troops to truly end any qualms he'd had about doing so.

"How could you even consider marriage to that . . . that . . ."

"That what, Mother?"

"Hellion." The countess spat out the word as if it was not to be said in polite society. Still, if one had to chose between Napoleon's troops and Lady Trent . . .

"Which hellion?" he said innocently.

She gasped. "You are involved with more than one?"

"I gather you are referring to Pandora Effington." He chuckled. "And no, Mother, one is quite enough."

"That one is entirely too much." She drew herself up to her full, if diminutive, height—she was no taller than Pandora—and cast him the glare that had haunted his childhood dreams. "Well, I will not allow it."

"You have nothing to say about it." He grinned, always amazed that his mother's ire amused him more than anything else.

Her eyes widened. "I forbid it!"

"Be that as it may," he shrugged, "I will

marry her. At this point I am confident of success."

"You're talking about that game you're playing with her, aren't you? That ridiculous bargain?" She folded her hands together in a stern fashion. "Everyone, simply everyone I know is talking about it. I have never been so humiliated."

He lifted a brow. "I was not aware of your involvement."

She continued as if he hadn't spoken. "My own son. Wagering his future like this. Risking something as important as whom should be the mother of his heirs. My grandchildren. It is simply too much." She brought the back of her hand to her forehead, closed her eyes and reached her other hand out to him beseechingly. "I cannot abide the very thought. I fear I shall swoon right here on the spot."

He tried not to laugh. He had seen this act many times before. "Then I should suggest moving to the vicinity of the sofa, Mother. It's much more comfortable for swooning."

She opened her eyes and glared. "Thank you for your concern, but the feeling has passed." She marched to the sofa and lowered herself on to the seat in the manner of a queen deigning to converse with the commoners. "Tell me one thing, Maximillian, why her? Of all the women in London, in England, why are you set on this one?"

He smiled, more to himself than to her. "I have my reasons, Mother. I doubt that you'd understand."

Her eyes narrowed and she studied him carefully. Finally she gasped. "God help us all, you're in love!" She collapsed deeper into the sofa and fanned herself with her hand. "Oh, I truly am going to swoon."

"What makes you think I'm in love?" He dropped Laurie's note on the desk and settled in the chair behind it.

She raised her head and glared. "I'm your mother. Like it or not, I know you. I can see it on your face."

"Really?" he murmured. "How interesting."

"It's not at all interesting." Her head dropped onto the sofa back. "It's devastating." She raised her head again. "She's one of *the* Effingtons, you know?"

"I do." His mother was rather a snob, if an amusing snob. "The granddaughter of a duke."

"Well, that's something, at any rate." She started to lower her head, then stopped. "Do you know what she's called?"

"You mean the Hellion of Grosvenor Square?"

She nodded.

"I'm well aware of that."

Once more his mother's head dropped back.

"She really hasn't done all that much to earn the title, Mother."

"Hah! There have been duels and wagers and, dear Lord, Maximillian." This time she didn't bother to raise her head and settled for fixing him with a pointed glare. "She's in her eighth season."

"Seventh, Mother," he said, and bit back a grin.

"Regardless." She waved a weary hand. "One has to wonder why she hasn't married before now if, as you say, she hasn't done all that much to earn her reputation."

"She hasn't married before now," he cast her a smug smile, "because she hadn't met me."

The countess's eyes widened as if she couldn't believe his arrogance; then, without warning, she laughed. "Maximillian, you are such an amusing devil. I daresay I can't blame the chit for restraining herself until she met you."

"Thank you, Mother."

She heaved a resigned sigh. "I also know that tone of yours. There is nothing I can do to stop you, is there?"

"Absolutely nothing."

"You are as stubborn as your father."

"You could wish me well."

"I could. But I'm not especially pleased about it." She sighed again. "I still don't understand how you can want to marry a women who's been scandalously involved with your dearest friend."

"My dearest friend?" Confusion knitted his brows. "Who are you talking about?"

"Oh, you know." She waved a dismissive hand. "Viscount Bolton. He's the one she ran off to Gretna Green with, when was it, now? Six years ago?"

"Five," he murmured. *Laurie*? Shock coursed through him. He'd known of the incident, of course, but had somehow failed to note the identity of the gentleman who'd accompanied her. It was of no importance at the time.

"He's the one who named her the Hellion

of Grosvenor Square. If I recall the gossip then, she quite broke his heart, poor dear." She struggled to sit upright and studied him. "You didn't know this, did you?"

"No." Of course. It all made sense now. Laurie's adamant objection to his relationship with Pandora. His strange comment about being humiliated whenever he was around the Effingtons. The way he and Pandora had acted in the country . . .

*Odd, how we seemed doomed to repeat the mistakes of the past.*

"The mistakes of the past?" His stomach turned and his heart caught in his throat.

"What was that?"

"Nothing, Mother." Or everything. He searched the desktop, snatched up Laurie's note, and read it twice more, focusing on the darker words. *Not-Traveling-Scotland-Return-Five-Days-Game-End.*

"If I can tell when you're in love I can certainly tell when something has overset you. Now, what is it?"

"Miss Effington has run off with Laurie," he muttered. *Marriage-Not-Planned-Only-a-Ruse.*

"Oh, really?" Her voice rang with delight. He cast her a sharp glance. Immediately she adopted a downcast expression. "What I meant to say was, oh," she sighed sympathetically, "really."

"Thank you for your concern." *Bath-nice-this-time-of-year-desperate-hellion-trying-to-escape.*

"Well, it's no doubt for the best, although I must say I am pleased you are finally interested in marriage. I know several eminently suitable, and really quite charming—"

"I'm going to marry Miss Effington, Mother." *Forgive-me-no-choice-follow-us.* "I'm going after them."

"Maximillian, you cannot be serious." She rose to her feet. "I for—" He shot her a quelling glance. "Well, I think it's a mistake. She has run off with Bolton to Gretna Green once before, and—"

"They're not going to Scotland." Laurie had done a damned fine job of relaying information. Still, why the subterfuge? Unless this was Laurie's way of dealing with what, at this point, must be divided loyalties. "I believe they're going to Bath."

"Bath?" Confusion creased her brow. "No one runs away to Bath to be married."

"They're not getting married." Should he start for Bath now? No. First he should stop at Pandora's house. If Laurie was clever enough to leave him a message, maybe he was clever enough to stall their departure.

She gasped. "That's deplorable! Scandalous! Maximillian, you cannot go after this . . . this hellion."

"As you pointed out, Mother, *that hellion* is the woman I love." He headed for the door. "And she's leaving, apparently to escape marriage to me."

If Max was too late . . . cold fear clutched at him. It would not be impossible for her to escape detection for the next five days. As long as she remained with Laurie she'd be safe, but knowing Pandora, he couldn't be certain she did not plan to go off on her own.

"Maximillian, wait." Genuine sympathy rang in his mother's voice. "Do you wish to

force a woman into marriage who is so desperate to avoid it—and forgive me, dear—or
avoid *you* that she would take the extreme
measure of running off with another man?
And further, do you really want such a
woman?"

"You have the question only half right,
mother. I'm afraid the crucial issue isn't if I
want her." He raked his fingers through his
hair.

"But if she will still have me."

Lady Harold swept down the wide stairway, clutching a note in her hand, Lord Harold a step behind.

Cynthia smiled up at them. "Is all arranged,
then? Are we ready to go?"

"Pandora has run off." Lady Harold
reached the bottom of the stairs and grabbed
a cloak off a nearby chair.

"With the twit," Lord Harold said.

Cynthia stared in disbelief. "What twit?"

"Bolton." Lord Harold's voice was grim.

Cynthia gasped. "My twit?"

"He shall not be your twit if we do not stop
them." Lady Harold swung the cloak over her
shoulders.

"What do you mean?" Cynthia's breath
caught.

Lady Harold heaved a deep sigh. "We think
they've gone to Gretna Green—"

"Again," Lord Harold interrupted.

*Again?*

"Pandora left a note." She waved the paper.
"She didn't say precisely that was where they

were going, but the implication was more than clear."

Lord Harold snorted. "The girl says she sees no other way to avoid marriage with Trent. I knew this game would come to a bad end. I should have stopped it when Bolton came to me."

"Lawrence spoke to you?" Cynthia's head reeled.

"That's of little consequence at the moment," Lady Harold snapped. "We have to stop them." She started toward the door.

"Wait." Cynthia shook her head. "I don't understand. What did you mean when you said they'd gone to Gretna Green *again*?"

"It was before you knew her. She and Bolton headed to Scotland during her second season. On a lark, Pandora said then, with two other couples. When they were caught, she adamantly refused to marry him."

Lord Harold shook his head. "I should have put my foot down then. Should have made her marry him. He's not a bad sort, really. Of course, he was the one who named her the Hellion of Grosvenor Square."

Lady Harold's eyes widened and she stared at Cynthia. "You didn't know?"

Misery washed through her and she shook her head slowly. "I knew the story but I didn't know Laur—Bolton was the twit."

"I am sorry, my dear." Lady Harold put her arm around her and gave her a quick hug. "All might still be resolved to everyone's satisfaction."

"Resolved?" At once anger swept away her distress. "The only satisfying resolution would be to slay Bolton on the spot. Strangle him with my bare hands. Stab him with something sharp and wicked. Or shoot him. But perhaps that wouldn't be painful enough."

"I like this girl, Grace." A smile quirked Lord Harold's lips. "By Jove, she sounds like an Effington."

"Poor thing," Lady Harold murmured. "Enough of this, we must go."

"Wait," Lord Harold said. "Why? It's a nasty night. Rain's coming down like a biblical retribution."

"Harry." Lady Harold's voice rang with impatience. "We have to save Pandora. Her reputation is at stake. Her very future."

"Why," he repeated stubbornly, "she's a grown woman. It's time we let her make her own mistakes."

"Harry," Lady Harold pinned him with a no nonsense glare. "We have always let her make her own mistakes. If we hadn't she wouldn't be in this situation now."

He shook his head. "I still don't—"

"If we don't stop her, she'll lose the man she really loves." A slight smile played on Lady Harold's lips. "You do remember how ridiculous people act when they're in love, don't you?"

He studied her for a moment, then smiled sheepishly. "Especially Effingtons."

Abruptly Cynthia realized Pandora's parents did not have to search their memories to recall those feelings. A pang of envy shot through her. Would she and Lawrence feel that way someday? If he didn't marry Pandora. And if Cynthia didn't shoot him.

"Very well, then, let's be off." He looked around. "Where in the name of all that's holy is my coat? And where is Peters?"

"Oh dear." Lady Harold winced. "I sent him on an errand right before I found Pandora's note. I do hope..." She shrugged. "Well, it can't be helped now." She stepped briskly toward the door. "Come along, both of you."

"I gather this means the kidnapping is off?" Cynthia couldn't quite hide her disappointment.

"It can't be helped," Lady Harold said over her shoulder.

"Kidnapping?" Lord Harold frowned. "What kidnapping?"

"It's of no significance at the moment, my love." She pulled open the door and stepped outside.

"There is a pistol in the bottom drawer of my desk should you need it," Lord Harold said under his breath to Cynthia.

"Is it very difficult to use?" she murmured.

"You should have no problem at all."

"Excellent." She smiled sweetly. In spite of her initial reaction, she didn't believe Pandora would really marry Lawrence although what the two truly had in mind escaped her. And she was confident she would have Lawrence back to do with as she pleased.

Shooting him sounded like a lovely idea.

Pandora shifted from one side of the seat to the other. The rain beat on the top of the carriage in an endless staccato that pulsed through her blood and directed the rhythm of her breathing. With every minute spent inside the cold, damp carriage, her spirits sank lower and her anxiety increased.

She leaned toward one of the open windows and drew in a deep breath of fresh air, ignoring the rain that slapped across her face. But even her discomfort at being in this black box of a carriage with the constant drumming of rain couldn't distract her from the ever-increasing jumble of emotions assaulting her.

Five days? It would be a lifetime. She changed positions on the seat and heaved a heartfelt sigh.

"Do you plan on making those pathetic sounds for the rest of the journey?" Laurie said pleasantly. "Or are they simply an accompaniment to your inability to sit still for more than a minute at a time?"

"Yes," she snapped, regretting her tone at once. He, of all people, did not deserve her ire. "I'm sorry. I'm rather—" She wrung her hands together. "I have a bit of difficulty being in a closed carriage in the rain."

He scoffed. "Bit of difficulty?"

"I feel . . . trapped. Actually, with the noise of the rain on the roof, I feel as though"—she cringed to herself at just how ridiculous it sounded—"I'm being buried alive." She'd never told anyone except Cynthia about this and waited for the inevitable laughter.

"And that's why you insist on all the windows being open," he said slowly.

"It helps." She shrugged and forced a laugh. "It's a ridiculous fear, I know. Not like heights or snakes or—"

"I don't think it's ridiculous at all," he said

quietly. "I suspect we all have absurd fears of one kind or another."

"Not Max."

"Even Max. Max is terrified of failing."

"Terrified? I knew he disliked failure . . ." She sighed once more and shifted yet again.

"Pandora, I must admit, I'm rather confused." He was silent for a moment, as if choosing his words. "When you told me your plan, I thought it made sense in terms of winning the game with Max. And it was clear to me something had happened between the two of you. Your usual, oh, spirit was noticeably absent. Why, you were almost nice to me."

"Was I?"

"It was quite unnerving." She could hear the grin in his voice. Was the man trying to cheer her up? She really had misjudged him.

She laughed softly. "Forgive me."

He sighed in an exaggerated manner. "I shall do my best." He leaned forward and his tone sobered. "Joking aside, Pandora, the question I can't figure out is, why?"

"To win the game, of course," she said lightly.

"I don't believe you."

"It's true. I want to win. I don't want to marry him simply as his reward for victory." Her voice caught and she forced a firm tone. "You reminded me of it yourself. All those years ago, I declared I wouldn't marry without love. My feelings haven't changed."

"Do *you* love *him*?"

She hesitated. She hadn't said it aloud. Not to anyone. She wasn't certain she could. "It's of no significance. He doesn't love me. I've given him every opportunity to tell me and he hasn't.''

''Even so, he—''

''Our bargain is the only thing that matters to him.'' Her anger returned and she welcomed it. Her voice hardened. ''All he wants is victory and he'll do anything he has to do to achieve it. Anything at all.''

''Come now, I can't imagine Max—''

''Really?'' Fury swept through her and the words she'd kept pent up inside tumbled free. ''You can't imagine Max saying, 'Now, you have to marry me'? Or, 'The game is over, now you have no choice'? Or, 'Marriage is the only way to salvage your honor.' Or, 'You're ruined now and I ru—' '' She sucked in a shocked breath and clapped her hand over her mouth.

''Oh, well, that explains a great deal,'' he said slowly.

''Bloody hell.'' She groaned and doubled over to bury her face in her hands. ''I am such a fool.''

''These things, um, happen.''

She jerked upright. ''Not to me. And there has been a fair amount of opportunity through the years.''

He paused for a long moment, as if deciding what to say next. Finally he drew a deep breath. ''He does love you. He told me.''

Her heart stilled. ''Are you certain?''

''I don't think he's ever lied to me. In addition, he's already acquired the golden apples for the last test.''

She wanted to believe him. ''Why didn't he tell me?''

"Why didn't you tell him?" Laurie said pointedly.

A hundred thoughts ran through her head most of them centering on the morning in the stables. Maybe she hadn't been wrong about his loving her, after all? Maybe it was more than just a need to win on his part? Maybe . . .

"He loves me," she said softly. She wanted to laugh and cry at the same time. *Max loves me. And I love him.* She sank back in the seat and grinned like an idiot. Like a complete and total fool. Like a stupid, impulsive—

She jerked upright in her seat. "Good Lord, Laurie, we have to go back. At once. Before Max learns of this."

"Excellent idea." He reached up and rapped on the carriage roof.

"Fortunately, Peters is not supposed to give Max my note until tomorrow."

"*Your* note?" Laurie said uneasily. "Ah yes, I had forgotten about your note."

"We can be back before he even knows we've gone." She couldn't wait to return. To Max. The man who loved her. The man she loved. "Why isn't the driver turning this thing around?" She pounded on the ceiling.

"Patience, Pandora." Laurie laughed.

"I have no patience, Laurie. Not now." She moved to the window and leaned out. Rain drenched her almost at once, but she didn't care. "Driver," she yelled, to be heard above the rain. "We need to go back. Now! Immediately!"

Without warning the carriage turned sharply, throwing her across the aisle onto Laurie's seat. For an instant she wondered if they'd tip over. Another abrupt move tossed her once again, this time onto his lap.

They stared, face to face, mere inches apart.

"Pandora?" His lips were a breath away from hers.

"Yes, Laurie." He didn't want to kiss her, did he?

"Do you feel anything whatsoever for me?"

She drew a deep breath. She had no desire to hurt him, but . . ."No. And you?"

"Nothing," he said, with a fair amount of relief.

"Nothing at all?" Why was she just a touch disappointed? "Not even a bit of lust?"

"Always a *bit* of lust." He grinned.

"Good." She grinned back and returned to her seat.

If Max was willing, she'd call off the game at once. She'd marry him tomorrow, if he wished. After all, she was ruined and he had ruined her.

And she couldn't wait until he ruined her again.

# Chapter 23
## *The Final Play*

$\sim\!\!\mathcal{O}\mathcal{O}\!\!\sim$

"**W**here is she?" Max stepped into the Effington foyer and shook his arms in a futile attempt to rid himself of the water on his sodden greatcoat. Droplets of rain flew in a wide arc around him.

The pudgy apple-cheeked woman who'd opened the door—the housekeeper, probably—stared at him as if he'd lost his mind.

"Well?" he snapped and pulled off his gloves, realizing between his impatience and his drenched appearance he probably looked quite mad.

The woman's eyes widened. "She who, my lord?"

He drew a deep breath and forced a measure of calm to his voice. There was no need to take out his anxieties on the poor woman. She already appeared scared half to death. "My apologies . . . ?"

"Mrs. Barnes." She bobbed a curtsey and reached for his gloves.

He passed his gloves to her, slipped off his coat, and handed it to her as well. "Thank you. Now then." He had wasted enough time on pleasantries. "Miss Effington. Is she in?"

Mrs. Barnes' brows knitted together. "I'm not sure I can say, my lord. I can check with Peters . . ." She glanced around as if expecting him to peer out from behind a column any minute.

"Please do. It's urgent I speak with her." He smiled to soften the sharpness of his tone.

She nodded and hurried off, vanishing into the shadowed recesses of the house.

Max paced across the circular foyer, then back, and again. He couldn't start for Bath without making certain she had already left. It was always possible her plans had gone awry or Laurie had managed to convince her to abandon whatever she had in mind—although he suspected his hopes were unrealistic. He'd had more than his share of luck regarding Pandora and her blasted game already and he doubted his good fortune would hold.

How could she run away from him? The question had pounded through his mind since he'd first understood the meaning of Laurie's message. Was she so angry she hadn't stopped to consider the consequences of her actions? Her reputation would be destroyed, her name synonymous with scandal. A scandal she would never live down.

Or perhaps it wasn't anger at all? Maybe she was simply determined to win for reasons beyond those of simple competition. Could it be the idea of marriage to him was so repellant she was desperate to avoid it? Would she rather face the future disgraced and dishonored than face it with him? Regardless of any bargain between them, he would never force marriage on Pandora against her will. But he had thought, no, he had been certain she loved him. And he had further believed she was enjoying the game as much as he was. An odd sort of courtship granted, but a courtship, nonetheless. Was he wrong?

He glared in the direction the housekeeper had disappeared. What was taking the woman so long? Surely determining Pandora's presence in the house was a matter both easy and quick. With every minute that passed, she could be farther and farther away from him.

At least his luck still held in one respect: she'd picked Laurie instead of some other man to accompany her on this farce. Laurie was like a brother to him. Max trusted him with his very life.

*But he could he trust him with Pandora?*

He stopped dead in the center of the foyer. Damnation, where had that come from? Aside from everything else, Laurie was in love with Miss Weatherly.

Still, he couldn't ignore Laurie's failure to tell him about his relationship with Pandora. Oh, certainly it had occurred during that period when Max had hidden himself away in the country. And it was not inconceivable that Laurie would neglect to mention it through the years. But why didn't he say something when he first noticed Max's interest in Pandora? Or when Max and Pandora had agreed to their game? Or even at the ball, when Laurie had encouraged Max to tell Pandora he loved her?

*Unless . . . Laurie loved her himself?*

No. It was a ridiculous idea. Max forced it from his mind. Laurie never would have left him a message if he truly intended to marry Pandora. The very thought was absurd. Laurie didn't even like Pandora. His suspicions were prompted by nothing more than jealousy.

He blew a long breath and shook his head in disbelief. He'd never experienced so much as a twinge of jealousy before.

Not jealousy, and not . . . fear. Oh, he'd known fear on the battlefield. Only a fool wouldn't. But his fate was in his own hands then. Now he was . . . helpless.

Damn love, anyway. Everything with Pandora had been proceeding so nicely until he realized winning her heart was far more important than winning her hand.

The door flew open and Peters stepped inside, accompanied by a gust of wind and a spray of rain. "Good evening, my lord."

"Peters," Max said with relief. Now he would get some answers. "Can you explain what is—"

"My lord." Peters stepped toward him, ignoring the rivulets pouring off his drenched clothing to puddle on the marble tiled flooring. "I was sent to deliver a message to you from Lady Harold. She wished for me to relate the information exactly as she prepared it." Peters cleared his throat. "My dear Lord Trent." Peters drew a deep breath and expelled it all at once. "Wehavebeenabductedby-

GreekconspiratorsdeterminedtoreturnGreek-
treasurestoGreecetheyhaveMissWeatherlytoo."

"Peters," Max snapped, holding out his
hands to ward off any further efforts at a nar-
rative he only vaguely understood. "Is this
about Miss Effington?"

"No, my lord."

"She is my only concern right now. Where
is she?"

"I'm not precisely certain, my lord." Peters
paused as if debating his next words. "She
did, however, ask me to deliver a letter to
you—"

"Excellent. May I have it?"

The butler's brow furrowed. "I'm not to
bring it until tomorrow."

Max bit back a sharp reply and forced himself to remain calm. "But I am here now and
it scarcely matters whether I get it today or
tomorrow."

"She was very insistent on that point, my
lord," Peters said stubbornly.

"Nonetheless." Max's jaw tightened and he
struggled to maintain a reasonable tone. "I'm
certain even Miss Effington would see the
logic of giving me the note now, thus saving
both of us time and effort that could be better
spent elsewhere."

Peters studied him carefully. "Miss Effington's happiness has long been a concern of
myself and the rest of the staff."

Max met his gaze with a direct unflinching
stare. "That's exactly what I want as well, Peters."

Peters nodded slowly. He stepped to a nar-

row table, opened a drawer, pulled out a
folded paper, and handed it to him.

"Thank you, Peters." Max stared at the note
in his hand, not at all sure, now that he had
it, that he wished to read it. "I gather this
means she isn't here."

"No, my lord," Peters said quietly.

"I see." What words had she left for him?
He didn't really believe she intended to marry
Laurie, although he couldn't dismiss the possibility entirely. No doubt everything in her
note was designed to make him want to turn
away from her forever. Falsehoods, probably,
one and all. Still, was he strong enough to read
them? Was he truly her hero? Or just a man
in love?

A pounding sounded outside. At once Max
slipped the note into his waistcoat. Peters
started toward the door, but before he could
reach the handle, it was flung open with a
force helped by the winds. Pandora nearly
flew into the foyer.

Max's breath caught and he took a step toward her.

Laurie followed close on Pandora's heels
and struggled against the rain and wind to
close the door behind them.

"Peters." Pandora stepped further into the
room, then stopped. "Why, you're drenched."

"As are you, Miss." Peters' tone was staid.

"Is it still raining, then?" Max said, in a casual manner that belied the way his heart
thudded in his chest at the sight of her. Or the
relief sweeping through him at the knowledge
that she was safe. Or the aching need to have
her always by his side.

"Max?" Her eyes widened and her gaze met his. A brilliant smile lit her face. "Max!"

In less than an instant she was in his arms.

"Hellion." His lips crushed hers and he couldn't kiss her hard enough or hold her close enough to reassure himself she was real and sound and with him now.

"Oh, Max." Her arms were around his neck and all she wanted was to touch him and feel his warmth against her and his lips on hers. Regardless of any bargain, any game, she knew this was where she belonged, where she'd always belonged. "I had to come back. I couldn't leave you."

"You're rather wet, you know." He grinned down at her.

She laughed with the sheer joy of the look in his eyes. "Do you mind?"

"Not at all." Again his lips met hers and any doubts she might have had were swept aside by the rush of happiness surging through her.

"She insisted on leaving the carriage windows open," Laurie said wryly.

Max pulled his lips from hers. His eyes narrowed and his gaze met hers, cool and considering. A chill skated up her spine. He released her in a deliberate manner and stepped back. "Did she?"

Laurie shook his head. "She has some ridiculous fear about carriages in the rain."

"Does she?" Max's voice was cool, and a distinct sense of unease washed away the delight of a moment ago.

"She does, indeed," Laurie said slowly, staring at Max. Did he too notice Max's subtle change of attitude?

Good Lord, did Max know of her scheme? Worse, did he think she truly intended to marry Laurie? Caution edged her voice. "Max?"

Tension thickened the air. Max's gaze locked with Laurie's. Pandora held her breath.

"I think you and I have a few things to discuss." Max's voice was level and unemotional. "About tonight and," he paused, "mistakes of the past."

Mistakes of the past? She stifled a gasp. Max obviously knew about she and Laurie and what had happened years ago. And if he knew about that night, what was he thinking about this night? She reached out to lay her hand on Max's arm. "Max, let me ex—"

Max cast a disdainful glance at her hand and she let it fall, his look a sting as sharp as any blow. His gaze returned to Laurie's.

"Pandora, this is between Max and me." Laurie's voice was calm and resigned. "And you're quite right, Max, such a talk is long overdue."

"If I may interrupt," Peters said. "I believe there is a rather pressing issue that needs to be attended to."

"Bloody hell." Max grit his teeth. "I'd forgotten." Concern sounded in his voice. His gaze met hers and apprehension shone in his eyes. "Pandora, I'm not entirely certain of the details. Your parents—"

"Harry and Grace?" Fear squeezed her stomach. "What's happened? What's wrong?"

"It's hard to explain, but apparently they're missing."

"Missing?" Panic seized her and she fought

to remain calm. "What do you mean, missing?"

Max glanced at Peters and the butler sighed, then pulled a deep breath. "TheyhavebeenabductedbyGreekconspiratorsdetermin—"

"Peters," Max said sharply. "Do slow down and tell it in your own words."

Peters raised a brow. "As you wish, my lord." He cleared his throat. "It seems Lord and Lady Harold have been abducted—"

"Abducted?" Pandora shook her head in shocked disbelief. "Who would wish to abduct them?"

"Greeks," Max said with a puzzled expression. "I think."

"Greek conspirators, to be exact, my lord," Peters said.

"We have to find them," Pandora said.

"Conspiring to do what?" Laurie's brow furrowed in confusion.

"We need to be off," Pandora said, her voice ringing with urgency.

"Return Greek treasures to Greece." Peters' voice was matter-of-fact, as though he dealt with such things every day.

"We don't have a minute to lose." Pandora glared. Why weren't they listening?

"That's the most ridiculous thing I've ever heard." Laurie slanted her a pointed glance. "Almost."

Max nodded. "Now that I can understand what Peters is saying, it does sound absurd."

"Regardless," she clenched her fists in frustration, "until we know exactly what this is all about we don't have a moment to waste."

Laurie shrugged. "Although I have heard of stranger things I suppose."

"Stranger than this?" Max scoffed. "Obviously Lady Harold left the message herself. People who are kidnapped rarely leave their own messages."

"Excellent point," Laurie murmured.

"Would you two cease debating how foolish this sounds?" Pandora's voice rose. "Harry and Grace, my parents, two people I care very much for, are not to be found. Frankly, I don't give a bloody damn if they've been carried off by natives from the jungles of South America or ancient Egyptian mummies come to life or—"

"They have Miss Weatherly as well," Peters said.

"Miss Weatherly?" Shock rang in Max's voice.

"My Miss Weatherly?" Laurie's tone mirrored his friend's.

Peters cast him a quelling glance. "*The* Miss Weatherly."

"That's quite enough. I, for one, am going after them. Immediately." She turned and started toward the door.

"Pandora!" Max's voice cracked behind her. He grabbed her arm and whipped her around to face him. "You're not going anywhere."

"Someone has to do something and apparently it's not you." She glared up at him.

"Don't be a fool. Of course we're going to do something," he said, the line of his jaw set. "We're just trying to determine what. Until we can make some sense of this all, it's stupid to go running out into the night, in a storm, I might add, without any idea of where we're going or why."

"Don't you understand?" Her breath came hard and fast, fueled by her fear. "We're talking about Harry and Grace and Cynthia. The three people who mean the most to me in the world. If anything were to happen to them . . ." The back of her throat ached with unshed tears and her voice broke. "You and Laurie keep saying this doesn't make any sense. You may be right. But right now, I don't care. I just want to find them. Don't you see how dangerous it all is? Anyone mad enough to hatch a plot like this wouldn't hesitate to . . ." She couldn't bring herself to say the words.

Max directed his comment to Laurie, but his gaze never left hers. "What do you think, Laurie? I suspect the docks might be a place to start."

Relief swept through her, and for a moment she thought her knees would buckle.

"It's as good a place as any," Laurie said briskly. "Let's go."

Max released her arm and started for the door, Pandora at his side.

"You're not coming," Laurie said. "Max, tell her."

"Of course I'm coming," she snapped.

"If it was any other female, I'd agree with you, but," Max sighed, "I wouldn't know how to stop her."

"Max, I would not put this woman in a carriage in the rain again to save my soul." Laurie stepped closer to him and lowered his voice, but she could still hear him. "It's something about the sound of the rain on the roof and an enclosed carriage. She was at her wits end earlier—''

"I was not!"

"She was restless, anxious, she could not sit in one place longer than a moment. And I don't even wish to remember the noises she made—''

"Laurie!"

"It's difficult to believe, I know," a serious note underlaid Laurie's voice, "but she was terrified.''

"Pandora?" Max studied her. "Is he right?"

"Yes, and I don't care." She grabbed the edges of his coat and stared into his eyes. "It's ridiculous. A silly little problem—''

"Silly little problem?" Laurie scoffed.

"A completely irrational fear I've had all my life." She paused, then plunged ahead. "The sound of the rain on the roof inside a closed carriage has always make me think of dirt hitting a coffin with me inside." She shuddered.

"You are willing to endure this, not once but *twice* tonight?" Max said slowly.

"Normally I would do anything to avoid it, but tonight I don't care. I'm going with you, or," she drew a deep breath, "I'm going on my own the moment you walk out the door.''

"Are you certain?" His gaze searched hers.

She swallowed hard. "Will you be with me?"

"Every moment." His gray eyes were as stormy as the night outside and just as dangerous.

"Then I shall be fine," she whispered.

Emotion flashed through his eyes so fast she

couldn't tell if it was joy or sorrow. "Good, let's be off then, Hellion."

"I still think it's a mist—"

The door slammed open, cutting off Laurie's words. Wind gusted through the foyer and a wave of raindrops splattered over the floor.

"Peters!" Harry's unmistakable bellow rang over the noise of the storm. Grace and Cynthia staggered into the foyer, clinging to each other, looking more like soaked rag dolls than anything remotely human. Peters leapt to help Harry force the door shut.

"Mother!" Pandora flew across the room and threw her arms around Grace.

"Dora, sweetheart." Grace hugged her hard, then drew back and placed her palms on either side of her daughter's face. "Are you quite all right?"

Pandora nodded and blinked hard. "I thought I might never see you again."

"Oh, dearest, we would never abandon you, no matter who you choose to marry. Or how." She leaned closer to whisper into her ear. "I assume your presence here means you have not married anyone."

"Not yet," she said softly.

"Miss Weatherly." Laurie stepped to Cynthia and swept a polished bow. "You are looking lovely tonight, as always."

Cynthia pushed a long strand of dripping hair away from her face, straightened her shoulders, and extended her hand in a regal manner. "Thank you, Lord Bolton."

Laurie took her hand and brought it to his lips as if it was not at all unusual for him to kiss the still wet hand of a drenched and dripping woman. He released her hand, straightened, and casually flicked the water off his fingertips. "Do tell me, Miss Weatherly, how you managed to escape the Greek conspirators."

"How?" Her expression didn't change, but unease flashed in her eyes and her gaze shot to Grace.

"I was wondering the same thing myself." Pandora studied her mother carefully. "How did you escape?"

"It wasn't at all easy," Grace murmured. "They were quite . . . oh, I'm not sure how to put it. Cynthia? How would you describe them?"

"Me?" Cynthia's eyes widened. "I would say they were . . . um . . . perhaps . . ."

"Vague? Elusive? Difficult to keep in sight?" Laurie raised a brow.

"Quite." Grace said in a lofty voice.

It was apparent, even to Pandora, that Max and Laurie's suspicions about the kidnapping were well founded.

"Do tell us more." Pandora folded her arms over her chest.

"There really isn't much to tell." Grace waved her hand in a casual manner, as if abduction was an everyday occurrence. "Greek conspirators are, well, Greek conspirators. And not at all unlike French conspirators, although not quite as rude, or German conspirators, even if they aren't quite as organized, or Italian conspirators, whom I've always felt—"

"What are you talking about?" Harry stared in complete confusion. "What conspirators? What Greeks? What Italians?"

"We were led to believe you were kidnapped by Greek conspirators," Max said mildly.

"Kidnapped?" He snorted in disbelief. "Whatever would give you that idea? We went after Dora. Again. Didn't get far, though. Blasted carriage wheel broke within the first quarter hour and we had to walk back." He narrowed his eyes and fixed his daughter with a hard stare. "This was the last time, Dora. Marry whom you want. Run off with whomever you please. Or don't. But no more chasing after you every time we turn around to save you from yourself."

"You didn't need to chase me. I was perfectly fine," Pandora said indignantly. "And I'd scarcely call once every five years every time you turn around."

"So, no Greek conspirators, after all, eh, Miss Weatherly?" Laurie grinned.

"I don't believe anyone said there weren't Greek conspirators." Cynthia wiped her wet forehead with the back of her hand. "Lord Harold simply pointed out . . ."

At once the room filled with any number of accusations and excuses and denials.

"Why would anyone, Greek or other—"

"I really don't think five years between—"

"You have spent entirely too much time—"

"But, Dora, our intentions were—"

"Quiet!" Max's voice echoed in the foyer with all the authority of a god on Olympus addressing the peasants. "While you have all been discussing conspirators, real or not, and elopements, again real or not, it strikes me that the only thing that has been accomplished tonight is the earning of my eleventh point."

Pandora's mouth dropped open. "How, in any conceivable manner, can you consider this a point?"

"It's quite simple. It seems that I and I alone was not involved in the various intrigues ongoing tonight, therefore it is up to me to sort them out.

"This test was to defeat the three-headed beast that guards the gates of hell. As I look at the group before me, it's apparent the heads of the various plots, escapades, and so forth," his gaze lingered on Pandora for barely an instant, then passed on, "are Pandora, and Cynthia in league with Lady Harold. No one can deny that all that has occurred this evening, for some of us, was indeed a taste of hell. Additionally, I was to rescue a friend from the Chair of Forgetfulness." He nodded at Laurie. "The mistakes of the past, whether forgotten or simply hidden, have now been revealed. "

"Brilliant, Lord Trent." Grace applauded. "Well done."

"Bravo, my lord." Cynthia beamed.

"I always knew he could do it." Harry grinned. "By Jove, the man will fit in with the Effingtons like he was born to it."

"That's only eleven." Pandora stepped toward him. "You still have one to go."

His gaze met hers. "Do I?"

"You do. The golden apples of the Hesperides. They belonged to Zeus. A gift from his wife." She pulled a steadying breath. "A wedding gift."

"I know." For a long moment he didn't say a word. "It's fortunate I still have a few days left. Golden apples, among other things, are exceedingly rare." He pulled his gaze from hers and addressed the rest of the gathering. "And, as it has been a long evening, I shall take my leave." He nodded to the assembly and stepped toward the door where Mrs. Barnes had magically appeared with his coat and gloves.

*He wasn't going to claim the final point?*

The realization slammed into her like a hard punch to her stomach and stole her breath. Laurie said Max already had the apples. If it weren't for the look in his eye, she'd think he was trying to be dramatic.

Perhaps he was waiting until the final moment to pass the final test. That was it, of course. It was silly of her to think otherwise. Besides, there was only one other reason why Max wouldn't present the apples. And as much as she couldn't, she wouldn't, consider that possibility she could not put it from her mind.

In spite of Laurie's assurances, Max didn't love her, after all.

# Chapter 24
## *The Spoils of Victory*

**"I** wondered when you'd deign to pay me a visit." Max sprawled in his chair before the fire in the library, his brandy glass dangling loosely from his fingers.

"I thought I'd give you a day to think things through." Laurie dropped into the other chair.

"I've done nothing but think," Max muttered.

"I doubt that." Laurie picked up the brandy decanter and eyed the level of the liquor. "I'd wager your servants keep refilling this too."

Max shrugged. "I haven't noticed."

Laurie poured a brandy for himself. "You look like hell."

"Thank you. It's always nice to know others appreciate your accomplishments. Appearing unsavory is an art." Max rubbed the day-old growth of beard on his chin. He knew full well how disreputable his appearance had become since the night before last. He simply didn't care. "Why didn't you tell me about you and Pandora?"

Laurie blew a resigned breath. "I don't know, really. You weren't around when it happened. When you finally regained your senses, well, the incident no longer mattered. I frankly never thought to mention it."

"That accounts for 1813 and all the intervening years until what, a month ago? Why didn't you tell me then? It would have been an excellent way to convince me not to pursue Pandora."

"If I had told you, would it have stopped you?"

Laurie's gaze locked with his and endless seconds passed in silence. Max laughed mirthlessly. "No."

"I didn't think so." Laurie took a sip of his drink. "Therefore it seemed pointless to bring it up."

Max swirled the brandy in his glass noting, in some part of his mind that cared about such things, that there was barely enough to coat the sides of the snifter. "Did you love her?"

Laurie hesitated, no doubt deciding what to say. Max's shoulders tensed. "For a moment, perhaps. At the time, I thought she'd broken my heart. All she really damaged was my pride."

Max tossed back his last swallow of brandy in an effort to hide his relief. He held his glass out for more. Laurie obliged without comment.

"Before I forget, this is yours." Laurie passed him a gold chain hung with an intricate pendant.

Max studied the finely wrought charm. "The goldsmith did an excellent job. It's exactly what I wanted."

"Why didn't you give it to her the other night? You could have ended the game right there and then."

"I suppose." The bauble winked and glittered in the light from the fire. Max stared, mesmerized. "Earlier that evening, I was asked, by my mother of all people, if I really wished to force a woman into marriage who was so desperate to avoid it, to avoid me, she would run away. You said she was scared in the carriage?"

"Well, yes, but—"

"A woman desperate enough to face her fears in her attempt to escape . . ." He shook his head. "I couldn't get the question out of my mind and I couldn't quite face the answer. I'm not entirely sure I can even now."

"But you do intend to give that to her, don't you?"

He handed the necklace back to him. "No."

"No?" Shock rang in Laurie's voice. "What do you mean, no? That's one of the stupidest things I've ever heard you say."

"Or one of the most intelligent." Max heaved a heavy sigh. "If I present that to Pandora, I win the game and she has no choice but to marry me."

"I thought that was the idea."

"I thought it was, too." He paused for a long moment. "If I don't, she wins."

"If she wins, she can pick your bride." Laurie's voice was indignant. "And you know full well she'll pick Cynthia. My Cynthia."

"Miss Weatherly's under no obligation," Max said mildly. "She's not part of the bargain and therefore is free to do exactly as she pleases."

"I certainly hope so," Laurie muttered, and shook his head. "But I still don't understand any of this. You've worked for nearly a month to win this game and Pandora. Why are you stopping now, when victory is within your reach?"

"Think about it, Laurie. I didn't really play fair, did I? My actions weren't always in the spirit of the game, as it were. More than half my points weren't earned so much as they were handed to me."

Laurie raised a brow. "How is that a problem?"

"When we made our bargain all I wanted was a suitable wife with a bit of spirit." Max chose his words carefully, trying to sort his feelings out for himself as much as for his friend. "Pandora was perfect. I didn't care what it took to win. In fact, I quite welcomed the challenging nature of her tests and her mind. It was all rather exhilarating and great fun. At some point, I realized I wanted—no, needed—more than her hand, I needed her heart. Her love.

"I don't want her to marry me because she has to," Max said harshly, "but because she wants to. Because she loves me."

"She does love you."

"Do you know that for certain?" Max narrowed his eyes. "Did she tell you? Did she say it as she was trying to get as far away from me as possible?"

"Not in so many words," Laurie said slowly. "But any fool can see she loves you."

"This fool can't. All I can see is a woman who would rather face ruin than marry me." Max nodded at a crumpled paper on the table next to the decanter. "That's the note she left me. She said our game was, how did she put it? Oh, yes, 'delightfully amusing,' but now that she had seen you again, all her old feelings had been rekindled."

"Hardly." Laurie snorted. "Although I don't think she detests me nearly as much now."

"It scarcely matters. I didn't believe anything she said about you." He picked up the note and crushed it into a tight ball. "But Pandora also said she'd decided long ago she wouldn't marry without love, and therefore she couldn't marry me."

"That doesn't necessarily mean she doesn't love you . . . only that she doesn't know you love her."

"We shall see." He tossed the note into the fireplace and it lay on the grate untouched. "She's the winner of the game. What happens now is entirely in her hands."

Flames licked at the edge of the paper. "You know, she never mentioned love when we each listed our requirements for a spouse. Of course, nether did I. It didn't matter at the time. I didn't realize it would be important to the Hellion of Grosvenor Square, and it certainly was not in the plans of a rake, a rogue, a scoundrel, and a beast."

Pandora's note caught in a bright, flaring flame. He couldn't tear his gaze away. A tongue of fire leapt, then died, leaving only a misshapen black ash that would crumple to nothingness at the slightest touch.

"Odd, how now that it's nearly over, it's the only thing that matters at all."

Pandora stared at the note in her hand, with its now familiar crest and message written in an equally familiar bold hand.

*My dear Miss Effington,*

*I concede defeat. As the game expires tomorrow, I shall call on you at five o'clock for your terms of victory.*

*Please respond as to whether that is satisfactory.*

> *Your servant,*
> *Trent*

"Miss?"

Pandora glanced up.

"The footman who delivered it said he was to wait for a reply," Peters said.

"Tell him it's quite satisfactory."

"Very well." Peters hesitated, as if there was something he wished to say, then nodded and took his leave.

Pandora's gaze returned to Max's terse message.

*I concede defeat.*

A horrible, aching loss swept through her, accompanied by the same pain that had driven her plan with Laurie. Max had the means to earn the final point, but he refused to do so.

He'd rather face whatever bride she chose to name than marry her.

How could Laurie have been so wrong? How could she? She crumpled the note in her hand. So be it. She would exercise her right as the victor, in accordance with their bargain, and claim her prize. She had until tomorrow afternoon to decide exactly who Max's bride should be. More than a full day to determine his fate, his future.

How much longer would it take to accept her own?

Time had run out.

Pandora paced the length of the parlor, still mildly amazed that she could do so without having to sidestep any number of artifacts or books or papers strewn wildly about. For some unknown reason, after Grace had learned of Max's concession, she'd been seized by a completely foreign desire to transform this room from its usual state of unrestrained confusion to a rather startling semblance of propriety. Maids had worked late into the night and most of the day. Now, nothing was out of place. It was the perfect picture of a perfectly proper parlor. And it only increased her apprehension.

Max would be here at any moment. Just watching the minutes tick by was enough to drive her mad. She wasn't at all sure what she wanted more: to get tonight's engagement over with as quickly as possible and with a minimum of emotion, or to avoid it for as long as she had breath left in her body.

This was it, then. The end of the game.

There would be no more adventures with Max. No more verbal sparring or shared laughter or searching gazes from remarkable gray eyes that seemed to see into her very soul. She'd never lost anything she'd truly wanted in her entire life before. What a pity she didn't realize sooner that she could win the game, yet lose what she wanted most.

"Pandora?" Cynthia stepped into the room and studied her friend. "I came as soon as I got your note. Are you certain you wouldn't prefer to see Lord Trent alone?"

"Quite certain." A meeting alone with Max was the very last thing she wanted. Pandora smiled wryly. "You may consider yourself my second. Besides, you've been in on the game since the beginning, it's only fitting you're here at the end."

"I still can't believe you've won."

"Neither can I."

Cynthia sank onto the settee, then jumped up immediately, her eyes wide. "What on earth has happened here?" She glanced around the room with a shocked expression. "It looks so . . . so . . ."

"Proper?"

"Exactly." Cynthia nodded.

Pandora shook her head. "I've only seen it like this once or twice and I can't say I particularly like it. It makes me rather uneasy."

"I can certainly understand why," Cynthia murmured. "It is unnerving."

Hercules eyed Cynthia from his perch on the gong. "Meow."

"Of course, he certainly would not have been missed," Cynthia said, returning the bird's beady-eyed glare.

The door opened. Peters stepped aside to allow Grace to enter, followed by Max, Laurie, and Harry.

"Never find another thing in this damn room ever again," Harry muttered, surveying the parlor with a disgusted air.

Peters stepped out of the room, discreetly closing the door in his wake, and Pandora considered calling him back. He would be so much more comfortable here than listening at the keyhole with Mrs. Barnes and Cook and no doubt the rest of the staff as well.

"Good evening, Miss Effington," Max said politely.

"Lord Trent, as always it's delightful to see you." Pandora favored him with her sweetest smile. "And you've brought a second as well."

"I hadn't quite thought of him that way." Max shrugged.

"I'm here as a curious bystander," Laurie said quickly. "An observer, nothing more."

"I daresay, in that you join most of London." Pandora struggled to keep her voice cool and aloof. "What a shame so many wagers will be lost tonight. I gather most of the money was on Lord Trent."

"They, like I, underestimated you." Max smiled in an unconcerned manner. "Now then, if we could get on with it?"

"Of course." Pandora forced a calm tone in spite of the racing of her heart and the hard, cold weight in the pit of her stomach. "As you no doubt remember, our bargain called for marriage between the two of us if you won, and your marriage to a bride of my choice if I won. I have given this decision a great deal of thought.

"I did promise I would not choose someone completely unsuitable, but rather a bride of the nature of Miss Weatherly—"

"I suspected as much," Laurie said indignantly. "I knew you were going to make him marry Cynthia."

Pandora shook her head. "Actually, I was—"

"Well, I'm not . . . I won't . . ." He furrowed his brow and clenched his teeth, looking every bit like a man deciding to plunge over a cliff and knowing full well the first step over the edge was irrevocable. "I won't allow it."

"You won't allow it?" Pandora said slowly.

Cynthia stared. "Why won't you?"

"Why?" He crossed the room to stand before Cynthia. "Because I want . . . I wish . . ."

"Yes?" Her eyes were wide.

"To let you push me around a dance floor for the rest of my days," Laurie said quickly.

Pandora bit back a grin. Max made an odd sort of choking sound and she glanced at him. "He can't say the word, can he?"

Max shook his head, his voice ragged with suppressed laughter. "Apparently not when it applies to him."

"I can say it," Laurie said sharply, and turned to Cynthia. "He can't marry you because I'm going to."

"Oh my." A stunned smile quirked the corners of her lips.

"Well?" An anxious note sounded in Laurie's voice.

"Well," Cynthia's eyes twinkled with delight. "We shall certainly have to discuss it."

"Discuss it?" Laurie's voice rose. "Are you saying you might not—"

"I wasn't going to name Cynthia," Pandora said at once. "I was saying someone *like* her would be suitable."

"Then who were you going to name?" Max's cool manner belied the intensity in his eyes.

She stared at him for a long moment. How could she live her life without Max in it? "I really can't—"

"I want this nonsense stopped right now." A buxom older woman, dressed in the height of fashion, swept into the room.

"Sophia," Harry said with delight. Grace shot him a reproachful glare. "Rather, I mean Lady Trent."

*Lady Trent?*

Max groaned. "Mother."

"Harry, it's been a very long time." Lady Trent nodded at Grace. "Lady Harold." She scanned the gathering and her gaze settled on Pandora. "Now then, Miss Effington, my son has been in his cups for the last few days, according to his servants."

"Mother." Max ground out the word.

She ignored him. "I have reason to believe it's because of you. I have further reason to believe you have been just as miserable."

"Do you?" Pandora's brow rose.

Lady Trent sighed as if it was obvious. "Your attempt to run off lasted barely two hours, if I understand correctly. That means either you were suddenly struck by the impropriety of what you were about to do— which, given all I have heard about you, seems inconceivable to me—or you realized you weren't with the gentleman you wished to be with. As much as I was not initially pleased with this match, even I can see the value of love. Now, don't be a silly twit—"

"Excuse me, Lady Trent, but I'm the twit." Laurie swept a bow.

"My twit," Cynthia said with a note of satisfaction in her voice.

"Pandora." Max stared at her intensely. "Why *did* you come back?"

Her mouth was abruptly dry. "Why?"

He stepped toward her. "What were you going to say before my mother arrived?"

She stepped back. "What?"

He took another step. "Who were you going to name?"

She matched his move. "Who?"

"Who?"

Pandora shook her head and squared her shoulders. "No one."

Max's eyes narrowed. "No one?"

He moved toward her. She moved back. "I decided the game, the bargain, all of it, was ridiculous and I shouldn't hold you to it." She shrugged as if it was of no consequence. "So I'm not."

"Why not?

"I just explained."

"I don't believe you."

"I don't care!"

"Why aren't you holding me to our arrangement?" His gaze was hard and searching.

"I told you!" she said through clenched teeth.

"Now, tell me the truth."

"It was the—" The restraint she'd struggled to maintain shattered. "Very well." She glared. "If you're going to marry anyone you're going to marry me. And I would rather be left to dangle by a fraying rope over a pit of deadly vipers than to agree to marry you."

"Why?"

"Because a horrible lingering death is preferable to marriage to you!"

"Not that part." Again Max moved toward her, and her breath caught at the look in his eye. "Why did you say if anyone was going to marry me it was going to be you?"

"Because I'm a fool! Your mother said it: a twit!" She didn't like that look one bit.

"What else?"

"Nothing!" She tried to retreat, but discovered she'd backed her way to within a hand's width of the closed parlor doors and there was nowhere left to go.

"Dora." He was a scant few inches from her.

"Don't call me Dora!"

He stared down at her. "What else?"

"Nothing!"

His voice was unyielding, demanding. "What else?"

"Nothing! Everything!" His gaze bored into hers, into her heart, her soul, and the words she'd held tight inside her broke free of their own accord. "Very well! I can't see you married to anyone else because I love you, you arrogant brute! I've probably loved you from the moment I told you what a rake, a rogue, and a scoundrel you were!"

"Don't forget beast," he said mildly, the corners of his lips twitching as if he stifled a smile.

"I could never forget beast!" She stared up at him. "You think this is amusing?"

"A bit."

She whirled to slip past him, but he pulled her back and trapped her against the door. "You do realize, as much as I appreciate your reluctance to compel me to marry someone else, you don't have that right."

"Of course I do. It was part of the bargain. If you won, I had to marry you. If I won, I got to pick your bride. You conceded defeat. I won."

"Not really." He shook his head. "At least, not yet."

"What do you mean, not yet?" The beat of her heart sounded in her ears.

"When we agreed to a time limit, you said it would start with the agreement of our bargain."

"Four weeks ago today." *And it's over now. All of it!*

Max shook his head. "Not exactly. When we agreed to our contest in the burying grounds—"

"Good God," Harry groaned. "Grace, did you hear that? They forged this bargain in a graveyard."

"Hush, dear," Grace murmured.

"It was well after midnight," Max said. "Which means the game does not expire now until after midnight."

She couldn't seem to breathe. "But you've already conceded."

"I've changed my mind." He glanced at

Laurie. "Did you by any chance . . ."

Laurie grinned, pulled something from his waistcoat pocket, and tossed it. Light glittered and gleamed off a golden object streaking in a high arc across the room, looking for all the world like a gilded star shooting across the heavens. Max caught it with one hand and wrapped his fingers around it. He turned to her and held out his fist. "The twelfth and final point."

His gaze trapped hers, and she wanted with all her heart to believe it was surely love she saw in his wonderful gray eyes. Her gaze slipped to his hand and his fist unfolded.

Tears blurred her vision and she reached for a tiny gold sphere hung on a delicate gold chain. Her hand trembled. No, not a sphere. Her breath caught. A solid gold apple rested within a slightly larger latticework apple, itself captured in an apple fashioned of gold wire, the entire piece no bigger than the first joint of her thumb.

"It's a wedding gift, you know." His voice was gentle.

She nodded, but couldn't bring herself to meet his eyes. Not yet. "From Hera to Zeus."

"No." He placed two fingers beneath her chin and lifted her head until her gaze met his. "From me to you. Max to Dora."

"Matched hounds." She sniffed back treacherous tears.

"Well matched, I think." He laughed. "By love." His voice sobered. "I do love you, you know."

"Do you?" She couldn't keep the wonder from her voice. "Are you certain?"

"Very certain. But I could prove it to you." He pulled her into his arms. "Test me, Pandora. Make me prove it to you."

"And if you should pass my test?" She could barely choke out the words.

"Then you will be my wife and I shall spend the rest of my life as your hero." His gaze searched hers, looking for the answer to a question he hadn't asked. "And your husband?"

"I wasn't especially looking for a husband." She gazed up at him. "But I think perhaps you may be preferable to a horrible lingering death, after all."

"And preferable to being torn apart by wild camels in the deserts of Egypt?"

She swallowed hard. "Possibly."

"Or tortured at the hands of naked savages in the wilds of America?" He grinned.

"Very likely."

"Then I claim my prize, as the game is indeed at an end." He lowered his head to hers, his lips barely a breath from hers. "And the rules are no longer necessary. Any of them."

"Every one," she murmured and his mouth covered hers.

Dimly, she noted applause from those gathered in the parlor and vague cheers from the servants on the other side of the door and marveled that she didn't care the tiniest bit who witnessed their embrace or who knew how very much she loved him. She wrapped her arms around his neck and reveled in the welcoming feel of his body close to hers and the crush of his lips and returned his kiss with the utter joy that welled up inside her.

A kiss that marked the end of a game played between a hellion and a hero and marked as well the end of a bargain struck for a husband and a wife. Or marked perhaps . . .

. . . Just the beginning.

# America Loves Lindsey!
## The Timeless Romances
## of #1 Bestselling Author